Zagader

Robert S Baker

Dedicated to

Dave and Dawn Harris

CHAPTER 1

Strange Sound

Stories of spaceships and little green men talked about in an old local newspaper, Jacob read laughing along with the mention of the coronavirus virus while enjoying his pint of home-brew. Jacob had resided on the Moor for years, the only green and white he had seen was discarded rubbish by holidaymakers, certainly not aliens. Jacob walked the same route for years attending his ewes, enjoying the occasional frosty evening with a clear sky glimpsing a shooting star. Sometimes, without warning, engulfed by misty fog from the sea, creating a strange sound, as if the bowels of the earth were howling.

Jacob lived alone since his wife had passed away some years back from breast cancer. He reminisced reliving holding her hand while she took her final breath. Rosalind slowly released the grip on his hand, leaving him alone in this uncertain world of misery without her. Jacob, wiping the tears from his cheek, could not bring himself to seek romance again; he'd had known Rosalind all his life from when they attended school. Jacob fondly gazed to the mantelpiece where her ashes sat in the urn above the fire. He didn't need much to sustain him; a hundred ewes would keep him occupied. Grazing is not an issue on the Moor, Jacob had earned his right of free grazing from his father before him. He would be the last generation, he hadn't sired a son, something else missing from his life, sat at his oak kitchen table with the good book opened on Revelations. Jacob had no time for these people with their telescopes gazing at the stars searching for spaceships, he had gone out with the good book; told in no uncertain terms to go away by some foul-mouthed yobs. He sighed despondent, believing he knew the truth according to the message in the good book. Jacob smiled everyone to their own opinion, providing they did not harm his sheep, they can waste their time staring into space.

Jacob patted his faithful sheepdog Jack laying close to the hearth, hearing a strange sound outside. Watching Jack's ears perk, looking to the door growling. Jacob grabbed his shepherd's crook and torch venturing outside into a blanket of fog. Hearing the strange sound he had heard many times before over the years. Jack glued to Jacob's heels, they carefully made their way to the sound of breaking water, striking the rocks on the shoreline below. The further they ventured from Jacob's thatched house, the darker the sky became, more mysterious than the Devils curse, not a star seen through the fog. If Jacob hadn't walked this route so many times before he wouldn't have ventured towards the cliff edge. The sound of breaking waves increased in volume, finally reaching the fence separating land from death, with a vertical drop to the rocky shoreline below. Jacob patted Jack reassuringly, although Jacob wasn't sure something wasn't happening. Perhaps God had come to take him to join Rosalind he loved dearly. Jacob squinted at a blinding light vanishing into the distance, presuming blistering hot fragments of a meteor penetrating the darkness.

He sighed heavily, slowly finding his way home hearing the sheep bleating as he entered the house. Both he and Jack, his dog, were soaked from the damp fog. Jacob glanced to wear his wife's ashes sat over the fireplace, stared in horror they were gone. He walked closer to the mantelpiece seeing a neat ring of dust where the urn sat for four years. Jacob would never touch the mantelpiece, a sacred place in his mind where Rosalind resided. He looked to Jack for answers! Jacob concluded ashes would be no use to anyone other than God; perhaps, he had taken them. The only explanation Jacob could accept, couldn't imagine a thief stealing ashes; although he never locked his door and his gun is still in the corner with a box of cartridges. Jacob checked his tin where he kept his cash in the kitchen cupboard, the money is still present.

Jacob made a coffee pouring a few dried biscuits into Jack's bowl, placed on the floor by his water dish. He returned to the front room staring at the mantelpiece again in case he is mistaken, lowering his cup in the hearth and throwing more blocks on the fire. Jacob flopped down in his old armchair staring at the mantelpiece, sipping his coffee. Jack returned laying down by Jacob's feet. Jacob nearly always slept in his armchair, hating the bed ever since Rosalind had passed on, wasn't the same.

Morning came too quickly, Jacob disturbed by the light coming through the window. Quickly making him some breakfast, a couple of fried eggs, a rasher of bacon and a slice of crusty bread. Jack would have any spare scraps his master passed to him. Jacob would freshen with a cold wash in the sink is sufficient to wake him; he'd had his shirt on for a week and decided it would last one more day. Jacob stepped out into a bright day; the wind is always strong by the coast. He strolled across the Moor, carrying a bale of hay on his shoulder and a little supplement for his sheep. Threw the hay in the hay rack looking at the sheep around him, reckoning they were all there without counting individuals. He walked amongst his sheep looking for lame ones or any that looked under the weather. A sheep's life is hard on the Moor, and only the fittest survived.

He made his way back to the barn, noticing the half-dozen hens had managed to lay eggs in the laying boxes for a change; he wouldn't have to go on a hunting spree to discover their hidden location. Jacob returned to the house, pushing a barrow load of logs, delivered some time ago. There were no trees on the Moor where he lived. They had to come from some distance, or if Jacob is lucky, he could drive his old tractor down to the shoreline and collect driftwood and use for a source of heating. He usually traded with another farmer to avoid spending hard-earned cash.

He pushed the barrow through the front door into the living room, stacking the wood in the hearth glancing to the mantelpiece. Jacob froze to the spot! Rosalind's urn is there in its usual place. He pushed the barrow out of the house, glancing back again to the mantelpiece to reassure himself he didn't imagine. He walked into the kitchen, making a cup of tea sitting in his armchair, staring at Rosalind's urn, could he possibly be hallucinating, something strange is happening! Jacob sat there for nearly one and a half hours, not quite sure what he is waiting for. He quite expected something to happen; only hearing the clock chime 4 o'clock on the wall. Jacob walked to the window, moving the net curtains last washed by Rosalind before she died, looked out not knowing what he is looking for, he needed a sign of some kind, hearing the strange sound that accompanied the fog. Jacob grabbed his crook, Jack, his faithful sheepdog, came to heal. They strolled out of the house heading in the direction of the sound coming from the clifftop.

Jack paused laying down, Jacob glanced back. "What's the matter, Jack?" Jacob asked calmly, sensing the fear in the dog's eyes. Jacob knew the wasn't much that would frighten Jack; he'd seen off one or two trespassers in his time, leaving them with a message they wouldn't forget.

Jacob continued walking puzzled by Jack's reaction, listening to the sound, the strange noise coming from the sea shrouded in fog. Jacob reached the fence, two more yards, certain death awaited you on the rocks below. He squinted, trying to focus on a bright light heading into the heavens disappearing from view, he sighed heavily, slowly making his way home to the house.

Jack, sitting by the front door shivering, not like him at all. Jacob wondered if he is unwell he's six years old, remembering Rosalind picking him from the litter on a neighbour's farm. Jacob opened the front door, they both entered, he hastily walked in the kitchen; quickly prepared a warm broth. Soaking Jack's dog biscuits in his bowl, placing by the hearth throwing on a few more logs to increase the heat, Jacob couldn't imagine life without Jack. Jacob glanced to the mantelpiece smiling to see Rosalind's urn is still there. Jacob decided he would pay any price, sell his soul to the devil to have Rosalind in his life. Sat down in his armchair by the fire after making a large mug of soup, holding in both hands watching Jack devour his food. Jacob drifted off to sleep in the armchair with Jack resting his head on his master's boot. Jack listened to the wind howling; rattling the tin on the neighbouring shed roof. Jacob snored, oblivious to what is taking place outside dreaming of Rosalind making him tea in a spotless house, she insisted keeping, frequently scolded for coming in with dirty boots.

Jacob awoke with a jolt, morning had arrived. He had his cup of tea and a thick crust of toast with marmalade, a jar he was saving for a special occasion that never came. Grabbed his crook by the door heading out into a windswept morning grabbing a bale of hay from the barn, he carried on his shoulder across the Moor to the sheep rack. Jacob caught an old ewe with his crook sitting on her backside using his foot clippers, he trimmed her feet, ending up catching six more with the same problem. Jack, his faithful sheepdog, sat quietly watching, eating the clippings known as dog chocolate. Jacob carried on walking across the Moor for some distance suspecting he had a sheep missing, standing on a large rock he looked back to his flock; counting carefully discovering they were all there. He struggled across the windy Moor for over five hours, returning to the house. Jacob opened the door stood there shocked, not believing his eyes. The house cleaned from top to bottom, the dust on the mantelpiece surrounding Rosalind's urn had gone. The crockery which had sat in the sink for weeks is washed up and stacked on the draining board. Jacob went into the bedroom, scratching his head clean sheets on the bed, he looked from his bedroom window, sheets hanging on the line they were washed. Fresh clothes for him in a neat pile with a note, he could barely think, trembling as he picked up the notepaper: "Jacob, wash and change your clothes, you smell, from your Rosalind."

Jacob reads the note 5 times before dashing into the bathroom, removing his dirty clothes, taking a bath the first one in six months. He stepped from the bath, the large bath towels were there waiting for him, quickly returned to the bedroom, changing into fresh clothes. Jacob studied the note, definitely Rosalind's handwriting. Perhaps God he surmised is allowing Rosalind to come from heaven and help him. Jacob never smiled so much, where every looked, no dust, he opened the fridge, cleaned, and with a plate of sandwiches wrapped in cling foil for him. He sat at the kitchen table; he had no idea what is happening? He didn't really care the thought that Rosalind is close is enough, made himself a pot of coffee, celebrating adding a little tot of whiskey. Jack sat beside him in his usual begging posture, Jacob smiled, casting a morsel of crust, Jack caught instantly.

Early the next morning Jacob attached his small trailer to his old Fordson N tractor, cranking the engine frantically until she spluttered into life. He turned the fuel onto TVO, he remembered his father acquiring this old tractor when he was a child, his father sitting him on his knee, allowing Jacob to try and steer. If it wasn't the fact his father had won the football pools, he entered on a whim one week, he wouldn't have this tractor; they could have never afforded in those days. Jacob kept her in memory of his father, he didn't use her very often, perhaps three or four times a year. He remembered courting Rosalind, she would love to drive this old tractor down onto the beach, the track is a little precarious; nevertheless, she managed, they would spend hours cutting and collecting firewood for the farm.

Jacob drove on with Jack sat in the trailer with the chainsaw and axe, steadily descended the old track taking them down onto the beach, which wasn't very big more stone than anything else. You could always guarantee after a good storm timber will have come ashore.

Winter approaching another week, and November is here, Jacob cut a load of timber watching a heavy mist approach from the sea. He quickly started his tractor heading up the track, returning to the farm. He unloaded the trailer into a small shed where he stored the wood to keep it sort of dry, removed his pocket watch the one his father gave him before he passed on. One o'clock lunchtime. Jacob sat at the kitchen table slicing a piece of bread, with a large portion of cheese and two pickled onions would do for lunch, smiling, remembering the times Rosalind would prepare him a lovely meal; he lived like a king in those days. He quickly washed the dishes something he hadn't done for some time, suspecting if Rosalind is watching, she would burn his ears if he didn't, after all the trouble she'd gone to-to tidy the house. He placed the dishes in the cupboard where they belonged. Jacob ventured outside, grabbing his old wheelbarrow loading with blocks, returning to stack by the hearth.

He smiled, hoping Rosalind wasn't watching, she would scold him frequently for pushing the wheelbarrow in the house with a dirty wheel. He quickly stacked the blocks against the wall, removing the barrow from the house checking there is no mud left on the flagstone floor. The misty fog is as thick as ever. Jacob heard the sound the weird sound of the earth in agony. He grabbed his crook, slipping on his waterproof coat; Jack, close to his heels. They set off towards the cliff fence, staying on the well-trodden path Jacob knew so well. For years he'd walked this path, hearing the same eerie sound hoping one day to discover where it's coming from. He stared into the mist, observing a bright light, almost beckoning him to step over the fence which he knew would be sudden death if he ventured further. Jack had come with him this time and not shied away from as before; Jacob bent down, patting him with reassurance. Jacob sighed heavily, slowly turning around walking to the house, finding the door open, quite suspected thieves, watching Jack run indoors barking, then silent, not a whimper. Jacob gripped his crook firmly anticipating trouble, although puzzled why Jack wasn't barking. He entered the property seeing Jack sitting in front of his chair, wagging his tail while Rosalind stroked him.

Jacob had prayed for this moment for as long as he could remember after Rosalind passed away. Common sense dictated, he is hallucinating, no one came home from heaven; she's in an urn on the mantelpiece. He watched Rosalind rise to her feet approaching him in her usual attire, knee-length skirt pinny tied around her waist with the blouse she loved so much, embroidered with roses. Jacob is frozen to the spot. "Jacob," Rosalind said calmly. "Your meal is in the oven I must go," she kissed him on the cheek vanishing into the mist.

Jacob came to his senses dashing outside, you could barely see a metre in front of you; he didn't know which direction to take. He called out, "Rosalind, Rosalind, come back, please!" Jacob quickly followed the trail to the cliff-top, watching the misty fog vanish as if sucked into a vacuum cleaner. He returned to the house opening the oven finding a beautiful meal, potatoes, meat and vegetables, with Rosalind's lovely gravy. Jacob would always profess to Rosalind, he'd only married her because of the gravy she made, which usually resulted in a wooden spoon around the ear. Jack sat patiently like a starving animal hoping his master would cast him the bone. Jacob is trying to understand what is happening; is this just his imagination, had he prepared the meal subconsciously.

Jacob loved Rosalind more than life itself, in fact, more than he loved God, which he thought a sin. He quite accepted the fact God could do anything. The Bible speaks of miracle after miracle; perhaps he sighed heavily suspecting he is wishful thinking. Why would God bother with him a simpleton? Jacob washed his plate, casting the bone to Jack, who dashed off to sit by the fireplace grinding away at the bone with nothing else on his mind. Jacob made a coffee sitting by the fire, watching Jack totally unconcerned Rosalind is here one minute and gone the next; nothing is making sense. Although Jacob didn't really care, providing she kept coming to see him, his life is complete with her. He through more wood on the fire still pondering events, he dared not say anything to anyone fearing incarceration; he doesn't believe what's happening, so why should others. Before Jacob realised, the morning is staring through the curtains quite a bright morning from what could be seen. He awoke to find a birthday card on his lap, wishing him a happy birthday from his beloved Rosalind.

Jacob ran into the kitchen checking the calendar, his birthday, and he'd forgotten, Rosalind hadn't. She'd remember things like that which he considered insignificant in the scheme of things. He only marked the calendar with market days. Jacob placed his card on the cupboard so he could look at it again and again with his mind returning to work. Jacob hoped the old Ram had sired all the ewes properly this year and were carrying twins. He'd changed the Ram which hadn't been quite so successful. He and Jack were eating him for the last six months a little like eating shoe leather; nevertheless, Jack didn't seem to mind.

Jacob grabbed his crook walking down the steep track to the waterline staring out to sea, he didn't know what he is looking for. Nevertheless, he surveyed for as far as he could see, walking towards the cliff face sitting on a large Boulder. Jacob is astounded watching a small area of misty fog appear about 5000 yards out from the shore, slowly approaching the beach. The misty fog couldn't have been more than 3 meters wide and perhaps as tall which he thought is exceptionally odd. The misty fog stopped at the shoreline; there is a sudden burst of brilliant light stepping from the light Rosalind. Jacob rose to his feet, immediately walking towards what appeared to be his wife, his deceased wife. She is dressed in a classic white boiler suit for a better description; there is not a dark piece of material on her figure apart from her footwear which is silver.

Rosalind smiled, holding out her hand. Jacob accepted without fear of consequence for his safety, allowing Rosalind to lead the way into the mist which appeared to have a door. Jack stayed by the rock laying down, Rosalind glanced back-patting her leg. Jack immediately ran to join them as the mist engulfed them all, taking Jacob and Jack on a journey of discovery as they were about to find out. The misty fog cleared, Jacob found himself standing in a large construction under the sea; he could see fish through the windows swimming unconcerned around whatever he is in. Other male and females appeared dressed the same as Rosalind walking around the vast expanse of whatever kept the water out and them safe. Jacob wanted to speak and found he couldn't, Jack had vanished, no longer with them. He stood there, holding his crook watching his clothes disappear and replaced with the same as Rosalind is wearing and everyone else.

Rosalind spoke: "I'm created as your deceased wife, Rosalind, we will explain why Jacob all will become clear to you in time."

Finally, his mouth would work. "This cannot be heaven under the sea; this is devil domain, God lives in heaven above the clouds?" Jacob expressed unsure of anything any more.

Rosalind and the others studied Jacob's expression while Rosalind led him into another part of the construction. Everything is white, even the furnishings which were not dissimilar in shape to anything you could buy on the High St, he concluded. Jacob encouraged to sit down studying another person enter joining him and Rosalind. "I suspect you have many questions Jacob all can not be answered at the moment, as time progresses, you will realise we are telling you the truth, you may call me Peter."

Jacob studied him rather suspiciously: "If this is not hell, where am I, and how can this person be my Rosalind, she was cremated and on my mantelpiece?" Jacob asked calmly.

"We have been here since the construction of earth, we created the life forms on the planet, and some have evolved, unfortunately, not the way we anticipated."

"Are you saying God does not exist? Something I have believed in all my life and my parents, millions of other people and me. How do you discredit miracles, they do occasionally happen to the lucky few?"

Peter and Rosalind glanced at each other. Peter answered with a demonstration holding his hand out, resting the back of his hand on the table. Jacob watched the wedding ring Rosalind had lost when they were first married originally belonged to his mother, and her mother before that appear in Peter's palm. Jacob speechless looking at Peter and Rosalind, for answers, explanations to his questions. "A miracle I can perform, I can raise people from the dead such as Rosalind who sits before you. We have records of everything, every-one, every animal, every insect, every hair on your head, Jacob, we are the creators."

Jacob laughed: "I've heard talk, we came swinging out of the trees! God created everything in six days, resting on the Sabbath."

"Rosalind, remind Jacob of something only you, and he would know," Peter suggested.

"What happened between us on John Hickory's hay-stack Jacob, and what did you ask of me?"

Jacob rose to his feet, he knew exactly what Rosalind is referring to; she permitted him to make love to her for the first time, he proposed, and Rosalind accepted. "We did you know what and I asked you to marry me, you kindly accepted one of my best ideas to have you in my life."

"You need further proof Jacob," Peter asked, chang-ing his appearance into Peter the fishermen from the Bible. Jacob collapsed into his chair. Rosalind held his hand. "You must believe what Peter discloses to you, I am Rosalind I'm created from her ashes, check her urn on the mantelpiece and see what you discover inside; although your Rosalind was cremated the traces of her essence, remain in our memory banks, and I'm her in every sense of the word."

"Are we to live together as man and wife," Jacob asked, puzzled by everything. He remembered watching a Star Trek movie at the pictures with Rosalind, there is someone called a shapeshifter on board could they really exist?

"If you wish Jacob or I would keep your house and provide your meals and assist you with any task of importance to you."

"What if someone sees you with me? My friends all know Rosalind died, I presume you don't want to become common knowledge; the world would be turned upside down, I should imagine if everyone discovered their religion is false. My next question what happens to me now I know? Am I to suddenly disappear, which wouldn't be such a bad thing, I would definitely be with Rosalind in heaven?"

"You are not to die until the allotted time Jacob, you are worrying over trivial matters. Anyone who observes Rosalind on your farm, may not remember her death, I can assure you; we control everything," Peter pointed to a large screen on the wall. "Watch the aeroplane Jacob 197 passengers will lose their lives today thanks to a terrorist bomb." Jacob watched the plane explode, he hadn't watched television for some years, since the one he had refused to work, never bothering to afford to replace seemed a waste of money. The only person that would watch television is Rosalind, and she's gone. "Couldn't you have saved them," Jacob asked, rather distraught.

"Of course, you are missing the point, the Bible was originally constructed as guidelines by my brothers and me, hoping the inhabitants of the earth would use the book as a guideline. Unfortunately, as you know your own history, we failed miserably; now we have nothing other than savages living on the earth."

"If you are truly the creators, this should be a minor problem for you to rectify. To be quite honest, I don't think you are the creators, you're probably an alien from somewhere," Jacob paused, remembering what is written in the Bible. "Although the Bible does not speak of any other beings; that would lead me to believe you are a government experiment, and you're hoping to trick a simpleton like me."

Peter projected a beam of light from his eyes, stunning Jacob. Jacob stood there, frozen to the spot. "I want you the first of every month to come to the beach with your tractor and manure spreader. You will wait for your manure spreader to be loaded. When the fog clears, you will take your machine to one of your grass pastures. You will spread the contents thinly over the ground you understand me, Jacob," Peter instructed in his firm tone.

"I understand," Jacob replied robotically. Rosalind glanced to Peter and nodded, walking Jacob along the corridor, she paused, waiting for the misty fog to engulf them both and they reappeared on the beach. Jacob stepped from the misty fog in his original clothes, Rosalind vanished, returning to where she'd come from. Peter is waiting for Rosalind to return. "That went better than I thought Rosalind," Peter advised. "He will comply, although he is extremely strong-willed; his love for Rosalind is his strongest thought, I read his mind easily."

"I agree Peter with your conclusion, I will have to repair the manure spreader; he hasn't used it for years since Rosalind died. He only has a hundred ewes, barely enough to sustain his living, I will have to improve the situation Peter. We must make him a little more efficient, he will never realise he is spreading cremated humans on his pastureland, excellent fertiliser."

Peters silver eyes shone, observed Rosalind's turned silver from the brown colour she projected while in the presence of Jacob. "Rosalind, proceed cautiously, he will not remember his visit here, I wiped his memory other than with you. You may experiment as you see fit with him. The human flesh we require for our home planets will be transported every month," Peter concluded, flashed his eyes, walking off.

Rosalind transported to Jacobs farm looking at the manure spreader, dressed in the same attire as Roslind would originally where when she is outside with Jacob, a brown boiler-suit. She started working on the old manure spreader far worse than she suspected. Jacob came over to join her surprised, although, for some reason, it seemed quite reasonable for Rosalind to be here. "We must have this working properly," Jacob, Rosalind insisted calmly.

"I am aware Rosalind, I have manure to collect from the beach every month it's free," he smiled. Rosalind grinned, trying to perform the same way as a human would in facial expressions. They spent the rest of the day working on the machine using spare parts from the old workshop. Jacob had an old Fordson major tractor, he used to use on the spreader. While he wasn't looking Rosalind touched the battery terminals charging the battery from her own life form. She walked over to the diesel tank in the corner of the shed drawing off 5 gallons and emptying in the fuel tank of the Fordson major. Jacob commented: "She'll not start, I suspect the battery is flat, I'll have to blow the tyres up, they look a little worse for wear," he complained.

"Jacob," Rosalind suggested, "I would like one of your coffees, you make me one, I'll finish off here join you in a minute," she smiled.

Jacob smiled, "you always were better with machines than me." He chuckled, walking to the house with Jack at his heels.

Rosalind waited until he is out of sight sitting on the driver's seat of the Fordson major. She pushed the starter lever, the tractor burst into life after the engine turned over several times, filling the shed full of smoke. She reversed the tractor to the manure spreader attaching along with the PTO shaft to discharge the machine in the field, allowing to spread and empty. The spreader would carry about five tons, which were ample for their requirements for the moment until the shipments increased in volume. Rosalind checked every tyre on the machine and tractor inflating to the correct pressure by touching with her hand.

Rosalind entered the house to discover Jacob with his large Bible on the kitchen table reading passages. He knew Jesus had restored life to Nazareth who was dead for four days, Jacob concluded four days or four years there would be no difference in Jesus's eyes; he could restore anything he wanted. Why bother with him a mere insignificant person in the scheme of things?

Jacob asked: "I presume you have met Jesus; he restored you to life, Rosalind?"

"Why ask the question if you already know the answer, Jacob? You have met Jesus, although you don't remember, do not concern yourself with trivialities we have a greater mission." Rosalind smiled confidently deciding to use Jacobs religious beliefs to work in her favour.

He exhaled closing the Bible, passing a mug of coffee to Rosalind sitting opposite. "I must say Rosalind you haven't aged a day; Jesus must have set your age at 20, you look no older, and I'm 43. Jesus has truly given me a present, we must not speak of this; something tells my mind you are to stay a secret? Is that correct Rosalind I can't show my friends you exist?"

"Think Jacob logically, how many widowers there are in the world today; why weren't one of them chosen? The world would be in turmoil if they learnt of my existence, I'm here for a special reason you are helping Jesus. Say no more please or he may take me away deciding you are undeserving of the gift." Rosalind knew Jacob wouldn't want that to happen, she had listened to his prayers begging God to return Rosalind for years.

Jacob is quiet for a moment, "I presume you will have to return to heaven in the evenings, we won't be like husband and wife again like the old days?"

"Sometimes I will have to return and others I will stay, depending on my duties, after all, I'm working for God you wouldn't want me to disobey him, Jacob, would you?"

Jacob shook his head: "No, you must not disobey his commands, I definitely don't want to lose you again, Rosalind. I heard the old Fordson major start I didn't think she would ever again, I heard you try the manure spreader I presume it works. December I have to collect

a load from the beach of fertiliser; Jesus is generous, helping me grow grass for my sheep."

"Isn't he always." Rosalind smiled, walking into the
bedroom, making the bed. Jacob nervously entered:
"Will you be sharing this with me tonight, Rosalind?"
Jacob asked, slightly worried, wondering what he should
and should not do; he didn't want to offend Jesus or God
or anybody for that matter and especially not Rosalind.

Rosalind smiled, "only if you take a bath, Jacob, I
have clean sheets on the bed; your beard looks like rats
tails, and your hair is not much better, wash thoroughly,
and I will clip before retiring to bed this evening." Jacob
smiled, she is speaking the truth, he hadn't bothered
with his appearance or cleanliness since Rosalind died.
He spent the next hour in the bath, scrubbing every
part of his body shampooing his hair and beard twice
for good measure. He wrapped a towel around himself, heading for the bedroom quickly dressing, finding
Rosalind in the kitchen with sharpened dagging shears.
Jacob sat on the chair, Rosalind carefully cut his hair and
tidied his beard. He actually looked like a human instead
of a Neanderthal. Rosalind quickly swept up the loose
hair throwing on the fire giving off an awful smell for a
moment. Jacob looked at himself in the mirror that had
a crack across from Rosalind, and he playing a childish
game in the kitchen when they first married, the ball
hit the mirror on the wall. Both retired to bed, Rosalind
placed her hand on Jacob's forehead, he immediately
relaxed in a deep sleep. Rosalind, leaving to return to
the spaceship, stepping into the misty fog outside the
front door. She vanished reappearing in the spaceship

concealed in a large crater, camouflaged so no vessel or radar could detect the ship. Peter is waiting for her arrival with Matthew, another brother of the 12 apostles as they name themselves thousands of years ago when creating the Bible; hoping to instil order in the humans, which failed as the centuries passed.

Rosalind, Peter and Matthew acknowledged each other with a flash of their eyes, which were silver now Rosalind had returned. They walked through the vast space ship watching human bodies processed into joints of meat, anything that wasn't to be used is incinerated by their engines and turned into powder, disposed of initially through their recycling chambers. However, human technology had progressed and would detect any discharge from the spaceship, now Jacob will solve the problem. Matthew asked: "Peter, we cannot permit the human race to continue destroying the planet. They are only good for feeding other creatures; let's destroy, our task will be finished and leave the Earth to regenerate and become what it was a beauty to behold."

"Stay positive, Matthew," Peter advised. "The human race has its uses such as feeding the young animals on other planets we are terraforming. Let us continue along this path for another five years, while we find a solution to transport the humans alive to our designated destinations. The animals can hunt tracked down the human and eat."

Rosalind remarked: "Five years is not long Matthew, we will find a solution to transporting humans alive over vast distances throughout the universe. Look what we've achieved, Jacob travelled with me and didn't die, we are making progress. Before if you remember Matthew when we tried to transport another living being, they were instantly destroyed because the transporter is only designed for us nothing else."

Matthew acknowledged with the flash of his eyes. "Difficult, we are trying various methods when I bring humans aboard for processing, none arrive here alive from Africa, our best hunting ground for humans. Of course, the odd aeroplane disaster and as long as humans keep fighting there will always be bodies to transport."

Peter flashed his eyes. "We will succeed Matthew remember when we came up with the idea of God's to control the humans. That worked very well for some considerable time. Rosalind returned to Jacob I fear he's realised you're missing." Rosalind flashed her eyes walking along the corridor she stepped into the misty fog. 6 o'clock in the morning she reappeared by the woodshed, splitting wood with the acts as Jacob stepped from the house, he smiled, observing her working. "I'll make the coffee and breakfast Rosalind," he called out laughing. She acknowledged his comment with a nod, continued splitting logs loading the wheelbarrow.

He returned to the house, bewildered by everything his life had changed from a routine of breakfast feed the animals go to bed, to catering for Rosalind again which is not a problem as far as he could see; he had something in his life he long for four years. Jacob looked from the window seeing the snow starting to fall. November and December were dismal on the Moor, he wondered if his old Land Rover would start, he hadn't used it all summer trying to save money. Jacob looked in his tin at the back of the cupboard realising he would have to grocery shop, he hadn't bothered to grow vegetables this year. He couldn't be bothered there was only him, quietly hoping he would die and join Rosalind. Things have turned out the other way round Rosalind has joined him which made him smile, opening his old sweet tin only to discover a wad of cash. Jacob had to look twice he couldn't believe what he saw, there were hundreds of pounds held fast by elastic bands; shopping certainly wouldn't be a problem he grinned. Suspecting God is trying to help him, although, couldn't remember God giving anybody money, he concluded puzzled. There again he'd never heard of anyone having their wife returned; perhaps God is operating differently now in the modern age.

Rosalind pushed the wheelbarrow to the front door, carrying armfuls of blocks, she stacked by the side of the hearth; not bringing the wheelbarrow inside as Jacob would. She closed the door on the weather, joining Jacob in the kitchen, sitting down to eggs on toast with a little bacon and a cup of coffee. Jack sat in his usual position, waiting for anything to fall off the table. Rosalind patted Jack tucking into her meal which she would discharge later in the day went Jacob wasn't watching, she didn't require food to sustain her essence. Rosalind, a member of the Zibyan collective, pure energy, something similar to radiation, although admitted no side effects to any other being unless provoked. A form of shapeshifter, they could take any form they wanted solid, or liquid made no difference. Their own planet situated behind Neptune several billion miles away, although with their propulsion system a simple matter of three or four days to their home planet, "Zagader."

Jacob cleared the table, Rosalind washed the dirty dishes heating the water with power from her hands. Jacob hadn't stoked the fire for the boiler to heat the water. Jacob heard a knock at the door. Jack ran in front of him barking, Jacob opened the door. Police officers were standing in the doorway in their wellington boots after walking across the Moor. "Jacob Walker this is your farm?"

Jacob answered abruptly, "correct." Jacob glanced over his shoulder, Rosalind is gone from sight. "We've had reports," the officer laughed, "of aliens, strange people wandering over the Moor have you seen anything?"

Jacob laughed, "three green men purchased a joint of lamb from me the other day."

The officer smiled: "Our sentiments exactly, we have more important issues; no little green men would come to this planet they would have to be mental," the officer laughed walking away.

Rosalind had returned to her spaceship meeting Peter and Matthew. "What's going on, Peter?" Rosalind asked.

Peter advised: "I watch the officers, a dozen of them scanning part of the moorland, none of our brothers and sisters have ventured onto the moor without my consent. I suspect it's what the humans call a hoax, someone's making up stories, continue as before Rosalind be on your guard."

Rosalind flashed her eyes to Matthew and Peter, checking the scanners aboard the spaceship, locating the police officers were some distance away from Jacobs farm. She reappeared by the old Land Rover where Jacob is standing with his head under the bonnet checking the oil. He glanced at her. "That was close, Rosalind! The old Land Rover won't start, the battery flat, I'll have to walk to the village," he frowned.

"Make the coffee Jacob leave the vehicle repairs to me, I hope you're driving across the Moor to the village otherwise the police will be arresting you. Your old Land Rover hasn't an MOT certificate or tax or insurance."

Jacob sighed, "as usual Rosalind you are correct I haven't bothered since you passed on. I can easily drive across the Moor. Is there anything you'd like from the shop if you can ever get the old beast working."

"Remember to say nothing to anyone Jacob about me, purchase essentials, say nothing out of the ordinary," Rosalind advised extremely concerned with recent events.

He returned to the house; Rosalind held the terminals on the Land Rover battery recharged, she climbed inside turning the key, the old diesel Land Rover burst into life. She drove to the diesel tank topping up parking the Land Rover outside the house. Jacob had made the coffee hearing the sound of his Land Rover he couldn't help but smile. Rosalind could always make things right, watching her enter the house; she'd left the engine running on the Land Rover to warm the cab for Jacob. He kissed Rosalind on the cheek finishing his coffee, holding his old shopping bag. He climbed into his Land Rover steadily driving along the old track, which is actually shorter than going by road, allowing him to study his sheep. Jacob finally parked walking the mile to the village shop, which had changed since the last time he visited, into a self-service affair. He walked along the shelves with his basket looking at the price of food; everything is expensive, promising himself to grow vegetables next year. Jacob is shocked if he wanted an extra shopping bag he would have to pay. Instead, he had an old box the shopkeeper gave him; even more of a shock the groceries come to £50.

Jacob struggled to carry the box, and shopping bag the mile to the Land Rover; he'd purchase far more than he intended. The bags of flour were quite cumbersome, needing them to make bread. Jacob finely placed his groceries in the back of the Land Rover, heading home slowly across the Moor. Rosalind helped him unload, putting everything in the cupboards. Jacob noticed she'd already made three loaves of bread, he didn't dare ask how considering they were out of flour. She cut Jacob a large crusty slice with the smearing of butter and jam. He sat there as if he'd won the lottery drinking coffee gazing into Rosalind's beautiful brown eyes.

Rosalind interrupted his thoughts: "Sheep, you must check them, Jacob, I wouldn't be surprised if some have lambed." Jacob smiled slipping on his coat with Jack following close to his heels, he left the house. Rosalind already knew there were lambs on the Moor and had prepared several pens in the barn. She is finding this whole experience quite enjoyable, although she could be anything she wanted. Playing the part of Jacobs wife and helping on the farm is very interesting and thanks to their ability to extract information from anyone's mind, she could perform flawlessly.

Jacob hadn't walked very far before he could see several ewes with lambs; he quickly returned to the barn, smiling, noticing the pens already prepared, Rosalind is always one step ahead of him. He grabbed a four-wheeled cart, he used to tow behind his quad bike before that broke, now he had to pull the cart by hand. He sighed slowly watching Rosalind come from the back of the buildings on his old quad bike; she parked in front of him with a smug grin practising human facial movements to try and blend in.

He stood there shaking his head in disbelief, wherever Rosalind had come from he didn't care, his life is turning into a bundle of fun again like it used to be before she passed away. Rosalind attached the little trailer patting Jacob on the cheek, "don't belong I'll make the coffee."-Jacob climbed aboard his old quad bike towing the small trailer, gathering three old ewes and six lambs placing in his trailer. He slowly returned to the barn placing the ewes and lambs in individual pens for the moment; giving each a little water, a few sheep nuts making sure the lambs could suckle before going in the house for his coffee.

Rosalind had already prepared lunch serving as Jacob walked in. He placed his hands either side of her face gently kissing Rosalind lovingly. Rosalind is somewhat surprised, she knew from the records Jacob and his deceased wife very rarely held each other or had physical contact. "Thank you for being in my life Rosalind," Jacob remarked, sitting at the table.

Rosalind smiled: "I'm pleased, Jesus allowed me to return." Maintaining her cover as an alien by making Jacob believe Jesus had returned her.

"Yes, praise the Lord," Jacob voiced. "I've never thanked God for a meal since you were gone, I'm surprised he even bothers to look down on me," he sighed slowly, enjoying his meal.

"Remember tomorrow what you must do, Jacob," Rosalind advised.

"I'll not forget Rosalind, I'll be on the beach at daybreak with the tractor and manure spreader; free fertiliser," he smiled.

"Tonight Jacob I have to return to heaven; only for one night then I will be with you by the time you've spread the manure tomorrow, breakfast will be on the table waiting for my husband."

"It's a long time since I've heard you call me your husband; warms my soul immensely Rosalind and you are my beautiful wife. I'm such a lucky man I must've really pleased God somewhere for him to return you to my life."

Jacob returned to his sheep to monitor and check if any more had lambed using his quad bike, and trailer pleased him immensely, saved a lot of walking. He watched the misty fog start to engulf the Moor. He dropped another bale of hay off in the sheep rack before heading to the buildings, hearing that strange sound coming from the clifftop. Jacob walked through the misty fog stopped by the fence on the top of the cliff, with Jack close by his heels, watching a bright light vanish.

Rosalind had returned to her spaceship discussing matters with Peter and Matthew. "I presume you are ready? Jacob will be on the beach around 8:30 PM in the morning."

Peter assured: "We are ready; he will have a full load, the maximum he can carry, five tons. We managed to acquire several hundred bodies, we processed and are on the way with the transport to the designated planets. What is the situation between you and Jacob; he appears to be extremely fond of you Rosalind."

"If all humans were like him, we wouldn't have a problem, I haven't detected unkind thoughts in his mind about me. Although at times he's a little suspicious, especially when I make things work and he cannot. I think the most difficult human thing to deal with is pretending to sleep; because we don't, I have to pretend until he's asleep then I can go about my business."

"I detect you are enjoying your assignment, Rosalind," Matthew remarked. "Don't become too attached, although I know highly unlikely; when we decide to eradicate the human race, he will be one of them remember that. Unless Peter and our other brothers and sisters find a way of instilling in humans, the necessity to work hand-in-hand with nature and not just greed and destroy."

"If that time comes before Jacob dies naturally, I may take him home, I enjoy his company," Rosalind remarked deep in thought.

Peter and Matthew glanced to one another considering Rosalind's remark. Peter responded, "he could not travel the vast distance in human form or withstand the prolonged acceleration. If we had solved the problem, we wouldn't be sending humans to feed the animals processed, would be far easier to ship them alive, for the animals to enjoy the chase, and add extra fertiliser to the planet's surface."

"I appreciate what you're saying Peter let's take one step at a time. I'm returning to the farm to ensure Jacob is on the beach ready for the consignment to be transferred." Rosalind flashed her eyes, stepping into the misty fog transporting to the farm. Although still dark outside their eyes shone like torches, she checked the tractor, and manure spreader is ready and returned to the house making breakfast. Jacob sat up in bed smelling bacon and eggs dressing quickly having a quick wash, he sat at the kitchen table enjoying his breakfast. "I haven't slept so peaceably for years now you're back in my life Rosalind, I couldn't wish for anything better," he smiled.

Rosalind kissed him on the cheek, "it's good to be home, don't forget fertiliser this morning Jacob."

"No, it's nearly 8 o'clock, I'll make my way down to the beach," standing up kissing Rosalind on the cheek heading out of the door to the tractor and spreader. The tractor started quickly much to Jacob surprise. Barely daylight the weather is overcast and beginning to snow, he pulled his coat tight trying to stay warm, standing up occasionally warming his hands on the exhaust pipe of the tractor. He finally made his way down onto the beach. He backed up to the water's edge standing by the tractor engine to stay warm the wind is quite vicious cutting along the coastline.

Jacob noticed the misty fog coming in off the sea, and the next minute engulfing the manure spreader and vanishing as if it never existed. He could see the spreader loaded to the brim with a powder. Jacob didn't bother to investigate the contents. He placed another piece of string around his coat, trying to stop the wind opening. He drove steadily up the steep track, the tractor struggling to gain traction, the stones were slippery coated in snow. Jacob breathed a sigh of relief, reaching the top travelling the short distance to the pastureland, spreading the fertiliser very thinly over the pasture. The tractor and spreader performed ideally much to Jacob surprise driving back to the shed. He parked throwing an old sheet over the bonnet of the tractor to keep the weather out of the engine.

Rosalind came from the house, grabbing Jacob's hand, he followed her indoors. "I fed the sheep Jacob and brought in another five ewes and their lambs. I think you should bring the rest of the flock in I've made room in the barn what do you think, husband?"

"I think you are a wonderful, clever wife." Jacob picking her up in his arms, kissing her gently on the lips. "We'll have a quick coffee; Jack and I will bring them in. You stay out of the cold, I don't want anything happening to you," he smiled reassuringly.

Rosalind is starting to enjoy the physical contact, some think totally unnecessary with her own brothers and sisters. They were pure energy created and programmed, mating is impossible in their pure form even if they shapeshifted, they could not participate in other species practices, strictly forbidden and futile.

Jacob patted Jack on the head. "Come on, let's have the sheep in while this weather persists, I don't want to lose any lambs." Rosalind watched them leave stepping out into the blizzarding snow sweeping across the Moor. Jack ran on finding the old ewes bunched behind large boulders. The sheep moved quickly; they knew they were heading for the buildings running on ahead of Jack. Jacob followed, shielding his eyes from the stinging snow. Rosalind had gone out, opening the gates watching the ewes run inside immediately starting to steam. She'd already placed a bale of hay in the rack and filled the troughs with fresh water at least the ewes could lambing comfort now. Jacob a few minutes later joined her at the barn. They both stood there watching whirlwinds curling into the air, twisting the snow in a never-ending dance. Jacob hugged Rosalind, "thanks for opening the gates I quite forgot; the ewes looked settled, it'll cost a bit to keep them in. I'll have to purchase some creep feed and nuts for the ewes; hopefully, the hay will last until spring. I'd make silage, but I don't have the equipment," he frowned disappointed with his own performance. They ran back into the house followed by Jack, who had turned white, caked in snow, he shook himself by the fire laying down. Rosalind made a coffee, commenting: "I've mended the television, Jacob."

Jacob didn't bother to comment, Rosalind could walk on water there is nothing she couldn't do, she'd always been the same. She placed a hand on his shoulder. "Jacob, you think we should buy a round baler, you can make silage perhaps another tractor." Rosalind had already read his thoughts to ascertain what he really wanted for the spring and summer?

Jacob smiled, "I wish, I'll keep the ewe lambs back, time to increase my flock. I have to change the Ram, as regards affording that sort of equipment only in my dreams," he sighed heavily.

"I'm returning to heaven this evening Jacob, I will talk to Jesus, perhaps he will assist, who knows," she remarked, passing a towel to Jacob to dry his hair and face.

He frowned: "You can't ask God or Jesus for anything else, I have you I will manage Rosalind," he insisted drinking his coffee.

"We shall see Jacob," Rosalind voiced, walking to the far end of the kitchen removing an old shoe-box bringing back to the table, she lifted the lid. Jacob stared in disbelief filled to the brim with money, he didn't realise the money is collected from corpses transported to the spaceship, which they usually burnt having no use for the currency themselves. "Rosalind! Where has it come from?"

"Oh, something I'd saved over the years since I was a child. This is my nest egg, our nest egg I should say. We must purchase out of our area, no one will be none the wiser don't you think husband?"

"I will not touch your savings as tempted as I am; you struggled all your life scrimping to accumulate. I'll not waste your money."

"It's our money, there's barely enough here to buy a second-hand baler and tractor not forgetting the bale wrapper. This is our future Jacob," she insisted firmly.

Jacob gently placed his hands around Rosalind's waist, easing her down onto his knee. "You are a woman to behold; giving without reservation. When the snow has cleared if you insist, I'll look in the farmers weekly and see what's about, the best time to buy is now. Nobody wants a round baler while it's snowing," he chuckled.

She kissed him on the cheek, moving to the kettle boiling the water to make another drink, she glanced from the window you could barely see a few yards in front of the house. After tea, Jacob went out to check on his ewes, discovering two more had lambs he placed them in pens, returning to the house shutting the door on a miserable evening. Rosalind and Jacob watched television for the first time together in four years until the clock struck 11 o'clock, they retired to the bedroom. Jacob drifting off to sleep after Rosalind had placed a hand on his forehead.

She changed quickly heading for the spaceship in the misty fog transporter, waiting for her at the front door. Rosalind walked into the bowels of the spaceship where humans were processed to be transported by another spaceship. Everything is automated the carcasses would come in stripped of any clothing left on the bodies, and laser cutters would remove the flesh away, leaving very few bones to travel with the meat. The rest of the material is incinerated turning into dust, ready for Jacob to spread on the field. Once the flesh is processed, entered an instantaneous blast freezer to keep fresh while they waited for the transport ship which came every month.

Rosalind imagined Jacob on the conveyor on his way to be processed. She jumped, bringing herself back to reality, this is the first time she'd suffered a scenario thought, which is most disturbing. She knew she is fond of Jacob, but couldn't bear the thought of him used as animal food. She is determined there would be a solution, although she feared her brothers and sisters had already read her mind and would be concerned with her thoughts.

Peter joined her, "Rosalind your thoughts are irrational for a Zibyan; you will have to accept the fact if I cannot find a solution, Jacob will die like the rest of the human race. They are little more than rodents, destroying everything of beauty. What makes matters worse, we created these monsters through meddling with the genetics of the chimpanzee. Now the chimpanzees suffer at the hands of these hybrids; we will stop them, Rosalind." Peter walked off, not waiting for Rosalind to reply. Rosalind thought she must not make her thoughts available to all, although it would be challenging to have anything private in the Zibyan culture, everyone is designed to read everyone else's opinions to prevent hostility amongst the collective.

Rosalind returned to the farm, remembering to change her appearance stepping from the misty fog transporter by the sheep pens, watching Jacob come from the house. He commented, "you ever sleep Rosalind you're always up before me," he chuckled.

"How'd you know I actually sleep Jacob," she remarked, patting his cheek. "I'll make breakfast while you feed the ewes and lambs, I see two more have lambed during the night." Rosalind walked off towards the house, she wondered how Jacob would react if he knew who she really is? She realised she is contemplating things she usually wouldn't. Zibyans never considered any other race to be of any significance; they were little more than a plaything, an experiment. When she was programmed, history showed, they had created everything, they were the beginning, and the end should it come to that. Rosalind remembered her first sense of consciousness, fully formed as pure energy. She remembered the computer instructing her on her abilities, considering, she was only an hour from creation. Rosalind quickly gathered her thoughts; her mind is wandering, she didn't know why Zibyans didn't behave similarly to her. Yes, they could think and solve problems, never pondered on the past very often she considered the computer has designed their thoughts never to look at history unless essential.

Except where planet Earth is concerned, created initially as a breeding ground for various types of lifeform, after several millions of years of development; mutating creatures until they made the grave mistake of humans. Many debates were held, some Zibyans wanted them exterminated immediately, and others wanted to see what the outcome would be. Now Zibyans know! Humans were in the same category as rabbits and rats and would have to be controlled. Rosalind thoughts returned to preparing egg and bacon with fried bread for Jacob; her mind kept wandering trying to solve issues if they were real issues. Jacob entered the house kissing Rosalind on the cheek fondly, sitting down to his breakfast with a large cup of coffee. "I'm afraid I put the Ram into early this year, a silly bloody mistake," he cursed, "at least will have early lambs but it does create an awful lot of hard work," he frowned.

Rosalind patted him on the shoulder, "We will survive Jacob, may add a few extra pounds towards our future. Look what I found last week's farmers weekly; I went for a walk along the cliff enjoying the fresh air from the sea, someone must have dropped the magazine, how lucky," she commented, placing on the table in front of Jacob. He glanced up grinning knowing Rosalind had somehow acquired this, she is not a patient woman when Rosalind wanted something, is now; which made him laugh even more. Rosalind had read his thoughts pretending to be surprised at his laughter, as he opened the farmers weekly looking down the for sale section.

CHAPTER 2

Rosalind's in Control

Jacob noticed to biro marks highlighting, one round baler and bale wrapper. A little further down the page, an old 188 Massey Ferguson tractor four-wheel-drive with eight thousand hours on the clock. In brackets, bale loader available for this tractor along with muck fork and bucket. Jacob glanced to Rosalind, "I presume you've already purchased?"

"No, Jacob it must be your decision as well, I have to admit, when I was in heaven, I made contact with the small dealership in South Wales asking their opinion of the machines. What would they do for a cash settlement? I didn't want us wasting our time travelling," she remarked casually.

Jacob burst out laughing, "I presume you've worked out how we're going to travel there, my Land Rover isn't road legal as you reminded me."

"Well yes sort of, Jesus has arranged this for us, a little risky," she remarked, slipping on her coat passing Jacob his. She held his hand, leading him out of the front door into a misty fog; wasn't there earlier. Jacob suddenly feeling ill with the speed of travel; this is one of the problems Zibyans were trying to resolve when transporting humans over vast distances alive. Humans physiology couldn't stand the acceleration. Lucky as the crow flies; only three hundred or so miles away from where they lived on the moor. Jacob started to recover as he stepped from the mist into brilliant sunshine with Rosalind. She held his hand tightly, guiding him in the direction of the machinery dealership. She'd already travelled herself, making sure the equipment is sound to purchase before ever considering mentioning to Jacob. They entered the storage yard Rosalind showing Jacob the equipment. "Looks wonderful Rosalind for its age, can we afford it," Jacob sighed?

"Lead the negotiations to me, Jacob," she smiled, kissing him on the cheek, she walked off to the sales office with her shoe-box tucked under her arm. Rosalind entered the office, holding the sales rep's hand. She is now in control; she agreed the price she thought is fair, plus delivery to the farm over the next couple of weeks. The sales rep wrote out a sale ticket with a six-month warranty on the pieces of equipment.

Rosalind left the sales office enjoying the ability to manipulate situations, she had generally taken for granted. "I paid the salesperson they will deliver in a couple of weeks, come on, let's go home out of this miserable weather, starting to look overcast again Jacob," Rosalind smiled. Her facial expressions were becoming more comfortable to perform these days. They walked off into a small woodland stepping into the misty fog and were immediately transported to the Moor, Jacobs farm. He stepped from the mist falling over, struggling to control his sense of balance. Rosalind realised what is killing the humans in transport; their brains were being turned inside out in their skulls, their balance couldn't handle the velocity of travel.

Peter aboard the spaceship is receiving the information from Rosalind, realising if they sedated the humans while travelling, this might solve the problem and a way of transporting to the home planet for distribution as animal feed.

Rosalind helped Jacob into the house, sitting him by the fire in his armchair, making him a coffee; while he gathered his thoughts. She hoped no permanent damage is caused to him during transport as it had killed so many other humans. Rosalind left Jacob to rest venturing outside in the snow to check on the sheep; lambing appeared to be in full swing; 10 ewes had lambed. She carefully checked the animals, placing in pens marking each lamb with its own number so it would never be lost.

Jacob glanced to the mantelpiece looking at the urn with Rosalind's Ashes. He rose to his feet suspicious of everything, he opened the top of the urn Rosalind's Ashes were gone? Had Jesus or God re-created his Rosalind? Perhaps he is irrational, he concluded, and shouldn't be questioning the gift of Rosalind. Jacob realised for the first time in years, he's smiling, that is thanks to Rosalind, she made his life perfect or as perfect as it can be living on the Moor. He watched Rosalind come in from the cold, not in the slightest bothered by the plummeting temperature. "Do you feel better, Jacob?" she asked, concerned.

"Yes, thank you, I presume we travelled the distance in seconds and my sense of balance couldn't cope although it never affected you, Rosalind?"

"You must remember Jacob, I am accustomed to travelling at high speed; when you live in heaven that is the way you travel. God wouldn't have subjected you to the speed if he didn't think you would survive Jacob. That would rather defeat his plans for you which there are many, he will enlighten you as time progresses. What did you really think of the equipment Jacob are you pleased?"

"Very pleased; you selected excellently, I hope we have operators manuals with the equipment? I've never used a round baler only a conventional one. I have used a tractor and loader before when my dad hired one from a friend. One year there was so much seaweed washed up on the shore, a golden opportunity for free fertiliser, my father and I trailered it and stockpiled," Jacob reminisced. Rosalind smiled, "you have nothing to worry about Jacob; I've used a round baler and a tractor and loader before we were married, on work experience, and the bale wrapper which virtually operates itself," she assured confidently.

"That was years ago Rosalind things have changed," Jacob smiled.

She patted Jacob on the head. "Why do you think I selected that particular round baler, bale wrapper tractor and loader; because those were the ones I'd driven before," Rosalind actually chuckled for the first time.

Jacob shook his head; venturing outside to check the ewes and lambs once more before retiring to bed, finding more ewes had delivered. He marked the individual lambs and mothers penning them together, running short of space he realised before returning to the house with Jack close to his heels. He and Rosalind sat together on the old settee watching television until 11:30 PM, before venturing into the bedroom. Rosalind lay in bed kissing Jacob on the forehead, touching him with her hand he fell into a deep sleep. She immediately changed her appearance stepping outside the front door into the misty fog transporting to the spaceship, flashing her eyes to Peter and Matthew with the usual greeting. "We are running tests after we heard the conversation between you and Jacob; you must be very careful Rosalind, I think he's quite suspicious of everything," Peter suggested.

"I have Jacob under my control Peter, he's blissfully unaware of who I really am; he believes Jesus and God sent me to him, he accepts that explanation wholeheartedly."

Matthew suggested: "While we are all together, I would strongly recommend our next shipment of humans should come from the Arab countries. I have seen the way they treat animals, I want animals to have the opportunity to return the compliment."

Both Rosalind and Peter glanced to Matthew, surprised at his suggestion. "Nothing has changed for centuries Matthew what suddenly brings this to your urgent attention?" Peter asked.

"I have been here the same length at you two for thousands of years, we are fortunate we never age, or our powers deplete. I have watched the animal activists, try to protect the creatures of burden from punishment. Our fault Peter we made the donkey special allowing Jesus to use him to ride into Bethlehem on you remember?"

Peter turned to look at Matthew: "We have made many errors Matthew, my brother; we could use this situation to our advantage. We know Jacob travelled merely three hundred miles in our transport, which made him ill, not fatally thankfully. I suggest you try and transport alive Arab to hear; if he survives sedate him, and accumulate sufficient for the transport vessel, we will send live food to the animals to enjoy the chase. I think that is what's called sweet revenge by humans."

Both Matthew and Rosalind flashed their eyes, approving Peter's suggestion. Rosalind commented, "if you can't transport them alive Matthew to hear, I would suggest you send out a stun ray and discreetly render the individual unconscious, transport them here, and sedate for the journey to the home planet for distribution."

Matthew flashed his eyes frantically almost excited by the approval, disappearing to the rear of the spaceship to make preparations. Peter looked at Rosalind flashing his eyes, "you must return to Jacob before he wakes, although you appear to have the situation under control Rosalind. We were fortunate your experiment with Jacob showed us the way forward. I hear our collective praising your name," Peter flashed his eyes walking off in human form.

Rosalind made her way along the corridor, stepping into the misty fog immediately changing her appearance, reappearing by the sheep in the barn. Much to her surprise, Jacob is already out there shining his torch checking on his sheep. Jacob jumped, "I came out looking for you Rosalind you weren't in bed. I presumed you were here with the sheep. Where have you been?"

"Well if you must know Jacob, I ran away with a little green man who came to earth in a spaceship. Actually, I went for a quiet walk to gather my thoughts," she assured. "That reminds me, we are short of groceries Jacob you will have to visit the local shop. I will write down the list of things I want you to purchase for me," she patted his cheek. "I'll make breakfast." Rosalind walked off before Jacob could make another comment. He couldn't help smiling; he could never remember Rosalind quite so outspoken, but he didn't care; she is here making his life perfect and fulfilled.

Jacob entered the house finding his breakfast on the table, 3 slices of fried bread, each with an egg on top coated with baked beans. Jacob smiled pleasantly grabbing a crusty slice of bread mopping his plate, making sure there wasn't a morsel left. Jack had sat there waiting for a scrap, Rosalind opened the front door throwing a bone outside. Jack ran out to retrieve from the snow realising he is conned. Rosalind had shut him outside with the bone so he couldn't make a mess on the floor. Jack wandered off, laying between bales of straw crunching on his bone.

Jacob kissed Rosalind on the cheek, "I hope my old Land Rover will make it across the Moor, the snow may have drifted in places on the track," he suggested quite concerned, watching Rosalind place her thick coat on and gloves.

"I'll come with you Jacob, I've already thrown a shovel in the back of the Land Rover just in case," she smiled, displaying a human expression.

"Don't be silly Rosalind your freeze out there; I don't want anything to happen to you," he assured firmly.

"In which case, I'd better drive," she grinned quite enjoying using human facial expressions which she is now becoming accustomed to. Jacob burst out laughing following Rosalind out of the door. She climbed into the driver's side of the Land Rover, checking her memory banks. Selected four-wheel-drive starting the old diesel engine, studying a G P S map in her computerised mind of exactly where the track is under the snow. There were no visible landmarks left apart from the odd rock. Jacob sat there, astounded by her skill. She knew the Moor like him, but he'd never imagined she could drive the Land Rover on the old track when you couldn't see where it is in places, another miracle to behold he thought.

Rosalind left the Moor, driving on the snow-covered road. Jacob is absolutely shocked, she preached to him the vehicle wasn't roadworthy, yet she is on the side road heading for the shop. Admittedly he thought the chances of seeing a police officer were very slim in these conditions. Rosalind parked outside the shop, Jacob said nothing. They both entered Rosalind grabbed the trolley, and by the time he'd reached the checkout, there wasn't room to put anything else in. Jacob dreaded the bill suspecting to be horrendous. Rosalind smiled at the cashier when the bill came to £120 which Rosalind paid for in cash. Jacob had already started stacking the groceries into boxes provided by the store, glad to be rid of them. He slowly carried each box outside into the blizzarding snow, placing in the back of his Land Rover, pulling down the tarpaulin to prevent the snow penetrating.

Rosalind sat in the driver's seat again, Jacob sat there grinning, watching Rosalind select four-wheel-drive, heading back the way they came. She left the road cutting across the Moor, she could see faint tracks from where they came across to the shop, which made it easier to find their way home. Jacob had to ask: "I see it's okay for you to drive on the road with a dodgy vehicle and not me?"

She grinned, patting Jacob's leg, "I'm in full control Jacob of any eventuality, you've known me long enough, I only take calculated risks. I shouldn't imagine a policeman is within a hundred miles of the shop in these conditions."

He didn't bother to reply, looked across the bleak Moor barely able to see a hundred yards in front of him and somewhat relieved to be home. Jacob quickly carried the boxes of groceries into the kitchen for Rosalind to disperse amongst the shelving. He kissed her on the cheek venturing outside again to check on the ewes; only to discover another 10 had lambed, Jacob quickly checked their health and marked with a number, realising he'd forgotten all about Christmas, already, 31 December. Rosalind hadn't reminded him which he thought is strange; she always used to like Christmas. Jacob sighed heavily walking back to the house, finding

Rosalind busily stacking shelves. "We didn't celebrate Christmas Rosalind," Jacob expressed concerned.

She smiled, "I thought I'm your Christmas present. Jesus wasn't born on 25 December, you know that is a made update for convenience Jacob, so why celebrate something false?"

He placed his hands in the air in the surrendering posture, kissing Rosalind on the cheek. She looked away continuing with her groceries, while Jacob sat by the fire with Jack by his chair.

Rosalind, enjoying living on the farm with Jacob immensely, in the thousands of years she'd been on earth; she had never ventured far from the spaceship only once betraying Mary Magdalene. She found humans extraordinarily boring and repetitive. They seem to be only interested in procreation, inflicting misery on another creature and destroying the planet, which supports their very existence. Jacob is different, she enjoyed his company, although he wasn't her own kind, he had good quality's, he is her pet to do as she pleased with. Although thought pet is being somewhat demeaning. She is quite surprised he hasn't tried to venture further than kissing, which male and female humans seem to enjoy participating in. Rosalind carried a mug of coffee to Jacob waking him, he'd fallen asleep in the chair. "Don't forget Jacob tomorrow fertiliser, I know the weather is foul if you like I will collect the fertiliser?"

"No, I can manage you sure it will arrive in these conditions, Rosalind?"

"Yes, the fertiliser will arrive, but this will be the last load for some time, I suspect it's nothing you've done Jacob there's a slight change of plans I believe."

"Oh well, we mustn't complain," he smiled, drinking his coffee quite suspicious of the whole operation.

Jacob and Rosalind retired to bed; she kissed him on the forehead holding his hand. Jacob immediately fell asleep. Rosalind slid out of bed, changing her appearance walking to the front door; she stepped into the misty fog transported to the spaceship. Peter is waiting for her, "we have success Rosalind, admittedly Matthew has to transmit a stun ray; he managed to wipe out a Sahara Desert tribe in one mission. They are sedated the transport ship is due here in the next hour. They will be shipped alive and make conscious before dispersed amongst the planets for the animals to enjoy the chase. The humans will learn what it's like to be ill-treated, they will finally experience my writings of hell."

"I hope Peter the home planet will record events, I want to see the humans suffer the way they made the animals in their charge."

"I agree with you sister, I will summon you when the information arrives; we should have within seven days. The seventh-day, the sabbath as I named in the Bible, which the humans fail to observe in most cases. What are these thoughts in your processor Rosalind of experimenting further with Jacob? There is no need for you to subject your systems to intercourse; serves no purpose we know all there is to know."

"Are you instructing me, Peter, not to experiment further with Jacob? Have any Zibyan's attempted such a task to find out the fascinations? We have watched and experimented with humans. Not one Zibyan has actually experienced the information. If I find it displeasing, I'm sure the central computer will rectify my memory banks."

Peter and Rosalind flashed their eyes at each other in respect. Peter moved away, changing his form into pure light. Rosalind walked down the corridor stepping into the misty fog, changing her appearance transported to the sheep, noticing there were more lambs born during the night. She quickly marked and separated into pens before returning to the house. Jacob yawning coming out of there bedroom, watching Rosalind start to prepare breakfast. "There's no need to go out Jacob, they're fine, more lambs," she smiled. "Oh yes, don't forget, have your breakfast and head down to the beach; be careful the rocks will be slippy on the track I don't want anything to happen to you," patting his cheek. Jacob quickly devoured his breakfast, not wishing to be late for the Lord's work.

"I'll be careful," slipping on his thick old army overcoat along with his woolly gloves and cap, he stepped out of the house. He shielded his eyes from the blizzard removing the old tarpaulin from the bonnet of his tractor, struggling to get her to start. Finally, with a cloud of black smoke from the exhaust pipe, the old Fordson major burst into life. He steadily drove along the track slowly descending, feeling the tractor slipping and sliding a very precarious descent. Eventually reaching the beach, he drove some distance and parked where he had before. Jacob left the tractor running; he dare not stop the engine in case she wouldn't start again. He noticed the thick misty fog approach from far out to sea, engulfing his manure spreader. Jacob felt the tractor shudder as the load is placed in the spreader. He watched the misty fog vanish into thin air as if it never existed, he glanced back to see the spreader loaded with a fine powder. Jacob drove steadily along the beach looking at the slope he would have to climb, he selected a lower gear and opened the tractor throttle considerably; he attempted to climb selecting differential lock to increase his traction.

Rosalind had turned herself invisible, watching everything from the clifftop; she could see the old tractor is struggling to acquire sufficient traction. Jacob finally levelled out on top of the cliff heading straight for the pastureland, immediately discharging the contents of the manure spreader across the covered grass, turning the snow a grey colour where he travelled.

Rosalind returned to the house, she quickly changed her appearance waiting for Jacob to return. She heard him parked the tractor by the barn. Jacob quickly checked the ewes to see if there were any more lambs before dashing into the house. Rosalind helped him remove his coat hanging on the back of the door where it could drip without causing too much mess. "I shan't be going down there again with the tractor for a while Rosalind to dangerous; I didn't think I'd make it back," he remarked, sitting at the kitchen table. Rosalind made the coffee passing a mug to Jacob, she sat quietly opposite receiving a telepathic message from Peter. "The transport ship had left Earth's atmosphere, heading home with a live consignment." Rosalind didn't flinch, she didn't want Jacob to realise someone is communicating with her. The wind started to howl drifting the snow, Jacob hoped the thatched roof would hold fast in these conditions. Rosalind realised Jacob is anxious after reading his thoughts. She placed her hand on his forehead; he drifted off to sleep. Jack laying by the fire, glanced to Rosalind and looked away. Rosalind carefully carried Jacob to his armchair, positioning him comfortably. She changed her appearance stepping from the house into the misty fog transported directly to the spaceship many fathoms below the sea.

"What are you not telling me, Peter," Rosalind asked.

"I am concealing nothing Rosalind, although I am concerned this will be the first live shipment of humans, unconscious they are harmless. When they are awake, they are dangerous as you've seen for yourself."

"You notified the ship commander Peter of his cargo, only a matter of a maximum of four days, depending on the weight he's carrying. I foresee no problems. Here's Matthew approaching. What is your view Matthew," Rosalind asked.

"Peter is right to be cautious; we are dealing with the unknown. We have never transported live humans before; although they are sedated at the moment. Once they're on the designated planets and revived, who knows what will happen? We will have to wait for the information to be transmitted to us."

Rosalind enquired: "How many humans are on board the transport ship? They are in sealed containers, I presume Matthew?"

"Yes Rosalind and with a force field in place, anyone who left the containment area would be exterminated. We've only sent 200 as a test."

"We must remember; the atmosphere they are entering, when they regain consciousness is very thin, not formed properly at the moment. The humans will struggle to perform if they can't breathe adequately. We are not affected by such restrictions, don't forget, we can destroy with one touch. They are insignificant in the scheme of things," Rosalind assured.

Peter and Matthew flashed their eyes at Rosalind. Peter spoke, "we gain strength from your positive thoughts, Rosalind, I'm sure Matthew will agree everything you have said is the truth; although I do detest violence, except against violent beings."

Rosalind flashed her eyes; Peter and Matthew responded vanishing. Rosalind stepped into the misty fog waiting for her at the end of the corridor. She changed her appearance while transported to the farm. She checked the ewes and lambs and the thatched roof before returning to the house, hoping she can allay Jacob's fears. She smiled, noticing he's drinking a pint of his home-brew, sitting at the kitchen table. "Where have you been," Jacob asked in a serious tone.

Rosalind realised, he'd had more than one pint of home-brew by the slur in his voice. "Checking the sheep not sitting here drinking the Devils poison. One glass is sufficient, more is sinful Jacob," Rosalind remarked. She Grabbed the glass pouring the remainder down the sink. Before Jacob could move, Rosalind touched his forehead, Jacob is unconscious, she carried him into the bedroom, casting on the bed in an unceremonious action, disgusted with Jacob's behaviour. Jack, the faithful sheepdog, stayed by the hearth sensing Rosalind could harm him.

Jacob awoke the next morning with a hangover, he dressed and wandered into the kitchen holding his head; discovering Rosalind about to make breakfast pouring him a coffee. Neither spoke; Jacob is ashamed of himself and decided to break the ice with the words: "I apologise for my behaviour Rosalind."

"I'll check the sheep Jacob," she remarked, heading for the door, slipping on her coat, leaving Jacob to make his own breakfast. Rosalind discovered lambs appeared to be everywhere. She spent some time sorting out which lambs belong to which ewe. She would be glad when lambing is finished, and thankfully the air is decidedly warmer this morning. Rosalind fed the sheep returning to the house to find Jacob had made breakfast for her, which she didn't really want.

Nevertheless, she would have to consume and dispose of at a later date when he wasn't looking. She knew if she discharged the unwanted food, Jack would gladly eat quickly. Jacob said nothing pouring the coffee slipping on his coat heading outside. Rosalind grinned, placing her plate on the floor quickly. Jack cleared within seconds. She put the plate in the sink along with the other dirty cutlery and started washing up before Jacob returned.

Jack started barking, he could hear something. Rosalind glanced to the door slightly concerned, Jack wouldn't bark if Jacob is approaching. Rosalind cautiously opened the door she could see nothing and sensed nothing. Jack ran between Rosalind's legs heading across the Moor barking. Jacob came running to the house, "what's upset, Jack?"

"I have no idea Jacob, I can't see anything, can you?"

Jacob scanned after grabbing his binoculars from the window sill, noticing some distance ahead, Jack herding a ewe and two lambs towards the buildings. Jacob chuckled, "that old dog doesn't miss a trick and can count the flock better than me. I hadn't realised a ewe was missing." He went outside opening the pen, placing some hay and sheep nuts for the old ewe; she'd come home with two beautiful lambs. He marked them with a number marking the old ewe with a unique mark, so he knew she would have to stay; whatever happened she is not to be sold to valuable. Jacob returned to the house, mixing a bowl of food for Jack. Patting him, placing the bowl on the floor. He hadn't realised this is a bonus meal for Jack he'd already had bacon and eggs. Jack looked in his bowl less than impressed with what is on offer after Rosalind had fed him. Jacob embraced Rosalind taking her entirely by surprise, she rather enjoyed the closeness sending strange sensations to her mind; for the first time since she'd returned Jacob passionately kissed her. This is definitely different; she knew what he is performing, she'd watched hundreds of humans do the same. Although never experienced the sensation herself until now.

A week had passed Rosalind received a telepathic message from Peter, "he'd received a transmission from the home planet; she is to return to the spaceship as soon as possible." Rosalind moved away, patting Jacob's cheek.

"I'm taking a walk Jacob down onto the beach, there isn't a chill in the air this morning. I need some fresh air," she smiled, slipping on her coat.

"I'll stay here Rosalind and look after the sheep; be careful on those slippy stones. I know the snow is starting to melt; we could still have more though, I don't think winters finished with us yet."

She smiled, leaving the house, walking to the end of the barn she stepped into the misty fog, transported aboard the spaceship. Peter and Matthew were waiting for her; they greeted each other with a flash of their eyes. Rosalind sat on something you couldn't see as if suspended without any support, Matthew and Peter sat similarly. They watched intently the whole wall became a film as if they were actually on the planet themselves. The naked humans were released from their unconsciousness, standing to look around. Firstly alarmed they were naked and secondly hearing the sound of what appeared to be ferocious animals growling in the vegetation. The human scattered into the undergrowth mothers and children alike; males grabbing sticks in their attempt to protect themselves from whatever they were facing. Not very long before screaming could be heard, they watched a woman torn apart by lions. Peter commented: "Excellent now the humans know what it's like to have pain in flicked it on them, without having any defence." They spent the next two hours watching humans torn apart by various animals. Matthew remarked, "a very successful mission, everything went according to plan. I must start and search for my next victims; finally, we have a use for humans not only feeding our pets but entertainment as well for our brothers and sisters."

Rosalind, Peter and Matthew glanced to one another, flashing their eyes, each going their separate ways. Rosalind changed and transported to the beach. She hadn't realised Jacob is stood on the cliff watching her step from the misty fog. Jacob quickly moved away, so she didn't see him walking back to the buildings with Jack. By the time Rosalind had joined him, Jacob is feeding the sheep and checking on the newly born lambs. Rosalind read his thoughts realising what he'd seen, deciding to say nothing for the moment and see what transpired. She could dismiss simply by saying that is the way she travelled from heaven. Whether he would, believe it or not, is another story. Rosalind returned to the house starting to prepare lunch. Jacob stayed outside with the sheep deciding to take a walk down onto the beach to make sure his eyes were not deceiving him. He slowly walked along the water's edge, the waves gently advanced towards the cliff. Jacob noticed Rosalind's footsteps suddenly appear in the sand heading to the track from the beach. He now had confirmation he didn't imagine things, he stood for a moment looking out to sea for any signs of a vessel. Jacob sighed heavily, slowly walking from the beach, returning to the farm buildings and his beloved sheep.

Rosalind called from the doorway. "Jacob lunch."

Jacob responded: "I'll be there in a minute." He wondered whether he should say anything concerning his suspicions; perhaps he should watch Rosalind a little closer before confronting her with his concerns. After all, he'd long to have his wife, why destroy something, he wanted by opening his mouth and probably saying the wrong thing. He entered the house sitting quietly at the table, enjoying his beautiful lunch. Rosalind reading his mind, understanding his past thoughts concerning what he saw. She knew this would fester in his mind; she decided to repel any suspicions he may have. "You noticed me returning from heaven, Jacob, and you never mentioned why? Are you keeping secrets from your wife now?"

He exhaled, lowering his knife and fork to the plate. "That's not what I envisage; when you go to heaven, I thought it would be vertical; not horizontal and coming in from the ocean in a misty fog."

"I should imagine, God and Jesus must be rolling about in heaven laughing at your comment Jacob; you have no idea what heaven is like. You only perceive what you think is right, not what God thinks is right. If I were you, I would dismiss your ignorant thoughts before I'm taken away from you again," Rosalind warned.

Jacob didn't reply; he continued to finish his lunch. "Thank you! I enjoyed immensely," Jacob moving from the table; slipping on his coat, grabbing his crook from by the door going outside. He jumped in his Land Rover heading across the Moor parked on the edge; he walked the mile to the shop. Jacob purchased a newspaper returning to his Land Rover, he sat catching up with world events, hoping there is something in there would give him a clue to what he didn't know. All he had his suspicions. Jacob noticed a small piece written about a tribe who lived in the Sahara Desert, had vanished without a trace; the only thing remaining is the animals roaming freely.

Rosalind reading his thoughts, Jacob wasn't the push-over she'd envisaged, she is convinced he is so in love with the Bible; he would believe anything she said to cover her tracks.

Jacob knew something didn't feel right; he just couldn't put his finger on what it is. Rosalind is correct how would he know how God operated? Why couldn't Rosalind come in from the sea in a misty fog, make no sense for her to travel here in full view? If she is seen by somebody, there would be an uproar. He exhaled, folding the newspaper placing on the passenger seat, he steadily drove home with more questions than answers. Jacob checked the ewes before venturing in the house. Rosalind sat watching television, Coronation Street, which made him smile; she used to be addicted to the program when they first married. Rosalind must be Rosalind, there could be no other explanation he concluded.

She smiled, placing the kettle on the stove, reading his thoughts as she made the tea passing Jacob a cup in his armchair by the fire. She returned to the settee turning the channel over on the television with the remote watching Emmerdale farm. Jacob nearly burst out laughing, this had to be Rosalind, another one of her favourite programs, although as far as he is concerned is an absolute load of tripe; the farming aspect is no longer there. Jacob fell asleep in the chair with Jack close by. Rosalind placed her hand gently on Jacob's forehead, changing her appearance, she walked out of the door stepping into the misty fog transporting her directly to the spaceship.

Peter is waiting, flashing his eyes: "You will have to be more careful Rosalind if you keep raising his suspicions, you could be in trouble. Although he couldn't harm you, he could direct the other humans to our spaceship location."

"Understood Peter, surprised he is suspicious or may have been just a stroke of luck as humans would describe."

"Now we can transport humans alive, you could actually dispose of him; we no longer need to spread human remains on land Rosalind."

"No, we don't know what will happen in the near future, I will keep him. I find the whole experience rather intriguing, he is quite unpredictable at times."

"I can't understand your fascination with one human male; he's not even what humans would call attractive. We certainly wouldn't rate him as anything other than animal food Rosalind. Perhaps you should stay away from the farm for a few weeks or permanently would be a better solution."

"Our brothers and sisters gave him to me, are you saying you have all changed your mind, I'm now to abandon my experiments, with Jacob?"

"Your brothers and sisters will not prevent you from carrying out whatever experiments you see fit. They are like me concerned you are becoming too involved with an inferior species of little value to the Zibyans. You are unlikely to discover anything we haven't already."

"That is why I am a higher grade scientist than you, Peter; that is how we discovered the best way to transport humans alive thanks to me, Peter!" She flashed her eyes, walking away, starting to understand why humans became annoyed, something she hadn't experienced before until now. Rosalind changed her appearance, stepping into the misty fog transporting to the beach. She stepped out onto the sand, slowly walking along the beach until she ascended the old track, carved in the cliffside hundreds of years ago by peasant farmers to transport seaweed for fertiliser. She finally reached the farm noticing Jacob checking the ewes, separating the final two ewes completing the lambing for this year. Jacob couldn't believe he hadn't lost a lamb a miracle in itself. Rosalind read his mind smiling at his thoughts not only of the sheep but her.

Jacob, without warning, scooped Rosalind up in his arms, she placed her arm quickly around his neck firmly, wondering what he's planning. She read his mind to ascertain if she is in danger or not. Rosalind smiled realising what he is trying to achieve now and had to make the decision did she want to go that far? She allowed Jacob to carry her into the house, he lowered her to her feet. Rosalind didn't know whether she is relieved or disappointed, he hadn't gone further. He kissed her very lovingly as he always did, there is nothing aggressive about Jacob in the slightest, which she quite admired. She quickly made two coffees while Jacob threw wood on the fire. She rejoined him carrying 2 cups; he sat in his armchair and Rosalind decided to sit on his lap, she never saw Jacob smile so much since she'd known him. Jacob started kissing her neck. Rosalind is intrigued she watched his fingers slowly unbutton her blouse, sliding his hand inside and caressing her. Rosalind had strange senses running through her, nothing is unpleasant. She jumped to her feet, holding Jacob's hand, leading him into the bedroom, she removed her clothes laying on the bed Jacob did likewise. Finally, Rosalind had experienced lovemaking which she didn't find an uncomfortable experience. However, from a Zibyans perspective, the sensation is similar to plugging yourself into the electric mains, she would receive the same tingling sensation, less the messy stuff.

They both showered and dressed, Jacob is now convinced this had to be Rosalind, Rosalind is reading his mind, pleased with the outcome, his suspicions had drifted off into the back of his mind. She made two more drinks sitting watching television for the rest of the evening; while Jacob went out to check on the ewes and lambs. When he finally returned, they retired to bed Rosalind placed her hand in his and Jacob entered into a deep sleep. She quickly changed her appearance heading for the door stepping in the misty fog transported to the spaceship. Peter and Matthew were both waiting for her arrival; they flash their eyes at each other in a pleasant manner. They sat side-by-side, watching more transmissions from the three planets they were slowly turning into replicas of earth. Rosalind noticed, the humans transported to the planets, still found time for sex, although they were likely to die soon ravaged by the wildlife. She couldn't understand the fascination and concluded it's because she wasn't human. She watched the two-hour transmission and about to leave. Peter commented, "have you finished experimenting Rosalind;

there isn't much else you can do with him now he might as well go on the next shipment."

"No, I have not finished with him and may keep him till he dies a natural death; unless I decide to send him as animal food." Rosalind walked off, which is rather rude not acknowledging Peter or Matthew with the courteous eye flash.

Matthew and Peter appeared in front of her, inhibiting her return to the farm. "You may not leave the spaceship until we receive a courteous acknowledgement; you are aware of the rules Rosalind, no Zibyan may dishonour another."

Rosalind knew she couldn't overpower two, wondered why the thought had ever entered her mind. She flashed her eyes at Peter and Matthew. They moved aside; Rosalind continued stepping into the misty fog transporting to the beach.

On the clifftop, Jacob watched Rosalind step from the misty fog onto the sand. He returned to the sheep realising he would have to accept the fact he didn't understand heaven, or God and how things worked. He's a mere mortal in the scheme of things little more than an insect in God's eyes. Rosalind read his thoughts as she walked from the beach. She concluded the more times he saw her step from the misty fog, the less suspicious he would become. He would eventually accept, she would have to travel to heaven occasionally.

Rosalind approached Jacob kissing him on the cheek. "I'll make breakfast," she continued walking to the house, preparing breakfast. She would make believe she had eaten something before Jacob arrived; saving her discharging on wanted food. Although Jack thought terrific, he'd never lived so high and mighty before, only had scraps and dog biscuits.

Jacob came into the house, sitting down for a lovely bacon and egg breakfast. "I saw you watching me from the cliff, Jacob. Does it bother you? I have to travel occasionally."

"I must admit Rosalind I find it strange; although its God's wish and I'm a lucky man to have his wife, I will have to accept what is. I'm in no position to question what God decides is right or wrong," Jacob expressed honestly.

Rosalind smiled: "God will be pleased with your attitude. Jacob, you will see many strange things God performs, you are a privileged one; except what is and enjoy his glorious gift of me."

He smiled glancing to Rosalind, "you are surely a gift, turning my life away from misery."

"You may receive a greater gift of travel through the heavens, to a place far beyond your imagination; no other human has visited until they are dead," she suggested conjuring another experiment.

Jacob stared bewildered: "you mean, I will visit heaven, surely not until my allotted time?"

"The journey will not be easy Jacob you may suffer from travel sickness," she chuckled.

"Who will look after the animals, you can't leave them to starve Rosalind, wait until they are on the moor again," Jacob suggested trying to stop smiling.

Rosalind cleared the table washing everything in the sink. She dried her hands on the tea towel, slipping on her coat. "let us walked Jacob across the Moor," she remarked, looking out of the window. "Not a bad morning, I remember when we first met; you nearly walked my legs off across the Moor," she laughed checking her memory banks for information on Rosalind and her likes and dislikes. He smiled slipping on his coat, grabbing his crook opening the door Rosalind stepped out followed by Jack. They followed the well-worn sheep tracks carved out by animals over the centuries. The air is brisk with the grey covered sky in places; at this time of year, the weather can change in seconds. They walked for two hours, noticing the grass is recovering as the snow cleared. Jacob is desperate to have the sheep outside again; the cost of feeding them indoors is draining his profits. The only thing that killed lambs more than anything else is wet weather, cold they can stand hiding behind their mothers or rocks. Rosalind and Jacob returned to the farm deciding to release half the flock with the eldest lambs. The old ewes were keen the thought of eating fresh grass appealed to them, the lambs followed quickly. Rosalind suggested, "let's walk down onto the beach, you never know there may be a surprise there for you, Jacob!"

"You keeping secrets from me again, woman," he patted her backside, holding her hand. They strolled off towards the beach down the rocky track cut into the cliff face, finally reaching the sand. The smell of the sea air is always fresh and inviting to the nostrils. Jacob had spent some time down here when he was younger fishing catching mackerel and plaice. Rosalind suggested, "you should come fishing Jacob; good protein, I remember you bringing me fishing once, and we ended up behind that rock over there," Rosalind displayed a grin.

He chuckled remembering what had taken place and he still managed to catch half a dozen fish. Jacob scooped Rosalind up in his arms, carrying her towards the rocks. She struggled to escape. "I prefer the bed," she smiled.

"I know the old bones there not what they used to be, I prefer a little comfort." Jacob noticed the misty fog coming in from the sea, a narrow strip no more than 3 meters wide. Rosalind smiled realising Peter had prepared a welcome for Jacob and had agreed with her thoughts of transporting him. Rosalind encouraged, "come along Jacob nothing will harm you. You are with me." They both walked into the misty fog; within seconds they were aboard the spaceship, Jacob looked watching the fish swim past unconcerned. Peter appeared in his robe along with Matthew. Jacob believed he is in the presence of disciples dropped to his knees in respect. "Stand Jacob, I am Peter one of the Lord's disciples, and this is Matthew, you read his Scriptures not so long ago; we watched you from heaven."

Jacob stood with his head, bowed: "Thank God for returning Rosalind to me. I was wandering in the history of despair until Rosalind returned to me by our Lord."

"Jesus considers you worthy Jacob, one of the few who have not turned their back on the Lord. The world has turned into Sodom and Gomorrah. God will not permit this behaviour to continue."

"What is the Lord's command and I will obey," Jacob assured.

"When the Lord has decided; Rosalind will bring you to me again, Jacob. I have many tasks to perform, Rosalind will take you home where you may enjoy each other's company with the Lord's blessing." Jacob watched what appeared to be an angel, floating, approach Peter carrying fishing rods. The angel passed the fishing tackle to Peter. "A gift from me Jacob, I am a fisherman of men, you may fish the sea with Rosalind." Peter passed the fishing rods and wicker basket to Jacob and Rosalind. Jacob bowed to Peter and Matthew. Rosalind flashed her eyes to Peter and Matthew, escorting Jacob along the corridor into the misty fog. In a second they were on the beach; Jacob held his head looking out to sea there is nothing, only the waves lapping against the shoreline. Jacob walked to the cliff face sitting on a rock looking at the fishing tackle. Rosalind joined him, she could see from his expression her plan is working; there is no doubt in Jacob's mind about Peter or Matthew. "What happens now, Rosalind?" Jacob asked.

"Nothing, we continue as we are enjoying each other's company running our small farm. Although I think we should fish for a while don't you Jacob," she smiled, checking her memory banks on how to set up a fishing rod correctly.

Jacob set up his fishing rod casting out to sea; they spent the next two hours fishing each catching a large plaice. As Rosalind wound in her line for the last time, she caught a large cod. Jacob surprised, although he did notice she could cast further out to sea then he could. Jacob gutted the fish leaving for the Seagulls; they strolled back to the farm carrying what they'd caught.

Rosalind started to prepare their evening meal while Jacob went outside, checking the remainder of his ewes and lambs. He sat on a bale of hay pondering what had taken place today, trying to imagine walking to the local pub telling his friends he is chatting to Peter and Matthew two disciples. Jacob envisaged the white van coming to collect him, laughed out loud with the old ewes looking at him suspiciously. Jacob slowly walked towards the house looking up into the clouds; the night is drawing in although a lot lighter than a few weeks ago.

Rosalind had prepared the large cod she caught. A banquet Jacob thought if he'd ever seen one. He tucked into his meal, enjoying every mouthful, bringing back memories of fresh fish when he used to spend a lot of his spare time on the beach fishing. Rosalind is reading his thoughts which were mostly about her and occasionally other things. After Rosalind had washed up, they sat together watching television until time to go to bed. Rosalind kissed him on the forehead, and Jacob is immediately asleep. She changed heading for the front door, she stepped into the misty fog transported to the spaceship. Peter and Matthew were waiting for her. They greeted each other with the flash of their eyes and sat watching the transmission of the way humans were behaving shipped to the newly terraformed planet. The males and females, along with some of the older children, had used large leaves to cover their modesty. The males had used rocks to sharpen bamboo into weapons.

Rosalind commented, "earth all over again remember the beginning?"

"Yes," Peter replied, "humans are certainly resourceful, especially the latest generation; they have learnt from their history books when undergoing education and are now putting it to practice."

Matthew suggested, "perhaps we should suspend shipments, we didn't intend the humans to kill the animals that rather defeats the object."

"They're not actually killing the animals," Rosalind advised. "They are only protecting themselves, their living quite happily on bananas and other fruits and catching fish from the stream. I don't think the adult animals are at risk at the moment."

Peter remarked firmly: "Humans are not wanted on these planets to colonise. They are merely food for the carnivores, I should have realised we have actually shipped carnivores; that's what humans are. I think we will return to the old ways; shipped them processed and dispose of the unwanted leftovers on Jacob's farm."

Matthew agreed: "Unfortunate I rather hoped the larger carnivores would have eliminated the humans by now, humans are cleverer than we thought even without superior weapons."

"My next question brothers? I would like to take Jacob to see our creations. I must comment on your excellent betrayal of Peter and Matthew from the Bible we wrote, Jacob is instantly convinced."

"I think it may be inadvisable to try and transport Jacob conscious to our planets. We had tried before and failed. The only way we can succeed is by sedating before take-off; I will give the matter some thought Rosalind.

You must return to Jacob, he is waiting for you on the cliff edge, you have been here for over six earth hours."

Rosalind flashed her eyes to Peter and Matthew. "Before you go, Rosalind," Matthew remarked, "humans are suffering from a new disease administered accidentally by their scientists; over 5000 have died already from the escaped virus. I have transported aboard before they are cremated. Arrange for Jacob to come to the beach in three days, I will have sufficient waste for his spreading machine to carry."

She flashed her eyes and continued walking stepping into the misty fog. She changed stepping out onto the beach to find Jacob had come down to meet her, which made her smile. He is becoming familiar with her coming and going from heaven Rosalind believed. She held his hand, watching him smile as they strolled along. "Jacob in three days, you are to come to the beach with the Fordson major and manure spreader; there will be a load of fertiliser for you, and in the near future you will be travelling into the heavens."

Jacob kissed Rosalind very passionately, which she hadn't received before from him. She eased away. "Jacob this early in the morning," she smiled, reading what is in his mind. Jacob placed his arm around her waist, they continued up the track cut into the cliffside. He looked at the other ewes and lambs desperate to be released and eat fresh grass. He looked up into the sky, deciding the weather is settled. "We'll let these go, Rosalind, they'll do better out on the grass than they will in here, save me feeding them every morning."

"You are correct Jacob sheep don't like restrictions." Rosalind opened the pens, she watched the ewes and lambs scurry off onto the Moor. Jacob looked at his second-hand tractor fitted with a loader and round baler and bale wrapper they had purchased for this season. "We must go shopping, Jacob," Rosalind advised holding his hand walking towards the house.

"I've never paid so many visits to a shop in my life Jacob," commented worrying about money.

Rosalind made the coffee reading his mind, she removed his old tin from behind the sugar. She'd already placed a large wad of cash in there, she passed the tin to Jacob. He almost spilt his coffee when he removed the lid; money jumped out onto the table so tightly packed in the tin. Jacob stared in disbelief, he is convinced he's short of cash, obviously not, he certainly wouldn't have to visit the bank which is a three-hour drive away. Jacob looked at Rosalind; she is the only explanation for the sudden influx of money. She shrugged her shoulders and grinned, Jacob burst out laughing. "We will go shopping Rosalind, perhaps buy you a pretty dress," he smiled.

"Jacob," she quickly reassured. "My clothes are made in heaven, should I require. Dresses are no good on the Moor, draughty, I prefer my jeans there more comfortable and overalls."

"As always you are practical Rosalind and I get to see your beautiful legs every night," he chuckled.

Rosalind smiled, slipping on her coat, Jacob patted Jack. "You stay and look after the farm, we won't belong." Rosalind drove the Land Rover slowly cutting across the Moor, checking the ewes and lambs on their journey to the shop, at least the snow had vanished apart from concealed crevices. Rosalind drove directly to the shop. Jacob is surprised considering the Land Rover wasn't taxed or insured to go on the road. Rosalind commented: "Don't worry Jacob, there is no police in the area."

Jacob wondered how she would know, guessed something to do with heaven, although he couldn't imagine Jesus being involved in breaking the law. He pushed the trolly; Rosalind plucked items from the shelves. The shop is quite busy considering there is a campsite not very far down the road. Otherwise, the shop probably wouldn't be here at all Jacob surmised. Rosalind had managed to spend over a hundred pounds, Jacob thought she is almost stocking up for world war three with the amount of flour she is purchasing. Jacob loaded everything into the back of the Land Rover, and Rosalind set off, leaving the road as a police car drove past on the main road. He watched Rosalind grin, she patted his leg, "you have nothing to worry about Jacob. Although I'm purchasing a second-hand Range Rover, you can use that to take me out, and the Land Rover can stay on the farm to be used across the Moor."

"And where is all the money coming from Rosalind, or shouldn't I ask?"

"You have a lot more money than you realise Jacob, you are like your father, a penny-pincher. Of course, if you're going to treat me horrible and not take your wife out. I can always return to heaven at least there, life is comfortable, and we want for nothing," she grinned.

"Where in the Bible does it say the wife takes control of your life; a wife is supposed to be dutiful to her husband," he smiled smugly.

"Don't you start quoting the Bible to me, Jacob Walker! Or you will be living on your own," Rosalind advised firmly, she parked outside the house, Jack is sat there in front of the door, daring anyone to try and pass him. Rosalind patted him, opening the door for Jacob to carry the boxes to the kitchen. Jacob is beginning to wonder whether this is actually his Rosalind; he could never remember her so strong-willed and determined to have what she wants. She still hadn't explained where the money is coming from. Rosalind read his thoughts, "the money is coming from my personal savings which you know nothing about, let that be the end of the subject Jacob, please." Rosalind quickly placed the groceries, grabbed her coat storming out of the house trying to behave like a female human would. She walked down to the beach, the misty fog approached, she stepped inside and immediately aboard the spaceship. Peter and Matthew were standing there waiting for her; they flash their eyes to one another with their greeting gesture. "Rosalind a few miles from your location on the farm, a mass grave discovered, you remember when the Romans disposed of the villagers. Now they are surveying the whole Moor in the hope of finding more graves and artefacts. This could become a serious problem for you at the farm."

"What do you suggest?" Rosalind asked.

"Matthew and I will frighten the archaeologist's make-believe the moor is haunted. One or two people will disappear, and become a food source for our animals and go on the next shipment. I know the police will search, and you will experience some disturbance. However, use your powers to blank their minds if you must," Peter suggested.

"I suggest Peter from what I can see from our scanners there are 10 people involved in the dig. We will take the whole 10 they will vanish. The police will immediately become involved, we will leave their clothes at the dig this will confuse the situation further. They may be led to believe this is a magical burial," Matthew suggested.

"Don't forget there will be helicopters flying searching the Moor, for signs of life," Rosalind suggested.

"One or two will have to have a malfunction, and their bodies will disappear. We will turn the Moor into the most undesirable place to live on earth if we must," Peter assured. "We cannot be beaten Rosalind the humans are nowhere near as advanced as we are."

"While you two are betraying God's; remember Jacobs flock of sheep, I don't want them harmed or him," Rosalind insisted. "Peter can you change the foreign currencies into sterling send a transformed sister or brother to a bank. They will exchange, remember not to take any more than £10,000 at a time. Otherwise, questions may be asked, never use the same bank twice," Rosalind cautioned. The three acknowledged each other flashing their eyes in respect. Rosalind walked into the misty fog at the end of the corridor and stepped out onto the sand, she glanced up to the top of the cliff seeing Jacob stood there, he came down the old track carrying two fishing rods and a basket. Rosalind smiled, she is becoming used to using human expressions, they appeared to come quite naturally now at the right moment. They smiled at each other, Jacob past her rod; within minutes she is casting way out to sea far further than Jacob could. Jacob presumed God is assisting with her cast. They stayed there for over two hours Rosalind catching another cod, and he managed three mackerel. Jacob gutted the fish on the beach, they packed their rods away, walking up the old track home to the farm. He and Rosalind watched a police helicopter flying overhead studying them for a moment and continued across the Moor. Jacob remarked: "I wonder what's happened somebody must be lost?"

"Probably," Rosalind opened the front door switching on the television in time to see the news, they sat and watched. The whole burial ground is taped off, forensics in their little white suits. A reporter is given a commentary: "Several people have gone missing excavating the burial ground, no one has any clues at the moment as to what has taken place here; the police are presently searching the Moor."

"There's your answer Jacob," Rosalind remarked, unconcerned, already knowing what had happened.

"I'll check the ewes and lambs, Rosalind, they're not used to disturbance like this."

"Okay, I'll have your tea ready in about two hours, don't be late," she smiled, watching Jack, the old sheepdog followed Jacob out the house.

CHAPTER 3

Keeping Control of the Situation

Jacob strolled with Jack close by his heels across the uneven ground, trying to avoid tripping on stones. Jacob could see the helicopter searching in the distance. Without warning the helicopter exploded descending to earth like a brick. Jacob stood there in shock, barely believing what he is seeing. There is no point in him trying to reach the helicopter it's miles ahead and the way it exploded, there would be no survivors he concluded. Jacob found his sheep huddled together, which usually meant there's a dog somewhere. He crouched down, holding Jack around the neck, he didn't want him running off until he knew what the problem is. Jacob noticed two police officers walking out of the gully. Jack barked, struggling to escape Jacobs grip. "Quiet Jack," Jacob ordered. Jack settled, although Jacob could feel him trembling. The police officers approached enquiring if he'd seen anyone and where he is from. Jacob pointed to where he lived. The officers smiled, continuing their search. Jacob steadily walked home via a different route to check all the ewes had stayed together; too difficult to count them while they were so unsettled.

Rosalind heard a knock at the door; she answered, standing there were two police officers the one female officer asked immediately. "Have you seen anyone suspicious around here recently, you probably heard, we are searching for missing persons."

"No, my husband is out on the moor tending his sheep; they tend to get a little upset when they hear loud noises, like helicopters. We saw on television what had happened."

The male officer looks strangely at Rosalind. "Jacob Walker! Didn't his wife die of cancer, who are you?"

Before the police officers could take another breath, Rosalind had stunned them both with a blast from her eyes. She watched the bodies vanish into thin air. She smiled realising Peter had transported them aboard the spaceship to be processed. Rosalind closed the door returning to prepare a meal for Jacob. Jacob removed his boots entering the house, patting Jack, "good dog."

Rosalind smiled, "how are the sheep, Jacob?"

"A little unsettled; I bumped into two officers; they're searching for those missing archaeologists or whatever they are. They have no business disturbing the dead; mind you, I wouldn't mind if they buried some of these yobbos, who come onto the Moor every year leaving, glass, tin and paper everywhere."

Rosalind glanced to him, "enjoy your meal Jacob; you never know what God has planned, you may see the evil ones disappear in your lifetime, who knows," she patted him on the shoulder.

"That would definitely be a sight for sore eyes. I haven't missed television, all you see is someone murdered; old folks assaulted and robbed of their money. Those people deserve to die. Sorry God for my outburst," Jacob continued eating his meal.

Rosalind made the coffee sitting on the settee, she switched on the television seeing a news reporter standing near the excavation, holding his microphone. "We've had an update from the police. Apparently, the archaeologists at the dig left their clothes behind when they were abducted or whatever happened. Now two police officers are missing searching the Moor for evidence of what has taken place. There have been reports from the public of spaceships and strange activity in the area. The last piece of news a police helicopter exploded; there are no survivors." Rosalind turned off the television.

"I suspect there will be more disturbance, Jacob. Don't forget in the morning, you must go to the beach there is a load of fertiliser coming for you," Rosalind advised; slightly concerned they would have to make sure there is sufficient fog to prevent helicopters from flying and spot Jacob.

"I hadn't forgotten Rosalind." They spent the rest of the evening watching television, not one of Jacob's favourite past times before they retired to bed. Rosalind incapacitated Jacob as usual by touching him. She immediately left the house stepping into the misty fog transported aboard the spaceship. Peter and Matthew were waiting for her to arrive; they flash their eyes to one another in a greeting. "Wise decision Rosalind disposing of the two police officers, adds more superstition to the already superstitious people in the area; they believe the Moor is haunted," Peter advised.

"I didn't have any choice, Peter, the officer, realised Rosalind is dead; he must have known Jacob to have remembered such an event."

Matthew confirmed, "there processed along with the archaeologists. I hope to process 500 humans before the next transport ship arrives. Perhaps we should invent an incurable disease and obliterate the human race."

"Patients Matthew, I'm sure the humans will destroy themselves by creating something they can't control," Peter advised. "I heard the conversation between you and Jacob, his attitude to his fellow humans, similar to ours when it comes to punishment for various crimes Rosalind."

"Yes, Peter, I think if he possessed the powers we do, he would annihilate most of the human race without hesitation; he is a good human."

Matthew confirmed: "Jacob is standing on the beach waiting for you Rosalind, you must go quickly and send him to the beach with the tractor and manure spreader. I will send the incinerated human waste before the search starts again for the missing humans, and they see Jacob." Rosalind flashed her eyes to Peter and Matthew, quickly moved along the corridor, stepping into the misty fog. Changing her appearance, she stepped onto the sand, Jacob held her hand. "Quickly Jacob the tractor and manure spreader; otherwise, the police may see you and ask a hundred and one questions you don't have answers for," she smiled reassuringly. They held hands running as quickly as they could to the farm. Jacob started the old

Fordson major driving down onto the beach; he watched the fog cover everything, he couldn't see 10 yards in front of him in any direction. He felt the manure spreader flex as it is loaded and the foggy mist vanished instantly. Jacob started the tractor heading up the track until reaching the top of the cliff, headed off for his flat pasture. He quickly spread the contents of the manure spreader and returned to the farm. Jacob parked the manure spreader close to where the penned sheep were lambing. He moved the hurdles, stacking them in a neat pile until they were needed again. Rosalind climbed aboard the tractor they'd purchased with the loader. She cleaned out the old barn loading on to the manure spreader. There wasn't much, the sheep weren't in there long, just one load. She parked the tractor in the barn as a police Range Rover arrived. Jacob watched two officers step from the vehicle making a beeline for him. Rosalind went off into the house out of the way.

"Jacob Walker, I believe, have you seen anything strange? Have you seen two officers today or yesterday?"

"Yes, when I was on the Moor there were two officers, I was checking on my lambs because of the disturbance; they're not used to a lot of noise. The two officers walked off in that direction," Jacob pointed, "I see no others, I wouldn't advise going over there with your vehicle it's boggy you'll be stuck."

The one officer smiled, "thanks for the information; you think someone could get into difficulties in the bog and disappear sucked under?"

"Probably at certain times of the year, but you'd have to be a real idiot to walk into the middle of a bog. Been there since the beginning of time, so what's been sucked underneath, God only knows. I shouldn't think police officers are that stupid; they would wander into the bog; even in wellingtons, you wouldn't get very far before they were full of water." Jacob watched the police officers drive off in the direction of the bog. Rosalind had listened to the conversation by turning herself invisible and is satisfied with what Jacob had said. She quickly entered the house, changing her shape into Rosalind, ready for Jacob to walk in.

Jacob ambled to the house, hoping the police wouldn't disturb his sheep, he opened the door to find Rosalind watching television holding up a cup of coffee for him to join her. They sat together watching the news, much as before the helicopter searching above. The presenter advised: "Tomorrow a hundred people were joining in the search walking the Moor and were under strict instructions not to bring dogs and disturb the wildlife or sheep."

He glanced to Rosalind, "I may bring my sheep back to the farm first thing in the morning Rosalind. I don't want them scattered over the Moor, in fact, I'll fetch them before night. I just about have time," placing his coffee on the table.

"Be careful, Jacob, can you manage?"

He smiled, "I can with Jack," he grabbed his crook from the door, slipped on his coat, heading out with Jack close at his heels. Jacob quickly set up a large pen inside the barn for his hundred sheep and lambs. He knew it would cost him money, but a better alternative than having them worried on the Moor by strangers, and could inadvertently herd them into another farmer section. Jacob grabbed a small sack with a few sheep nuts left inside. He started calling the sheep as he walked across the Moor. He could hear them calling; Jacob sent Jack off in a wide arc to gather the ewes and lambs. Wasn't many minutes before the ewes and lambs appeared to be together and quite happy to follow Jacob rattling the bag of nuts. They entered the barn without any trouble. Jacob emptied his bag of nuts in the trough at the end, making sure the water is turned on. He stood outside the pen, counting making sure he hadn't missed one; almost dark, placed a bale of hay in the sheep rack, he is only keeping them in tomorrow; while the crazy people walked across the Moor. Jacob is pretty convinced they wouldn't be found; the Moor had a strange way of making things disappear. This wasn't the first time someone had gone missing he recalled over the years and never found.

Rosalind came from the house, she stood there counting faster than Jacob could think, with her computerised brain. "They are all there, Jacob and the lambs," she smiled.

Jacob patted Jack, "good dog." Jacob scooped Rosalind up in his arms, carrying her to the house. "Put me down, you fool," she insisted. They retired to bed after having a large mug of cocoa. Rosalind kissed him on the forehead, he immediately drifted off into a deep sleep. She left the house, changing her appearance stepping into the misty fog immediately transported to the spaceship. Peter and Matthew greeted her with a flash of their eyes. "What are your plans, Peter?" Rosalind asked.

"I think I will send a thick fog and they will have to call off the search; however, they will only wait for a clear day to resume the search," Peter concluded.

"Have the humans we transported to the new planets been exterminated by the animals?" Rosalind asked.

"Yes," Matthew answered, "we won't make that mistake again. I prefer to send dead humans, we can freeze and keep fresh during transport and store on the home planet and distribute as necessary."

"Back to our present problem," Peter advised: "Permit tomorrow to go ahead, let them search the Moor, they will find nothing. Perhaps everything will calm down, and if it doesn't, we will have to take further steps."

"Agreed," Rosalind voiced. "Matthew, I think rather than unnerve humans by taking a large number from one area. You should have a snatch pattern around the planet. We should snatch one or two people from each town around the world; that way, it will look as if they are runaways, missing persons. Humans are always looking for those sorts of people on television until we decide to destroy the humans completely."

Peter intervened, "a sensible idea, however as much as we long to destroy the humans; our brothers and sisters on the home planet, are considering encouraging life on two more planets; once we have finished with the two were working on at the moment. I'm afraid which means we will need humans to continue feeding the animals for a while longer; probably no more than 200 years, we will have to see."

"Do we really need more leisure planets, Peter?" Rosalind asked.

"The collective has decided to increase our populace by 1 million; although we don't die. The collective wants to be prepared in case of an invasion. At present, we cannot be destroyed, the collective is thinking ahead in preparation for the unknown."

Matthew commented, "with four planets constructed similarly to early Earth; before we tampered with the DNA of chimpanzees, would be quite easy to hide in an emergency Peter if we were invaded."

"You must remember Rosalind, there are not many of us. Look at how many humans there are, their sexual appetite, leading to more procreation is swamping the planet, I suspect before long there will be another war. Hopefully this time they will wipe each other out; perhaps not completely but enough for them to realise their mistakes," Matthew suggested. He moved to the wall looking at a screen the size of a mobile phone he transmitted his thoughts. Peter and Rosalind watched on the screen on the other wall, individual humans and couples snatched from around the world and processed aboard the spaceship within seconds. The humans were joints of meat still quivering as they entered the freezer unit. Rosalind noticed Jacob is on the beach fishing waiting for her return. Rosalind smiled which Peter and Matthew thought is a strange and unnecessary distortion of the face. "I must return to the farm Jacob is fishing waiting for me."

Peter remarked, "you are becoming more human by the day Rosalind." They flash their eyes at each other, Rosalind walked down the corridor stepping into the misty fog. She changed her appearance stepping out onto the beach. Jacob picked up Rosalind's fishing rod, "I thought you could catch lunch while you are here," he chuckled, kissing her on the lips. He watched Rosalind cast her line out to sea, he thought for a moment, there'd be insufficient line on the real she'd cast so far out. "I wish I could cast like that Rosalind," he chuckled.

"It's all in the wrist action Jacob," she grinned, reeling her line in. Jacob watched a large cod, trying to break free. All he'd managed to catch with three miserable mackerel barely worth keeping. Jacob removed his pen-knife, killing the fish the minute ashore, gutting at the same time. The seagulls were hovering overhead they weren't going to miss the chance of an easy meal. Rosalind carried the fishing rods and basket Jacob struggled to carry the fish; he didn't think cod existed this big any more. He's pleased to return to the house and finally placed the fish on the kitchen table. He kissed Rosalind on the cheek going outside to check on his ewes and lambs again. Jacob could hear people he looked off into the distance across the Moor, watching them search for the missing archaeologists and the police officers. He's pleased he penned his sheep last night, at least they wouldn't be disturbed out there and possibly frightened into jumping in the bog or breaking a leg trying to run. Rosalind came out looking in the same direction as Jacob. "We are collecting our second-hand Range Rover today Jacob. God will transport us when there is no one watching."

"What about tax and insurance Rosalind, you haven't even told me what colour it is?"

"The colour is white, tax and insurance are taken care of, you have nothing to worry about. The vehicle is three years old ex-police vehicle and cheap. I will expect you to take your wife out for a Sunday drive occasionally," she smiled.

"Does it come with a blue flashing light," Jacob laughed.

Rosalind walked to the end of the building, watching the search parties, she could see further than Jacob or any human could. Rosalind returned to the house Jacob jumped on his old Fordson major transporting the manure they loaded the other day to his pasture and spread very thinly. People seem to be everywhere, helping with the search for clues for the missing persons. Jacob slowly drove back to the farm, parking his tractor and spreader, he entered the house. Rosalind immediately instructed: "You hold me tight Jacob, do not let go, it's time." Jacob gripped Rosalind kissing her neck, which she hadn't anticipated him doing, "stop it, Jacob, not now, be serious." In the blink of an eye, they were transported to Exeter to waste ground where no one is present. Jacob fell over, releasing his grip from Rosalind; he shook his head, feeling extremely dizzy. He struggled to his feet, holding Rosalind's hand. "This way, Jacob," she smiled, leading the way to the garage.

Rosalind collected the keys while Jacob looked around the vehicle, wasn't in pristine condition, after all, it's ex-police. Jacob slid onto the passenger seat suspecting Rosalind would drive which he didn't mind. Rosalind slid onto the driver's seat, starting the vehicle they headed for home. She called in at the shop, making Jacob push the trolley spending another hundred pounds on groceries. Jacob couldn't believe the amount of money they were spending, and still, they weren't short; the only conclusion he could come to is God is approving of everything taking place. Jacob loaded the groceries into the back of the Range Rover, hitting his ankle on the towing hitch; he glanced down, he hadn't noticed it before, at least he could tow the old trailer and take his lambs to market himself. They headed off across the Moor, Jacob asked, "why didn't you go the long way around on the side road?"

"I want to be nosy and see if those idiots have finished disturbing the Moor. We can release the ewes and lambs Jacob."

"Hadn't thought of that Rosalind," he replied quietly.

"Plus I can test the four-wheel-drive on our new vehicle," she smiled reassuringly.

"Not a bad ride Rosalind certainly more comfortable than the old Land Rover," he chuckled.

They finally reached the farm, Jacob carried the groceries into the house; while Rosalind placed in cupboards and in the fridge. She made them both a coffee while Jacob stoked the fire. He stepped outside, grabbing the wheelbarrow fetching another barrowload of blocks, leaving the barrow outside the door stacking the blocks by the fire. They sat together on the settee, drinking their coffee, watching the news on television. A reporter advised: "nothing has changed the search across the Moor had revealed no new clues, the police were baffled as to what had happened."

Rosalind smiled, "probably aliens Jacob we can blame them for everything," she patted his leg standing up, turning off the television.

He grinned, finding her comments rather amusing. "I'll release the ewes and lambs, Rosalind, I think they will do no good in a barn."

"I agree with you, Jacob can you manage," she asked.

He smiled, "yes, thanks."

Jacob and Jack went outside, he moved one of the hurdles, the sheep and lambs quickly left the barn heading out onto the Moor. They could freely roam, their only restriction, the pastureland which is set aside to make hay for the sheep to feed through the winter, totalling some 25 acres. Which Jacob like to get two cuts if he could. This year he hoped to have silage and hay now they had the equipment.

Rosalind had looked over the cliff noticing large quantities of seaweed had accumulated on the shore. She made her way to the barn finding Jacob stacking hurdles. "Jacob on the beach there appears to be a considerable amount of seaweed. I'll go down with the loader tractor, and you bring the manure spreader. We might as well take advantage, Jacob, you could chop it up into little bits with the manure spreader and leave it to rot in a pile; we can utilise it later then don't you think?"

"Sounds like my wife has an idea." He watched her sitting in the nice cab of their latest acquisition. She started the engine heading for the beach. Jacob started the old Fordson major feeling the wind cutting across the Moor, he hadn't a tractor cab to sit in to keep him dry and warm like Rosalind. Jacob sighed, thinking never mind and followed her down onto the beach.

Rosalind carefully using the forks on the end of the loader loaded the seaweed into the spreader. Jacob had to make four trips; there is more there than looked originally. Rosalind followed Jacob off the beach, she headed for the barn, and he continued to where he is stockpiling the seaweed. He started the manure spreader, he pulverised the seaweed leaving it in a neat manure heap; to be reloaded on the spreader at a later date when it had really rotted. Jacob returned to the barn leaving the tractor, he went inside the house, finding a coffee waiting for him on the kitchen table. He sat in his armchair by the fire and Rosalind perched on the arm, placing her arm around his shoulders. Jack started barking, which usually meant he had heard someone.

Rosalind look to the door quickly moving, and Jacob stood up. Jack is really upset by the way he is behaving, Jacob had determined, he couldn't wait to get out of the door. Jacob held Jack's collar carefully opening the door, another dog is wandering around without an owner or on a lead from what Jacob could see. "Hold Jack," Jacob instructed Rosalind. He ran over to his gun Cabinet removing the shotgun loading with cartridges; he'd had stray dogs before tearing his ewes a part or kill half a dozen lambs. Jacob about to destroy the stray dog. The owner shouted, "don't shoot! Don't shoot! Sorry, he got away from me," the young woman shouted, grabbing her dog, attaching his lead. Jacob lowered his shotgun. "How many of my animals has he killed," Jacob shouted, annoyed.

"None, my dog, isn't like that thank you," she stormed off towards the beach with her dog now on a lead. She obviously understood the message by the speed they were walking, he would shoot any animal that threatened his flock.

This is the first time Rosalind had seen Jacob angry to such an extent he would kill. She removed the shotgun from his hand placing back in the Cabinet. Jack sat by his master's heels, receiving a pat on the ribs. Jacob and Jack walked across the Moor, finding the ewes and lambs unharmed although bunched together. Jacob breathed a sigh of relief, slowly walking to the house. He looked across the Moor in the distance; he's about a mile from the road, which he drove to along an old track cut in the Moor some years ago. If you hadn't a Land Rover, you wouldn't venture from the road, Jacob had left it in that state to stop unwanted visitors. Jacob smiled realising he hadn't visited his post box, positioned by the road, no postman would venture to the house the road is so rough, their vehicles wouldn't make it. Jack jumped in the back of the Land Rover, Jacob drove the mile to his post box, discovering several brown envelopes, usually meant trouble. He didn't bother to open, slowly driving home to the farm, he entered the house carrying the post throwing the letters on the kitchen table. Rosalind immediately opened using her ability to translate into her own language, so she understood correctly what is written. "This one from Inland Revenue. They are warning you not to be late with your accounts this year; otherwise, you will be severely penalised, Jacob."

Jacob shrugged his shoulders, "I don't make anything anyway, I'm no good at accounting; Rosalind always used to do the books," he sighed realising what he'd said.

Rosalind removed an old book from the cupboard draw, sitting down while Jacob wasn't looking, she blinked her eyes twice and the accounts were up to date. "Leave it to me, Jacob, I'm Rosalind, I'm sorry I died I couldn't help it, not my fault the books were not kept in good order. Now they will be I'm back and back to stay," she commented trying to display an annoyed voice, which is not natural for a Zibyan.

"Sorry, Rosalind, my mouth is working without my brain in gear," Jacob gave her a hug.

"We have plenty of time, Jacob, you won't be paying any tax, don't worry, leave everything to Rosalind," she smiled. "Jacob put your coat on come with me. I'm taking you to see Peter; he has some questions for you."

"For me, a mere mortal, not much brighter than the sheep I raise," Jacob looked absolutely astounded at her remark.

Rosalind held his hand, they step from the doorway into the misty fog and within seconds they were aboard the spaceship. Jacob smiled, remembering his last visit. He saw Peter and Matthew approaching floating in the air. Jacob bowed in respect keeping his eyes fixed on the floor not daring to look at Peter or Matthew. Rosalind flashed her eyes to Peter and Matthew. "I have brought my husband, Peter, as you requested. Look upon Peter Jacob, you are not committing a sin." Jacob slowly raised his eyes looking at Peter the disciple in his robes, pictures he'd seen in churches and in books Peter looked exactly like that. Peter waved his hand, and seating appeared, Jacob is absolutely petrified. Peter invited him to sit down with the gesture of his hand, Rosalind guided Jacob to sit down by her. Peter asked: "Jacob, in the years you have lived on earth. How would you assess the human race?"

"The Bible says who among you is without sin cast the first stone. Although from my point of view, I think the people who hurt little children, murder without due cause and drunk drivers not forgetting the merciless terrorists, they should be exterminated. That's a personal point of view, not Gods."

Peter and Matthew looked at each other, Jacob thought he's now in serious trouble for speaking his mind; Rosalind gripped his hand reassuringly. "Jacob," Peter voiced calmly, "why did you not mention themes?"

Jacob shrugged his shoulders: "Possessions can be replaced, although I don't agree with stealing; you're not actually physically hurting anyone by taking their possessions; not a pleasant experience. I have had things stolen from the barn some years ago, only hand tools, but they were expensive to replace," he sighed heavily.

Matthew spoke: "Have you forgiven those who stole your possessions, Jacob?"

Jacob sighed. "They'll not return again to the farm hopefully, once I could forgive, twice I would not, I would like compensation if I could catch them of course," Jacob smiled.

"Wise words Jacob," Peter commented. "I can make this our rule for thieving, you can be forgiven once, twice will not be forgiven and your other remarks regarding punishment, will be applied, we agree entirely with your assessment Jacob."

Jacob didn't know what to say other than, "God's decision what happens to people, not mine, he created the world within six days, let him decide on the punishment."

Peter and Matthew vanished, Jacob jumped to his feet in shock. Rosalind grabbed his arm, "don't be alarmed Jacob they've gone to talk to God and discuss what they intend to do next. The world cannot continue the way it is Jacob, the human race is destroying everything. The planet was never designed to cater for skyscrapers or polluting vehicles to the extent it's suffering at the moment. Greed is prevalent among humans; you must see that surely, Jacob?" Rosalind held Jacobs hand leading him down the corridor, stepping into the misty fog. Jacob fell over as he stepped onto the sand, gasping for breath. Rosalind is hoping the more he travelled in their transporter, the easier the trips would become. She helped him to his feet, they held hands slowly walking along the beach to the top of the cliff, returning to the house where Rosalind made coffee for them both. Jacob sat deep in thought had he unleashed hell on earth through his own stupid comments; surely God would take no notice of what he thought?

Rosalind placed the cup of coffee in his hand, reading his mind and his worried thoughts. "Jacob, you have nothing to fear, Peter and Matthew are only God's disciples; he will make the final decision on what is to happen on earth, not them."

"Thank you, Rosalind, I'm a sinner like anybody else, I once found a £20 note on the Moor and kept it. I didn't hand it into the police," he frowned.

Rosalind actually laughed: "I don't think God would worry about such a trivial matter, Jacob. If that's your only sin, you have nothing to worry about, I know for a fact, you are a good man; otherwise, I would not have married you."

"I am blessed to have you with me Rosalind let God be the judge of the human race, not me. I'm going to check my ewes and lambs Rosalind."

Jacob slipped on his coat, grabbing his crook from by the door, Jack is by his heels. They left the house walking across the moor with a red sky in the distance, promising a better day tomorrow. Jacob walked for about half an hour, checking on his ewes and lambs, everything appeared to be in order. He hastily made his way home night is closing in, the Moor is nowhere you wanted to be in the dark there were so many trip hazards, even if you knew the place like the back of your hand. He breathed a sigh of relief, opening the front door with Jack his faithful sheepdog scurrying to lay by the hearth. Jacob removed his coat hanging on the back of the door along with his crook. Rosalind watching television the end of the news usually consisted of who'd been bombed today or who is murdered. She turned off the tv, pouring Jacob a cup of coffee and herself. They sat together, enjoying the final drink of the evening before they retired. They lay in bed together, Rosalind placed her hand on Jacobs, he immediately fell asleep.

Rosalind changed her appearance leaving the house transporting to the spaceship. Matthew and Peter were waiting for her. They flash their eyes at one another in the greeting ceremony. Matthew advised: "Jacob sees things in black and white Rosalind; however, we are implementing a snatch program using the information from the courts around the world to select from."

Rosalind commented: "The way I see crime soaring on television you will not have a shortage of candidates. I would advise the home planet to proceed with their plans and terraform two more planets. We certainly have sufficient food here for the animals to survive on until they become self-sufficient."

Peter look to the far wall, a screen displayed of two equally sized planets slightly larger than Earth. "Our brothers and sisters are creating a sun to warm the two planets. They can share the same sun. Once they have finished construction, we will send seeds we have collected over the years before some of the species became extinct thanks to humans. They will be planted on the new planets, once they are established, animals will thrive."

Peter and Rosalind followed Matthew to another part of the spaceship, a screen displayed on the wall listing the court cases pending of criminals. Matthew programmed his computer to snatch the named people if they were convicted by the court, once they were out of sight of anyone and transport them directly to the food processor. Matthew advised: "From what I can see and the calculations the computer has made, we should easily have a minimum of 300 humans, a week if not more.

Rosalind I may need you to send Jacob down with the manure spreader at least twice a month until humans realise criminals are going missing. If our plan works should encourage humans not to participate in criminal activity."

Rosalind laughed, Peter and Matthew looked at her and the way she distorted her appearance, making the sound. "Jacob will never realise he may have resolved the crimewave on earth by his few heartfelt comments."

The three of them stood there, watching the conveyor system start behind a transparent shield. Humans were arriving convicted of their crimes by a human court. The on-board computer read their minds before eliminating to ensure they were guilty of the crime charged before transportation and processing. Rosalind smiled again, which Peter and Matthew found totally unnecessary to display in their presents. Rosalind flashed her eyes at them both. "Jacob has come to the beach with the fishing rods I must go." Rosalind walked along the corridor, stepping into the misty fog stepping out onto the sand. She picked up her fishing rod watching Jacob smile. "Come on, Rosalind, I've caught three already," he chuckled.

Rosalind looked to see what he caught, three mackerel. She cast her fishing line. Jacob watched it travel through the air until he lost sight suspecting it would end up in America or somewhere. Rosalind grinned reeling in laughing; she found the whole process very amusing and enjoyable, which is something the Zibyans never concern themselves with as a rule. Rosalind fighting whatever is on the end of the line, something significant that's for sure; finally, she brought it ashore a large tuna. Jacob could not pick it up; he immediately dispatched the fish and gutted. He ran up to the farm coming back with the Land Rover struggling to lift the pieces of fish in the back of the vehicle. "You were saying Jacob, you caught three fish?"

"I hope you know how to preserve Rosalind, six months worth of fish here?"

"Of course, you will have to go to the shop and purchased white vinegar for me lots," she smiled.

They returned to the farm Rosalind passed a wad of cash. Jacob shook his head in disbelief but didn't bother to question where it came from. He jumped in the Range Rover heading for the shop; this is the first time he'd driven this vehicle and very impressed, he enjoyed the comfort immensely saved his old bones from being shaken about. He cut across the moor rather than using the road it gave him a chance to look at his sheep. Jacob entered the shop; the shopkeepers smiled, recognising him. "Jacob, we usually see you twice a year what brings you here today."

"White vinegar, we have a large fish to pickle, I don't suppose you have large quantities of that?"

"I have 5. 1-gallon containers that's all I have in stock at the moment."

"That will do thank you." Jacob, paid placing the gallon containers in the back of the Range Rover. He steadily drove across the moor in no particular hurry enjoying his comfortable ride. Jacob parked outside the house carrying the white vinegar into the house. Rosalind had gone down into the cellar finding suitable jars to store the fish in. She is stood there waiting for him. "I presume you walk to the shop Jacob," she remarked sarcastically.

"No, I took the opportunity to check on the sheep," he grabbed her quickly, kissing passionately on the lips; she is taken entirely by surprise. "Don't pick on me wife," he chuckled, stepping outside to close the tailgate on the Range Rover. Rosalind topped the jars with white vinegar carrying them down into the cellar where they would stay cool at a constant temperature.

She looked around avoiding the cobwebs that had accumulated, evident to her Jacob never ventured down here since his wife Rosalind had died four years ago. Rosalind made her way up into the kitchen on the stone stairs. Jacob is in the kitchen, making coffee for them both.

Rosalind felt a sensation run through her circuitry in her mind; she had the urge to hold and kiss Jacob. She didn't resist and proceeded to satisfy her urge. Jacob is taken by surprise, enjoying her closeness to him. They sat smiling at each other, enjoying their coffee, watching the television occasionally glancing to the depressing news. Rosalind suddenly listened along with Jacob, the newsreader remarked: "Something strange is happening around the world; there is not an unaffected country. People convicted of crimes are vanishing without a trace."

Jacob jumped to his feet, clapping his hands, "wonderful God acts in mysterious ways," he laughed.

Rosalind had never seen Jacob so happy over humans going missing. If he only knew the truth, she thought.

Although the experiment may be beneficial to see if crime is reduced around the world, she doubted. Rosalind received a telepathic message in her mind. "Jacob is required on the beach in the morning, Matthew had processed so many humans, he'd run out of storage for the incinerated parts," Peter advised.

"Come on now we must retire, you have a busy day tomorrow. You must go to the beach first thing with the manure spreader there is a load of fertiliser for you," she smiled confidently.

"How do you know Rosalind who told you?"

Rosalind pointed her finger upwards and her eyes. "Oh understood," he grabbed Rosalind's hand, leading her to the bedroom.

Rosalind immediately put Jacob to sleep, she changed her appearance leaving the house, transported to the spaceship. Matthew and Peter were waiting for her; they flashed their eyes in the greeting process. "You have been busy," Matthew Rosalind remarked, "you have a consignment already?"

"We did not realise how many court cases are held each day around the world, and how many humans are actually convicted, 99% of the time, the courts make the correct decision according to our computer; the transport ship will arrive in the early hours. Matthew has processed over 5000 humans. We have the seed for the new terraforming planets to travel on the return journey. Would you advise Jacob there will be two loads to spread today on his pastureland Rosalind? God has been extremely busy," he watched Rosalind laugh a strange expression for a Zibyan.

Rosalind looked to the scanner observing Jacob on the beach with the Land Rover it is raining heavily, she smiled, making Peter and Matthew look at each other bewildered such an unnecessary movement of her construction. Rosalind flashed her eyes stepping into the misty fog, stepping out on the beach climbing straight into the waiting Land Rover. "Jacob, you must come down to the beach with the manure spreader, there will be two loads today," she said with some urgency.

He smiled, driving off the beach quickly up the track to the top of the cliff and home. He ran in the house, slipping on his overcoat, returned to the barn starting the old Fordson major heading down to the beach; he parked waiting, turning his collar up, trying to shield his face from the bitter wind. Peter sent the first load of fertiliser carefully filling the manure spreader. The misty fog vanished. Jacob drove up the old track to his pasture, spreading the fertiliser and returning to the beach quickly. He saw the misty fog approach dropping another load in the manure spreader. Jacob absolutely soaked by the time he'd emptied the spreader and returned home parking the tractor. He ran in the house into his bedroom, changing quickly out of his wet clothes, fearing he may catch a chill. Rosalind made his breakfast adding a few secret ingredients of her own to ensure Jacob wouldn't catch a chill from the adverse weather conditions. Rosalind had cooked in fried bread with three rashers of bacon and three eggs and a whole tin of baked beans. Jacob enjoyed every mouthful sipping his coffee with Jack sat beside him. Jacob smiled, removing a piece of fat from the bacon, Jack swallowed without even tasting, which made Jacob laugh.

He commented: "Rosalind we can't spread any more manure on the pasture, I want the grass to grow ready for mowing; with any luck, we will be able to have one cut of silage and one of hay. If I had a trailer, I could stockpile the fertiliser God is providing and apply after the first cut of silage," he sighed heavily.

"That isn't a problem, Jacob," Rosalind advised calmly. "I will purchase you one leave everything to Rosalind, God knows what you need before you do Jacob," she assured. "Now I think about it Jacob you should have another second-hand tractor with a cab, you'll catch your death if you keep driving that old tractor."

"We've already had a tractor this year, I still don't know where the money came from to pay for it. I certainly couldn't afford a trailer or another tractor Rosalind; be serious otherwise, you will have a sin debt up to our neck, and the last thing I want to do is lose my farm, it's been in our family for four generations."

"Yes Jacob you will be the last generation, you have no children to carry on when you die."

Jacob flopped back down realising Rosalind is speaking the truth. "However, we may be able to change things, I will talk to God on my next visit to heaven and see what miracle he can perform," she smiled reassuringly. "In the meantime, you will have a second-hand tractor and trailer so don't argue Jacob. leave everything to your wife; she knows exactly what she's doing, you will not lose the farm you have my word."

He sat there very quietly; the tractor and trailer were quite possible. Offspring definitely not on the cards, he didn't think, short of a miracle. He and Rosalind had tried to conceive a child when they were first married, and nothing happened. Jacob suddenly smiled, remembering a story from the Bible about a woman conceiving in her old age. He decided to say no more on the subject in case he put his foot in it as he usually did. He would wait to see what plans Rosalind came up with to resolve the issue.

Rosalind slipped on her raincoat, stepping outside into sleet and rain cutting across the Moor. She stepped into the misty fog transported to Exeter. She changed her appearance into Jacob, walking along the road to the machinery dealership. Rosalind looked around selecting a 10-ton trailer three years old and another Ford tractor four-wheel-drive 125 hp which she thought would be ample for their needs. Still, in the form of Jacob, she approached the sales office paying for her purchases in cash, which she removed from her raincoat pockets. The salesman is quite shocked to see the amount of money she is carrying. She left their address for delivery, placing the sale ticket in her pocket. The salesman shook Jacob's hand, "will be delivered early next week our lorries coming your way. Thank you once again, Mr Jacob Walker, for your business."

Rosalind walked off down the road stepping behind a derelict building into the misty fog and vanished in seconds. She changed her appearance into her natural form transported aboard the spaceship. Peter is waiting for her arrival. "Rosalind your brothers and sisters are concerned with your plans. They are not concerned you are spending earth money which would only be burnt and turned into fertiliser if not spent. However, they are intrigued to know how you intend to introduce a human baby into your life with Jacob. It does not matter how you transform; you will not be able to carry a child?"

Rosalind laughed. Peter thought, totally unnecessary movement of her physique. "I am aware I cannot conceive, we were not designed that way an unnecessary process Peter. I intended to substitute a Zibyan for the purpose. You know we can transform and copy any shape we desire large or small."

Matthew joined in the conversation. "Your plan could be beneficial Rosalind; went Jacob dies there will be a Zibyan male already in place to take over and will eliminate the necessity for secrecy."

"Now I understand," Peter remarked. "A well thought out plan Rosalind. No human would be suspicious of events; everything would happen as they would expect. The only part that may cause a problem is introducing an infant without you actually giving birth."

"I will have to mate with Jacob once more, which is a disgusting process; pretend to conceive and convince him I am carrying a child. I will simply create the illusion of a bulge on my stomach. Jacob won't question anything as long as he believes God has intervened to make it happen," Rosalind smiled.

"You appear to have everything under control Rosalind," Matthew commented, flashing his eyes along with Peter acknowledging each other. Rosalind walked along the corridor, stepping into the misty fog transported to the front door of the house, she quickly went inside. Jacob is watching television drinking coffee; he looked up at her slightly concerned, "where have you been?"

"To purchase a tractor and trailer. I saw Peter concerning having a child, which I had failed to do over the years before I died. Apparently, there is something wrong inside of me. Peter has spoken to God, he will provide you with a son when we decide the time is right. There is no rush there is no time limit," she smiled patting Jacob on the head, making herself a coffee, sitting on the settee with him watching television. Jacob is grinning from ear to ear; he would have a son to carry on his farm; he kissed Rosalind on the cheek. They both sat back watching television listening to the baffled report of what had happened to the archaeologists; there is still no explanation for their disappearance. The case would have to remain an unsolved mystery for the moment the reporter advised. Jacob and Rosalind retired to bed she put Jacob to sleep, leaving the bedroom returning to her spaceship.

Peter greeted Rosalind with the flashing of his eyes. They sat quietly, watching a transmission from the home planet of developments and improvements, they would all benefit from in time. Matthew joined them. "Jacobs suggestion of how to select humans is turning out more successful than I anticipated Rosalind, the rate of crime is reduced by half unbelievable."

"We still need another transport vessel early next week. I'm pleased you found another way of transporting the fertiliser to the farm. The reports I'm having from the home planet are very favourable Rosalind, the animals are thriving on the flesh there receiving."

"Good, I must return to the farm; Jacob is waiting on the beach with the Land Rover. He is a very honourable human if the rest of the inhabitants were like him; we wouldn't have a problem. Although we wouldn't have a food source either," she commented deep in thought. She flashed her eyes to Peter and Matthew walking down the corridor stepping into the misty fog onto the beach and into the Land Rover. Jacob patted her leg, "If you weren't seeing St Peter Rosalind, I could be extremely jealous," he chuckled driving off. "What is the outcome over you carrying the child is it possible?"

Rosalind smiled looking at him, "anything is possible with God there is nothing he can't do; so why are such a silly question Jacob, you will have a son when he considers the time is right."

"That reminds me, Rosalind, what have you actually purchase; I shan't ask where the money is coming from, I suspect it's something to do with St Peter and Matthew."

"I have purchased a Ford tractor 125 hp four-wheel-drive, along with a second-hand Marshall trailer capable of carrying 10 tons with high sides. You will have to stockpile the fertiliser until you can use on the field, Jacob," Rosalind advised.

"Unfortunate I only have 25 acres of good pasture-land to grow hay on."

"Don't worry Jacob," Rosalind assured. "You will easily acquire two cuts from the field this year with the amount of fertiliser you are applying; the first cut will be silage the second will be hay."

"I'll not argue with you, your usually right," he smiled looking forward to having a cab to sit in, rather than just his old coat to prevent the wind cutting him in half. They arrived at the house entered, Rosalind made coffee for them both while Jacob watched the news on television. The ancient burial ground the archaeologists were investigating is a crime scene and closed until the police had time to investigate further; not considered a priority, although people were missing. They weren't buried, they'd vanished according to the reporter. Jacob sat there, holding his coffee. "You had better check the sheep this morning Jacob, perhaps, take a bale of hay out," Rosalind suggested sipping her coffee. Jacob glanced to her surprise at her comment sort of implying he wasn't looking after the animals properly; nevertheless, he decided not to comment. He finished his drink slipping on his coat, walking out of the door holding his crook with Jack beside him. They walked for about 2 miles watching the steam rise from the old bog.

Jack started barking; Jacob scanned the perimeter close to him, noticing an old ewe and lamb adventured to close and stuck in the mud. Jacob patted Jack for finding. Jacob using his crook, hooked the ewe around the neck, easing her to safety. He retrieved the lamb, trembling with the cold. Jacob quickly rubbed the lamb, creating circulation before releasing to its mother, bleating furiously. Jacob stood there, smiling with satisfaction; he wondered if Rosalind had been informed by St Peter, one of his sheep were in trouble. He shook his head, smiling at his own daft thoughts, continuing to walk around the bog which is about 2 acres in size at certain times of the year, with thick rushes in places and bracken which sheep loved to get tangled in. Much to his relief, there were no more sheep in difficulty. Deciding to walk to where the old burial ground is, he walked across the Moor, wouldn't take him long and would give him the chance to look at his neighbour's sheep to see if they were any better than his. Jacob walked for an hour, finally approaching the burial ground fenced off by the police. He stood there for a while, wondering what happened to the archaeologists. There again, according to the news, people were vanishing from everywhere all around the world. The only part that made him smile, they were criminals which he thought a just punishment the less of them there are, the better he concluded.

He took a deep breath walking back across the Moor looking at his sheep; hoping to increase the flock by a hundred this year. Since Rosalind had returned, Jacob had no idea how much money he had. He left everything to her quietly praying she didn't make a mistake, she's spending thousands of pounds on equipment he didn't know he had. Jacob noticed in the distance standing on a small rise in the ground a tractor and trailer unloaded at the end of his track. Jacob cut across almost running with excitement. The machine looked virtually brand-new, and the trailer wasn't in bad condition at all; barely a scratch on the paintwork. The lorry drivers smiled as Jacob approached, "Jacob Walker, I presume," the driver asked.

"Yes," shaking the driver's hand, "I thought this wasn't due here until next week?"

"Slight change of plan, I have a machine to collect from the next town, you were on route, so it only seems sensible to drop your tractor and trailer off on the way."

Jacob signed for the equipment, Jack had already jumped into the tractor cab. The lorry driver set off to his next destination blasting his klaxons as he drove away. Jacob grinning from ear to ear climbed into the cab of his new to him tractor; massive compared to what he'd owned before. The only Fordson he had is the Fordson major, and the first track to his father purchased the old Fordson N petrol paraffin which he kept for sentimental purposes. Little use in this day and age; other than for joyriding and minor jobs and pulling an old wooden donkey cart trailer that would barely hold a wheelbarrow full of manure; he'd have to load by hand in those days.

Jacob worked out how to start the tractor. He set off with a jolt after releasing the handbrake, he closed the cab door deciding how quiet it is. He looked in the distance seeing Rosalind stood at the end of the track which he travelled down extremely steady, to avoid being shaken to bits by the ruts. Jacob had never had so many new toys on the farm in all his life. He realised he's getting on in years, he certainly wouldn't be able to continue with the hard work, that accompanied farming without assistance, from either people or machinery. Machinery, the better option they didn't argue you only paid for them once apart from if they broke down, very rare.

He parked the tractor and trailer by the barn. Rosalind stood there grinning, she is quite enjoying using human facial expressions. She could tell by the smile on Jacob's face he's thrilled with what she'd purchased for him. Jacob opened the cab door. Jack jumped out followed by Jacob, he immediately picked up Rosalind in his arms, carrying her into the house. She'd already made the coffee he lowered her to her feet grabbing his mug sitting on the settee. "You certainly know what to purchase Rosalind, the tractor sounds beautiful and the trailer is ideal for what we need, especially if the fertiliser keeps coming from God."

"I should think the fertiliser will keep coming at least for two more years if not longer, Jacob. Perhaps we should look closer to the farm and see if we can increase your pasture land, I appreciate it may mean moving the fence," Rosalind remarked.

"We wouldn't be allowed, Rosalind there are certain restrictions, although I own some of the land, and I have grazing rights on the rest like one or two other farmers. I think if we start stirring up trouble or try and bend the rules, they'll jump on us like a ton of bricks," he expressed concerned. Rosalind produced a map of what Jacob owned, she placed it on the kitchen table. "I found this in the records in one of your grandfather's old boxes. If you look at the 25 acres of pasture marked on the map here, and you do the calculations your find you are 5 acres short; you are actually entitled to 30 acres of pasture. You own that land, Jacob," she expressed firmly.

Jacob finished his coffee, looking at the map, he grabbed a piece of paper doing the maths. Rosalind burst out laughing, she'd never seen such a primitive way of working things out. She had calculated everything in her own mind in seconds. Jacob spent 10 minutes double-checking his calculations. "You're correct, Rosalind,

I'll fence the area off tomorrow morning will you help me measure. If the authorities try to be difficult, we have the proof on paper, and you've accurately measured."

"Of course Jacob, you realise the solution would be; once we've measured. Move the right-hand perimeter fence to the new location, and we'd only have to use new wire on either end, two short distances because of the shape of the pasture."

He nodded, smiled in agreement, he remembered he had the old post-rammer around the back of the shed. He kissed Rosalind on the cheek ran outside; taking the old Fordson major off the manure spreader and attaching it to his old post- rammer. This would certainly make it easier to push posts in the ground; admittedly, after all the rain, they should go in quite easily. Jacob walked to the old air-raid shelter looking inside, finding the buildings still dry. He hadn't looked in here for years; discovering a stack of fence stakes. There must be a hundred or more, and roles of sheep wire, which he couldn't recall buying. Perhaps his father had and never told him, that went for the stakes as well. Jacob noticed a box on the floor covered in dust with a piece of paper trapped beneath. He removed the paper, the delivery note for the stakes and wire plus staples the date on the delivery note was the day before his father died. Jacob exhaled reliving memories of working with his father. Rosalind joined him patting him on the shoulder. Jacob nearly jumped out of his skin. "We appear to have everything Jacob to complete our task tomorrow, come on an early night a busy day tomorrow."

He smiled, placing his arm around Rosalind's waist, giving her a squeeze. They both retired to bed Rosalind immediately put Jacob to sleep. She changed her appearance going outside the only one that knew what she is up to is Jack, the sheepdog, he could say nothing to anyone. Rosalind set about loading the trailer with the fence stakes and wire; Rosalind is determined they would finish the project by the end of the day. She drove the tractor to the pastureland marking out in the dark day or night made no difference, she could see just the same. Rosalind placed the post ready to be driven in the ground in a few hours. She walked back to the farm, leaving the tractor and trailer there. Rosalind climbed aboard the old Fordson major with the post rammer attached taking to the paddock. She thought about starting work and realised Jacob would hear the noise, he would realise she wasn't the real Rosalind.

She returned to the farm at 6 o'clock in the morning, she started cooking breakfast and making the coffee, making sure she made sufficient noise to wake him. Jacob quickly washed and dressed coming in the kitchen kissing Rosalind on the cheek, sitting down to his breakfast, "you're keen this morning Mrs," he chuckled.

"Come on Jacob eat up, a busy day I want this job finished by 5 o'clock."

Jacob started laughing, "you know we can't complete that, probably take a week."

Rosalind placed her hands on her hips; she'd seen female humans do that when they wanted to make a point. "Jacob the fence posts are already there, so is the post rammer. The only thing stopping us completing the task is you sat there doing nothing. Daylight in the next 15 minutes, I expect you to be there with me working."

He stared in disbelief at her comment, watching her throw her pinny on the back of the chair, slipping on her boots and coat. There is no doubt in his mind she meant business and he better hurry up, or she'd be scolding him for the rest of the day. Jacob quickly drank the remains of his coffee, slipping on his boots and coat. He stepped out into the fresh morning, not quite a frost close enough. Jacob looked to the barn the tractor and trailer were missing and the post rammer, he looked to the pastureland some distance away there were the tractors sat waiting for him. Rosalind had walked on ahead, she wasn't going to be delayed by him, he ran to catch up with her. "Did you sleep at all last night, Rosalind?"

"Of course," she replied, holding the first post in place, while Jacob started the old Fordson major tractor positioning the post rammer. He drove the first post in the ground which didn't take many hits. Before lunchtime, they had all the posts in; quickly removed the staples from the old sheep wire on the original fence. They pulled across the field to the new boundary fence. They stretch the sheep wire to make it tight and re-stapled. Jacob looked at his wristwatch 4:45pm; the only thing left to do is lift the old posts out from the original fence, which would open the area up to 30 acres. Jacob breathed a sigh of relief, he's shattered, Rosalind looked as if she'd just made a cup of tea, not in the slightest tired from the day's events. "Tomorrow Jacob we can use the hydraulics on the old major, wrap a chain around the posts and lift them out the ground. If there are any good ones, we will save them. If not they can go on the saw bench and use for firewood," She ordered taking charge of the situation. Jacob didn't bother to argue, he's pleased to put his feet up; even Jack looked like he'd had enough of the day. They soon retired to bed, Jacob immediately went to sleep with Rosalind's assistants. Rosalind changed her appearance detaching the post rammer from the Fordson major. She grabbed a chain from the workshop and drove to the pasture land. She wrapped the heavy-duty chain around the first post, decided she couldn't be bothered it's dark no one would see what she is engaged in. Rosalind pulled out the unwanted fence posts by hand, taking a few seconds, leaving them lay on the ground. Jacob could collect them tomorrow and sort through what is right to keep, and what should be used as firewood. She drove the tractor back to the barn leaving their stepping into the foggy mist, she transported herself to the spaceship.

CHAPTER 4

Jacob Suspicions

Jacob woke up suddenly looking at the clock on the bedside Cabinet barely 3 o'clock in the morning Rosalind is missing. Jacob suspected St Peter may have called upon her or God to return to heaven. He quickly dressed grabbing a torch he left the house noticing the Fordson major no longer had the post rammer attached, a chain wrapped around the hydraulic arms. Jacob walked to the pastureland seeing the posts were laying on the ground. He shone his torch on his wristwatch just to confirm he wasn't dreaming 3:20 AM. "He muttered doesn't the woman ever sleep?" Jacob hadn't realised Rosalind had appeared behind him from the misty fog touched his shoulders, he's unconscious. She picked him up in her arms, carrying him to the farm, quickly undressed him placing back in bed and climbing in herself. Rosalind would simply say it Jacob said anything to her he must have been dreaming. Jacob opened his eyes, shaking his head, finding Rosalind laying beside him, he's in his pyjamas. Rosalind pretended to be asleep, Jacob decided to say nothing suspecting he's dreaming. He

113

looked at the clock by the bed 5 AM sighing heavily he tried to go to sleep for another couple of hours at least. Rosalind touched his arm, Jacob is in a deep sleep again. She went out into the kitchen, changing her appearance she transported to the spaceship. Peter is waiting with Matthew, both looking extremely concerned, Jacob may become conscious while she's away. "I have no idea what happened or why Jacob managed to escape my control."

Peter suggested, "I would put Jacob in a deep sleep at least until 10 o'clock in the morning, that way you can return to the farm to collect the posts yourself, and make-believe he overslept. Rather than jog his memory, he'd already seen the posts removed, Rosalind."

"Yes, I agree." Rosalind flashed her eyes at Peter and Jacob returning to the farm, she held Jacobs hand until she is convinced he wouldn't stir until at least 10 o'clock. She went outside taking the tractor and trailer across the field, not bothering to switch the lights on the tractor. Rosalind didn't need them; she could see perfectly well enough. Rosalind threw the old fence posts on the trailer checking the fencing once more, making sure they'd missed nothing. She checked the new pastureland for any signs of stones that would damage the farm equipment. She sent out blasts from her eyes, destroying any stone into insignificant fragments to prevent damage to the farm equipment in the future. She spent nearly 2 hours checking the newly added 5 acres. Now daylight, she drove back to the farm, rather pleased with her accomplishment. Rosalind went into the house and made breakfast and give Jack his bowl of treats.

Jacob came staggering out of his bedroom. "I have a stinking headache this morning, Rosalind," plonking down at the kitchen table looking at his lovely breakfast. He glanced at the clock, "you let me stay in bed, and we have all this work to do Rosalind?"

Rosalind shrugged her shoulders, "easier to do it myself Jacob than wait for you," she chuckled.

He grunted finishing his breakfast, slipping on his coat he went outside to find the trailer with the old fence posts loaded on the back. He recalled his dream remembering dreaming they were out of the ground last night now they're on a trailer? Jacob shook his head in disbelief; the woman is unstoppable; he could never remember Rosalind working so hard before. She came out to join him, "if I were you, Jacob, I would put the saw bench on the back of the old Fordson major and cut up some of these old posts; they will do for the fire," she smiled, patting his cheek walking over to find eggs laid by the hens overnight. Jacob asked, "Rosalind has God, Peter, or Jesus made you stronger than normal people?"

Rosalind turned to face him holding half a dozen eggs in her pinny, "he must have Jacob look I'm holding six eggs all on my own," she smiled walking back to the house realising, she'd been sarcastic.

Jacob attached the saw bench to his old Fordson major spending the rest of the day, sorting through what he wanted to keep and cut up the rest ready for the fire. He noticed two men looking at his pasture boundary alterations, suspecting officials. He walked down his old track cutting across as they'd finished measuring his extension to the pastureland. "Good afternoon

Mr Walker," one official said politely, "we see you have extended your boundary; we've checked the measurements, you are within limits, but you must not go any further."

"How did you find out," Jacob asked puzzled. He watched the other official point his finger into the sky. "Satellite! Big Brother is watching you all the time," the official chuckled. Jacob watched them walk off, jumping in their Land Rover, driving off across the Moor, joining his old track and onto the road. Jacob suspected if the satellite is scanning the Moor, it would have seen Rosalind he wondered if the satellite worked in the dark, as he walked to the house. Rosalind is there to greet him on the doorstep, "officials Jacob?" she asked directly.

"Yes, apparently there's a satellite above us, perhaps they are trying to use that to find out what happened to the archaeologists." He shrugged his shoulders, sitting on the settee in time to hear the news. The reporter looked extremely stressed: "Governments are bewildered, people are going missing, once convicted of a crime. Some people think it's Gods way of removing evil from the earth; others believe it's aliens." There is a pause: "Just in! A group of terrorists have vanished engaged in a battle with Armed Forces on the Syrian border, no one has an explanation?" Rosalind calmly passed Jacob a coffee, trying not to smile. "I've already eaten Jacob; would you settle for cheese and onion sandwiches tonight, we need to use the cheese before it spoils and that goes for the onions," she commented walking into the kitchen.

"That will do fine Rosalind." Jacob turned off the television, walking into the kitchen sitting at the table.

Rosalind commented, "tomorrow morning first thing Jacob; you must go to the beach, two loads of fertiliser take your new tractor and trailer, at least if the weather is bad you won't be affected your be nice and warm," Rosalind smiled.

"I presume you will be talking to St Peter or Matthew?"

"Why do you ask Jacob? Are you concerned, I'm here by God's will only. You must remember I descended from heaven, I have to receive spiritual instruction. If you wish to live alone again, Jacob, I can return to heaven and never come back to see you if that's what you really want?"

He lowered his sandwich to the plate, "whatever gave you that silly idea Rosalind; my life has never been so fulfilled until you returned. I'm inquisitive that's all, you must remember I am a mere mortal. I'm unsure of what you are, you look like my wife, you behave like my wife some of the time. Things happen around here that I find suspicious, you must understand Rosalind, I'm waiting to wake up from a dream," Jacob spluttered in somewhat of a panic, thinking he may be losing Rosalind.

"Finish your sandwiched Jacob," Rosalind advised pouring him another coffee. "As long as you want me to stay, I will stay," she smiled reassuringly.

"That will be forever until I die," he sighed heavily dreading the thought of passing on now he had Rosalind in his life. He wondered would he rejoin Rosalind in heaven, although the Bible states quite clearly until death do you part, so technically you are single once you're dead. That thought did not impress him in the slightest. Rosalind is reading his mind, she had become accustomed to Jacob in the short time she'd known him; there definitely is a familiarity. They both retired to bed Rosalind immediately put Jacob to sleep. She stepped from the house into the misty fog transported to the spaceship, greeted by Matthew and Peter, with the flash of their eyes. They sat watching the wall turning into a screen; their brothers and sisters on the home planet selected to speak, for the mass, a hundred in total.

"Peter is your earth name which we will continue to use as a reference, including your brother and sister, Matthew and Rosalind. You realise Peter, Matthew and Rosalind you have resided on earth since its conception to be colonised. You watched and encouraged some species to exist. The humans were a gross error of judgement on our part; we should have left everything alone and not interfered with the chimpanzees and created a hybrid."

Matthew advised: "They are serving a purpose, food for the terror formed planets, the animals seem to survive quite well on human flesh until they are established and can regulate their own numbers."

"You, Rosalind you are providing a valuable service, associating with the human for the purposes of disposing of waste. Noted in the interest of our advancement, you have made plans for a Zibyan to play the part as offspring for the human Jacob. Excellent in theory, a vote is yet to be cast by the collective to approve. Although once we have a Zibyan in charge of the farm, this will open up new opportunities which we can explore at a later date. This will have to be discussed, with the firstborn.

He is presently engaged in the search for fragments of our creators on another planet."

The screen vanished. Peter remarked, "from the information I've received from the home planet. There are plans not only for two more planets to be terror formed. Now they are considering six more planets. I do not see the purpose, although I am one of the many, my opinion is ignored on the grounds, I am too close to the subject they considered."

Matthew expressed, "I agree with your analysis. We appear to be copying the humans, one earth government, destroying thousands of acres of land to construct a railway line from one end of the country to the other. What will they do when there is nowhere to grow anything to eat. People are starving now, and still, they destroy the ground that feeds them; perhaps the humans are on a suicide mission, Peter?"

"We will have to wait and see. Jacob has come to the beach, prepared to transport waste products fertiliser onto the trailer. I can actually see him smiling a strange facial expression sat in his cab while the rain pours down and for once, he's not getting wet," Peter commented.

Rosalind smiled, flashing her eyes to Peter and Matthew walking to the misty fog stepping inside. She changed her appearance stepping onto the beach, opening the cab door on Jacob's Ford tractor sitting on the passenger seat. Jacob had discovered the tractor had a heater and six years old it still worked. He kissed Rosalind on the cheek, feeling the trailer loaded. She patted his leg, "come along Jacob you have two loads, we are so lucky to have fertiliser, it's given to us many farmers have to purchase their own."

He nodded in agreement, backing up to where he'd tipped the seaweed to rot, he released the tale board on the trailer running back into the cab, he tipped the fertiliser in a pile, quickly lowered the trailer and shut the tailgate. Rosalind jumped out of the cab running for the house to prepare breakfast for Jacob. Jacob drove down on the beach again enjoying every moment of driving his tractor, no wind screaming around his ears, he wasn't wet apart from when he ran to open the back of the trailer. The window wiper work so Jacob could see where he is going; there's certainly nothing wrong with today so far. He waited patiently watching a misty fog come from miles away across the sea and empty fertiliser in his trailer. Jacob drove to the manure pile again, emptying his newly acquired trailer driving to the farm parking, dashed in the house looking forward to his breakfast. Rosalind had really laid on a lavish breakfast, fried tomatoes, fried bread three rashers of bacon and three eggs and two sausages. Jacob exhaled, "I'll be as fat as a pig when I've eaten this lot Rosalind, but I'm not complaining."

"Jacob, I purchased a hundred ewe lambs 12 months old the farmer is retiring. I sort of jumped in and purchased the whole lot; you said to me the other day you wanted to increase the flock well we have."

Jacob, drinking his coffee, almost choked. Rosalind patted his back. "Are you, insane woman!" He shouted. "We haven't that sort of money to spend especially after you purchased equipment recently."

"I wish you'd stop panicking about money, we can easily afford, remember I do the accounts, not you and I wasn't going to miss a golden opportunity to increase the flock. Plus the ewe lambs you're bringing on yourself this year. Anyway, the lorries arriving at midday."

He continued eating his breakfast. "I'm sorry for shouting at you Rosalind. Do I know the farmer?" He asked calmly.

"Mr Clydesdale, he specialises in white-faced. Mr Clydesdale suggested you bring our flock off the Moor when the others arrive, while they sort themselves out and recognise each other and hopefully stay out of trouble."

"After a breakfast like that, I don't think I could walk across the Moor," Jacob expressed tapping Rosalind's backside as she walked past which made her grin. She knew a loving gesture by a human. Jacob stood up, walking to the door, slipping on his coat, grabbing his crook. "Come on, Jack, we've work to do don't blame me; it's Rosalind's fault," he chuckled. Jacob and Jack walked across the Moor until he located his sheep and lambs. "Away, Jack," Jacob ordered. Jacob watched Jack bunch the sheep, they slowly followed Jacob to the farm buildings. Rosalind had already set up a large pen to hold the sheep and lambs. He smiled, watching Rosalind empty a bag of sheep nuts in a trough at the far end to encourage the sheep to enter. The sheep and lambs run past him more interested in food than they were trapped. Rosalind came out, he shut the gate on the pen. Jacob commented, "we have several lame ewes and lambs, I'll clip their feet while we have them tightly penned."

Rosalind watched how careful Jacob is handling his sheep, clipping their feet, spraying each one with a disinfectant to try and keep the foot rot away, the same applied for the lambs. Rosalind noticed the lorry carrying their new flock slowly making its way up the rutted track, nothing the driver wouldn't be used to around here. The lorry parked, the driver climbed out quickly, opening the rear of the lorry dropping the ramp watching the ewe lambs run for freedom; they immediately started to eat the grass. Jacob released his own flock; there's an awful lot of bleating, which is expected. The lorry driver past Jacob some paperwork and left the farm in a hurry for his next destination. Jacob exhaled watching the sheep and lambs slowly walk off into the distance, munching every blade of grass they could find. He prayed the new flock would stay with the others. He placed his arm around Rosalind's waist, giving her a kiss on the cheek. "There are some nice you lambs you chose wisely, I couldn't have done better myself," he smiled. They walked across the Moor to the enlarged pastureland. Jacob noticed how much difference the fertiliser had made to the one section before they extended the pasture. "Perhaps I should spread a couple of loads of fertiliser on the 5 acres, you can see the difference plainly; the other 25 acres are coming on nicely," he remarked.

"Yes Jacob," Rosalind agreed looking into the air, "it will rain later today help wash the fertiliser in the ground."

They returned to the farm attaching the manure spreader to Jacobs ford tractor. Rosalind using the loader on the other tractor loaded the manure spreader. Jacob spread everything he'd stockpiled on the 5 acres extended pasture including the seaweed. They both stepped from their machines in the farmyard. Jacob commented, "with any luck, we'll get an early crop of silage." Rosalind smiled in agreement rather enjoying operating farm machinery and working with the animals. For thousands of years, she'd stayed aboard the spaceship apart from travelling to the home planet occasionally and betraying Mary Magdalene, thousands of years ago. She had never experienced earth and its real beauty until she shaped shifted into the form of Rosalind and became Jacobs wife. Rosalind checked her memory banks, discovering, she once had a vegetable garden. She walked around the back of the house to a fenced-off piece of ground realising it hadn't been touched by Jacob. He joined her. "Sorry, Rosalind I know you used to love growing vegetables. I'll see if I can start the old Rototiller and prepare the ground for you," he sighed, feeling disgusted with himself for allowing Rosalind's garden to deteriorate.

"I will start the Rototiller you never could; you and that machine have a love-hate relationship," she grinned walking to the garden shed. Rosalind removed the Rototiller quickly reading the manual from the database, so she knew exactly what to do. Jacob stood there watching; Rosalind is correct she opened a tin of petrol tipping a little in the machine, pulled the starter cord, it burst into life after sitting there for four years, Jacob couldn't believe it. She allowed the machine to warm for a minute. "There, you are Jacob." She watched him start to rotavate her garden, she grabbed a rake from the shed, removing any weeds left on top of the soil to the compost heap, where they could rot. Rosalind is determined to experience growing things herself, rather than allow her technology to perform the task for her. Peter and Matthew aboard the spaceship, were tuned into her thoughts along with the home planet, intrigued by her insistence to experience the way humans performed first hand rather than watch.

Jacob spent an hour going over and over Rosalind's garden until he'd pulverised the soil into submission, extremely fertile because of its peat content. Jacob placed the rototiller in the shed pleased to see the garden the way Rosalind always kept it pristine. "Sunday Jacob, you can take me out to a garden centre, and we will see what's available to purchase. I don't have any seeds or plants. I definitely want to grow a few rows of potatoes so don't suddenly have a bad back," she chuckled, enjoying the human form of teasing; she had studied from her memory banks and watching humans perform. Jacob is thrilled, he loved Rosalind beyond measure the first time around. Since she had returned from heaven, she's even more perfect in his eyes. "You will have whatever you want Rosalind," he smiled contentedly, closing the little gate on her garden as they left. Jacob and Rosalind returned to the house sitting by the fire watching television. A newsflash: "A hundred prisoners from New Orleans have vanished without a trace from their cells. Prison officers have carried out a thorough search and can find no trace of an escape." Rosalind watched Jacob smile; she already knew where the prisoners had gone, and Jacob would spread their remains in due course.

Jacob made Rosalind a cup of coffee, leaving her to watch the television. He returned shortly passing her a cup. "I'll check the sheep Rosalind I don't want them wandering off too far," he smiled. She smiled, watching him slip on his coat, grabbed his crook and Jack joined him at the door. He stepped out into a breezy late afternoon spending the next two hours finding his new ewe lambs. They'd all ventured some distance trying to find fresh grass. Jacob would willingly fertilise, although not permitted on the Moor. He walked back to the farm taking two bales of hay and a bag of sheep nuts on the back of his quad and trailer, driving across the Moor to where he'd left the sheep rack. Jacob came to a conclusion, his sheep were psychic. Jacob had barely cut the bales of hay and placed in the sheep rack before he's swamped by bleating ewes and lambs. He grabbed the bag of sheep nuts, making little piles walking across the Moor for a short distance encircling the sheep rack. Jacob watched the ewes and lambs devouring everything placed on the grass, what little there is of it.

He climbed aboard his quad with Jack jumping on the carrier, slowly drove away, deciding to visit the post box at the end of his track and see what the postman had left him. Jacob opened the box, a handful of letters mainly brown, which usually meant official. He sighed slowly placing the letters in his coat pocket heading back to the farm parking the quad bike in the barn. Jacob and Jack went into the house, Jacob removed the letters from his coat pocket, passing to Rosalind. She opened each letter studying the contents. Rosalind smiled, lifting a cheque. "The Inland Revenue is refunding you

£10,000 Jacob, there's been an error over the years in their accounting."

"About time I had something out of that lot," he smiled sipping his coffee. "I suppose that means a trip to the bank in Exeter, they've shut all the little branches where father used to go. We might as well have the day out and see if we can find you some plants and seeds for your garden," he smiled.

"That's the first idea you had today I like," Rosalind smiled. "Will go first thing in the morning, Jacob, we can leave Jack in charge your look after everything, won't you, Jack."

Jack barked as if he knew what Rosalind is saying wagging his tail frantically. Jacob and Rosalind spent the rest of the evening watching a little television and deciding what they would grow in her garden. They had agreed before retiring to bed they would purchase two rose bushes to brighten the place. Rosalind always wanted roses at the front of the house and died before she'd achieved her goal according to Zibyan records. Rosalind placed her hand on Jacob's forehead as he lay in bed. Rosalind left the room, changing stepping into the misty fog transported aboard the spaceship. Peter and Matthew were waiting. Matthew advised: "I am to return on the next transport ship to Zagader, I am summoned by our brothers and sisters. Peter will stay with you, I am to stay on Zagader for one earth calendar month to lecture our brothers and sisters in person. They want to see for themselves staying on earth for thousands of years has not altered any of our abilities and conviction to Zagader."

Rosalind displayed a human frown which is observed by Matthew and Peter. "I find that request rather strange Matthew, why now when we arrived thousands of years ago. If the request had been made, say after the first thousand years, I could understand, but after 9000 years or more," she paused.

"You sound like a human suspicious of everything, perhaps we should send you. You appear to be in greater need of attention then Matthew," Peter advised.

"You mean we cannot think Peter individually? What happens if there's a crisis, and we operate as a collective? Some are affected, some are not? We will not survive if you have no individuality. The collective is good; although we must operate individually, should the emergency arise," Rosalind suggested.

A large screen appeared on the wall members were listening from the home planet. "Rosalind, your intelligence has surpassed our expectations. We presume your association with Jacob has assisted you in thinking as an individual and not as a collective?"

"Yes, brothers and sisters, I have to think and assess the situation on my own. Waiting to consult Matthew or Peter or the home planet would take too long; Jacob would notice the delay in my decision-making processes, and so would anyone else. You all know the human brain is not dissimilar to our own; other than totally inefficiently used. They are not so stupid as to realise something isn't quite right if you don't answer your question quickly; unless you can think of a reason for delaying." A delayed response from the collective while they assessed everything Rosalind had said. "You have merit in your assessment, we will reprogram so we can all operate individually if necessary in an emergency. Otherwise, we will stay and operate as a collective and enjoy the warmth of each other's thoughts," The screen vanished from the wall. Rosalind watched Peter and Matthew stand to attention, while hoods engulfed their brain, giving them the ability to operate outside the collective without reprisals should the emergency arise.

Matthew and Peter look to one another after the hoods were removed and Rosalind. "Sister, you're not bothered by thinking and acting on your own?"

"You will find rather strange, I certainly have I'm still adjusting but the more you practice, the easier it becomes; I still prefer to be connected to the collective."

"Now I understand," Peter remarked, "why you have embraced the facial expressions of a human and participated in other activities. I see the merits of your actions, and so do the home planet now. Our programming is slightly altered; we can understand why you behave the way you do to be more efficient in the task you have set yourself."

Rosalind flashed her eyes, walking down the corridor stepping into the misty fog, stepping out by the front door. She glanced across the Moor, although not totally daylight, she could see walker's with their rucksacks following the path. She entered the house to find Jacob, making breakfast. "Rosalind, I'm 43years old, you know; how old I'll be before I die?"

"Why do you ask?"

"What is the point in having a son if I'm too old to teach him anything. I don't mean to be pushy, I will be about 49 before he is five years old and approaching 60 before he will be willing to learn. If I'm lucky enough to make 70, he will be barely old enough to take over the farm legally."

"Considering I won't die, I will be here to teach him. I know as much as you if not more Jacob; do not concern yourself. You could even live to 100 with my assistance," she smiled reassuringly.

"I suppose you're right Rosalind, although I would really love some time to play with my son and show him the way of the world, as you rightly pointed out you know more than me. You have God on your side. I will have to accept what is given I don't have any choice," he sighed slowly sitting in his old armchair. "I promise you, Jacob, you will have a son long before you pass away into history. Maybe the case you don't pass away at all. God may have other plans for you," she smiled.

Jacob grinned, "that would certainly be a miracle to behold, although I suspect society would soon realise something strange is going on if I outlived everyone else."

Rosalind kissed Jacob on the cheek flicking through the television channels until she found Emmerdale. Jacob laughed; he couldn't stand the programme going into the kitchen to have a glass of home-brew. He sat contentedly pondering on all that is said; contented with the thought, he would eventually have a son and perhaps a daughter if he is lucky.

Rosalind is reading his mind, she hadn't realised he may want a daughter as well, which quite surprised her, nevertheless nothing that couldn't be achieved she decided. Jacob had one more glass of home-brew;

deciding that's enough, he remembered the last time Rosalind had scolded him. He finished his drink kissing Rosalind on the cheek and retired early to bed. Jack, the faithful sheepdog, stayed by the fire, enjoying the warmth.

Rosalind switched off the television going into the bedroom. She kissed Jacob on the forehead rendering him unconscious. She walked from the bedroom, changing her appearance, Jack watched curiously for a moment then turned his head away, resting on his paws. Rosalind stepped out of the front door into the misty fog transported to the spaceship in seconds. Matthew and Peter greeted Rosalind with the flashing of their eyes, and Rosalind responded likewise. "Well, Peter, I'm sure you've read my mind, and Jacob's regarding children?"

"Yes, you can understand his concerns; he's ageing like all humans, thankfully. Otherwise, the world would be swamped; we are fortunate they haven't worked out what is wrong with their DNA sequence; otherwise, they would live forever, perish the thought."

Matthew commented: "I've ordered a transport ship, should be here within three days, I have more human corpses than I know what to do with, send Jacob with the trailer tomorrow Rosalind there will be two loads."

Rosalind cautioned: "How many humans have you processed this month, Matthew. Don't forget humans are not stupid; they are searching now trying to discover where the missing humans are going. We do not need them searching the sea where our spaceship is located. If we are discovered, although we can defend ourselves, it could possibly ruin everything."

"I have processed 5000 snatched from all over the world, most prisoners convicted of murder."

Peter insisted. "No more Matthew suspend operations for a month, allow the humans chance to calm down. The home planet has stockpiles of flesh for the animals, and with this consignment, you shouldn't need to do anything for two months."

Matthew suggested: "Peter if you listened to the transmissions of governments around the world, although they are concerned people are missing; they are rather pleased we are taking prisoners. Not only is it lowering the crime rate; but emptying the overcrowded prisons. The humans will not search very hard providing we don't take any of their leaders. I think we have nothing to be concerned about."

Peter glanced to the wall screen appeared displaying an aircraft carrier 20 miles to the south of them with helicopters flying with sonar scanning the seabed. "I think you are mistaken Matthew in your assessment."

Matthew looked at the screen. "This does not compute, the information I am receiving state something different from what we see, why?"

"Because Matthew," Rosalind answered. "Humans have tricked you into believing one thing and doing the opposite. Haven't you learnt any think Matthew in the time we have studied humans? They are devious, not trustworthy; they are hunting for us, something has given them a lead to our location; check your computers, Matthew."

Matthew vanished. Peter looked at Rosalind. "You are more experienced Rosalind at thinking as an individual, do you have any suggestions?"

"Yes, programme a Russian launch computer to send a missile towards the USA, and allow it to explode short of reaching land. The carrier will head for home or the Russian border it doesn't matter which way it goes providing it leaves this location."

Peter immediately turned: "Computer, you heard the conversation implement."

The computer spoke: "Missile launched from Russian submarine close to the Russian border. The aircraft carrier Abraham Lincoln has received orders to head North effective immediately."

Peter and Rosalind looked at the screen on the wall noticing the helicopters returning to the aircraft carrier, watching the ship change direction. Rosalind flashed her eyes at Peter walking down the corridor stepping into the misty fog, stepping out onto the beach seconds later. Rosalind smiled, seeing Jacob coming down the track on the beach with the old Land Rover, he stopped passing Rosalind a fishing rod and kissed her on the lips. She smiled in appreciation, casting out to sea as far as she could. Jacob tried to cast as far as Rosalind and failed miserably. She tried not to grin. Jacob commented, "if you catch a shark Rosalind, you can deal with him." Jacob watched Rosalind's rod bend under the strain of hooking something; he watched her reeling in another large cod, he sighed profoundly realising he stood no chance against her. Jacob dispatched the fish and Rosalind grabbed Jacob's fishing rod. She cast passing it to him, "now reel in slowly and see what you catch Jacob," kissing him on the cheek.

Jacob laughed, "you cheat Rosalind, you have the strength of God with you." Jacob found his rod bending and something on the line he reeled in slowly struggling, unlike Rosalind, he spent the next 20 minutes trying to land whatever is on the end of his fishing line, only to discover a conger eel. Jacob immediately cut off its head using the shovel in the back of the Land Rover. Rosalind laughing watching Jacob throw the eel in the back of the Land Rover along with her cod. Jacob drove to the farm with Rosalind still expressing a smile, he carried the still wiggling conger eel into the kitchen along with the cod. "Jacob there will be two loads of fertiliser tomorrow morning. Now off to the shop purchase more pickling jars if you can and more white vinegar please." Jacob didn't argue he kissed Rosalind on the cheek dashing out of the house, leaving Jack with Rosalind. He climbed in his Range Rover driving across the Moor, checking on the sheep as he travelled, relieved to see the flock is staying together and not separated. He finally reached the road driving the mile to the shop, entering to the sound of a buzzer on the door going straight to the counter. "Do you happen to have any pickling jars and more white vinegar?"

"I haven't been asked for pickling jars for years, these modern people wouldn't know how to pickle, I have three boxes left. I thought I would never sell how many do you want?"

Jacob smiled, "I will take the lot at the right price and another gallon of white vinegar, I'm pickling fish."

"There are 10 jars and lids in each box if we say £10 a box that's £30 for the lot plus the vinegar?"

"That's a fair price, I know they cost more than that, we're doing each other a favour here," Jacob smiled handing over the money, carrying the boxes to the back of his Range Rover, plus another gallon of white vinegar. Jacob drove off steadily watching people walking across the Moor, at least they were sticking to the correct pathways and not wandering amongst his sheep. Jacob parked outside the house. Rosalind came out opening the tailgate on the Range Rover, carrying a box of jars inside, while Jacob moved the other two returning for the vinegar. Rosalind had already prepared some of the cod and the conger eel. She quickly filled the jars after washing them thoroughly in the sink. Rosalind topped up with vinegar she finally sealed preparing them for the next stage before going into storage. "Jacob, after you've dealt with the two loads of manure tomorrow you can take me shopping, we can pay the £10,000 cheque into the bank and go to a garden centre," she smiled.

He didn't respond, the thought of driving to Exeter is not his idea of a good time, although he appreciated he'd have to pay the cheque in at the bank. Jacob went outside, taking a walk to his pasture land surprised the way the grass is growing, almost on steroids, he thought. Even the 5-acre extension, the grass had caught up and is the same length as the other. Whatever God is sending down is exceptionally potent, if the loads kept coming the way they were, he'd have ample to spread on the 30 acres; once he'd taken a cut of silage which the way things were looking would be in a couple of weeks if not sooner. Jacob smiled, walking across the Moor, finding his flock of 200 ewes, plus lambs. The lambs were progressing nicely and wouldn't be long before they were in the market. Jacob continued walking finding himself looking at the old burial ground where the archaeologist vanished. He couldn't believe they were all evil and taken by God, there must be other forces involved? If they were all females, they could have been kidnapped, but a mixed group. Jacob started walking back to the farm, dropping to the floor like a stone as an Air Force jet appeared to try and cut his head off; the noise is horrendous. The pilot shouldn't be flying this low with sheep on the moor, they would scatter every direction in a panic. Jacob picked himself up, heading for his flock of ewes discovering they'd all bunched together by the bog. He and Jack pushed them away to safer ground; Jacob is relieved none were harmed. He and Jack made their way home stepping inside the house, Rosalind already knew what had taken place. "You heard the jet, Rosalind?"

"Yes, Jacob, I thought he is taking the thatch off the roof, I didn't think they were permitted to fly that low?"

"Not at this time of year anyway, they occasionally do but not that low," Jacob advised calmly deeply concerned.

Rosalind switched on the television. The diversion peter and she set up in the spaceship to occupy the carrier had worked; ships were travelling north on a heightened alert basis. Jacob commented: "One of these days somebody's going to do something they regret and nothing will be left but ashes. Perhaps that's the way God is going to cleanse the earth," he frowned.

"If you were God Jacob how would you resolve the issue, all people seem to do is bicker and argue, seems to be the greatest pastime and to see who can inflict the most pain on the other," Rosalind remarked making a coffee.

Peter and Matthew were both listening to the conversation transmitted by Rosalind's mind, intrigued to see how Jacob would resolve the issue. "I think the first thing if I had the power," he chuckled. "I would melt their electronic equipment that controlled the nuclear weapons, make them inactive; no idiot could press the button and inflict pain and suffering on innocent people."

"You mean something like a virus Jacob?"

Jacob looked to Rosalind: "virus what you mean how would that work?"

"Haven't you ever seen or operated a computer Jacob?"

"No I've seen them in the bank, I watch the typist at work, in some offices at the cattle market."

"A virus is like having a cold, or the flu makes you inactive unwell. You know I died of cancer that's a sort of virus to explain in simple terms."

Jacob smiled, kissing her on the cheek. "Yes give the bloody computers cancer virus, then they couldn't launch the doomsday devices around the world. I think all countries should be affected they'd be in the same pickle," he chuckled.

Peter and Matthew aboard the spaceship had listened to the conversation realising Jacob simplistic idea may be beneficial; they would wait to speak to Rosalind when she came aboard the spaceship in the evening.

Jacob and Rosalind watched television for the rest of the evening before retiring to bed, where she put Jacob to sleep. She stepped from the house into the misty fog boarding the spaceship. Peter and Matthew were waiting. They had already worked out a plan and were waiting to discuss matters with Rosalind. They greeted each other with the flash of their eyes. "Rosalind, we have formulated a plan it would serve two purposes. One to immobilise nuclear weapons and the other to keep countries busy trying to solve the problem and not look for us or worry about people going missing."

"Explain your plan," She said cautiously.

"We can use their own Internet against them; not only will we paralyse nuclear weapons on land at sea and ships and submarines. To enhance Jacobs idea further, we would also include the banks where their money is kept. We estimate it would take them at least two Earth years to resolve the problem; the virus will also affect their satellites."

"Where would you insert the virus whichever country you choose will automatically be blamed and could start more confrontation."

Peter look to Matthew as if they were short of an answer. "Where would you suggest," Peter remarked.

Rosalind smiled, Peter and Matthew looked at her, strangely displaying a human expression. "Insert the virus in satellites simultaneously. We should have a world-wide effect in a matter of minutes. Their antivirus software will not recognise what is sent as a threat until it is too late, and the computers destroyed along with the microchips. If they attempt to launch the nuclear devices will explode before take off."

Peter instructed the computer: "Implement Rosalind's instructions effective immediately."

The computer responded: "Implemented."

"I'm returning to Jacob he is outside filling his tractor with diesel, preparing to come to the beach." Rosalind flashed her eyes to Peter and Matthew they responded likewise. Rosalind stepped into the misty fog transported to the farm. Rosalind shouted across the yard, "Jacob, I'm making coffee before you go."

"Okay," he smiled, walking to the house seeing the television is on with newsflash written across the screen. He sat quickly, watching. Rosalind joined him with the cups of coffee the presenter advised: "Most countries around the world have suffered a catastrophic computer failure on their weapon systems, even ships at sea are suffering from the same virus. The Ministry of Defence has no explanation at the moment."

Jacob smiled glancing to Rosalind: "That will give them a headache for a few weeks" he chuckled, "if they spent the money on curing cancer and other illnesses rather than on weapons; the world would be a better place."

"Off you go, Jacob God is waiting, don't forget you have two loads this morning, he is generous do not upset him," Rosalind smiled.

Jacob placed his cup on the table, walking briskly out of the door, followed by Jack. Jacob opened the cab door Jack jumped in followed by Jacob. He drove down onto the beach, parked, seeing the misty fog approach feeling a load of fertiliser shake the trailer as it loaded. Jacob drove to where he is stockpiling, tipped the load, returning collecting the next load emptying and finally parking by the barn. He returned to the house with Jack finding Rosalind had changed into a pastoral blue dress, wearing her fur-lined coat holding her favourite handbag. "Hurry Jacob, change you're taking me out, I have the cheque for the bank." Jacob stared in disbelief; he'd never seen Rosalind look so beautiful. He quickly ran into the bedroom, finding a suit already laid out on the bed for him; he hadn't worn that one for about five years he thought, changing quickly. Jacob opened the front door for Rosalind and the Range Rover passenger door. "I'm driving Jacob thank you." Jacob laughed, climbing in the passenger side while Rosalind walked around to the driver's door. Rosalind set off slowly down the drive, Jacob glanced to the front door of the house seeing Jack sat there quietly.

Rosalind drove very steadily they were in no rush, and Jacob felt like a trussed up chicken in a suit. Rosalind could see him looking at her; she is reading his thoughts. Some she thought rather explicit what he would like to do with her. After travelling for some time, Rosalind found a parking space. They walked to the bank paying in the £10,000. Continued walking down the road, Jacob holding her hand, which she found quite a pleasing sensation. She steered Jacob into a large garden centre where she purchased a variety of seeds two rose bushes, plus some winter vegetables and seeds. Jacob loaded their purchases into the back of the Range Rover. Rosalind steadily drove home, finding Jack still laying on the front doorstep. Rosalind parked the Range Rover leaving Jacob to unload while she made the coffee and changed into her working clothes.

Jacob grabbed the spade digging two holes one either side of the front door, placing a little manure in each and planting Rosalind roses. She came outside, holding a mug of coffee looking at his handiwork smiling. He accepted the coffee leaving Rosalind to sort out her own vegetable garden that is a taboo area for him, other than preparing the ground. Rosalind planted everything she wanted. She received a telepathic message from Peter, "To bring Jacob to the spaceship; he is to travel to visit Zagader. The inhabitants would stay invisible and betray themselves as spirits, such as suggested in the Bible to avoid any confusion."

Rosalind quickly asked telepathically, "what about the animals, Peter?"

He responded telepathically, "I will shapeshift into Jacob and Matthew will become you for the few days you are away, a new experience for us both."

Rosalind returned to the house, washing her hands in the sink. "Jacob, you are travelling to heaven tonight. Peter and Matthew will look after the farm you have nothing to worry about," she smiled confidently.

Jacob looked shocked, "what do I wear? How long will we be gone?" He asked, extremely concerned.

"You need nothing, miracles will take place the minute we start to travel; your clothes will be replaced; you only need to stay by me, and you will be safe. You will be the first person alive to see the other worlds God has created," she advised with confidence.

Jacob sat down in his armchair. "The first cut of silage in two weeks Rosalind, who will feed Jack? Look after my sheep," he panicked slightly.

"Leave everything to Rosalind; you really think I would allow everything you've worked for to be destroyed. Ye of little faith. I can feel God's displeasure already at your comments Jacob, you should be ashamed."

Jacob bowed his head. "Sorry Lord; earthly possessions have no place in heaven in your eyes; excuse this poor mortals stupidity."

"Time to go, Jacob, hold my hand. Stay here, Jack." Rosalind opened the door they stepped into the misty fog and within seconds were aboard the spaceship. In the seconds they had travelled, Jacobs clothes had changed into a spacesuit, he looked about himself puzzled not expecting to be wearing anything other than a robe as he'd seen in the Bible pictures. Jacob said nothing, Rosalind held his hand, leading him through the vast spaceship lying beneath the water. Suddenly they travelled vertical boarding another spaceship. Rosalind immediately placed her hand on Jacob's forehead rendering him unconscious, suspecting if she didn't, he would be dead within a few minutes. Rosalind awoke Jacob after three days; the spaceship is slowing down, preparing to dock on Zagader. She supported Jacob's arm, steadying him to his feet. He looked from one of the windows observing an Earth-like planet. "Are we home already?"

"No, this is one of God's planets where animals and vegetation are not destroyed by interfering humans. When a creature or human cease to exist on their own planet, they are transported here in spirit form to live in tranquillity, and other planets designated by God the creator."

Jacob exhaled trying to understand everything Rosalind had said, seeing stars in the distance. Rosalind felt the spaceship moving to land on the planet; she quickly rendered Jacob unconscious again until they'd landed safely, she feared the sudden acceleration and deceleration would destroy him if he is conscious. Rosalind felt the spaceship settle, watching her brothers and sisters unload the containers of flesh for storage and turned themselves invisible, so Jacob would not see them. Rosalind awoke Jacob stepping into a misty fog. They travelled away from the spaceship, stepping from the mist on a shoreline. Their spacesuits had gone, they were now wearing robes which made Jacob smile, convincing him this is definitely God's country. Zagaders atmosphere slightly thinner than Earths, Jacob struggled for a while to breathe properly. "Where is everybody," Jacob asked, looking to a starry sky although, daylight.

"All around us Jacob they are in spirit form, you cannot see them because you are alive; if you were dead you would be one of them," She answered calmly.

Jacob watched a lion come running from the jungle, he quickly picked up a rock in a panic taking a defensive posture. Rosalind grabbed his hand: "No, Jacob, the lion won't hurt you. You must remember this is heaven, and God controls the animals." The lion growled walking off into the jungle, Jacob breathed a sigh of relief, noticing a coconut fall striking a rock. He ran over quickly, drinking the milk laughing. He split the coconut completely in half, passing one half to Rosalind. She smiled pleasantly watching Jacob eating. Jacob asked, "Rosalind, are we permitted to swim? I haven't for years the water is always freezing at home."

She nodded, watching Jacob remove his robe running into the sea completely naked. The water extremely warm, Jacob found himself surrounded by dolphins. He could never remember being so happy before other than when he married Rosalind. He looked into the water, watching the fish nibbling at his feet which tickled. "Come on, Rosalind," he shouted, waving his arm for her to join him. Rosalind checked her memory banks immediately understanding how to swim, receiving concerned messages from her brothers and sisters; they never ventured into water other than for experimental purposes.

Rosalind stepped out of her robe, running into the water naked swimming to join Jacob. Her Zibyan, brothers and sisters watched intrigued, they'd seen humans perform in water many times before and considered a way of cleansing the body of bacteria, which Zibyans didn't possess. Rosalind and Jacob spent half an hour swimming around finally returning to the beach. Both laying on the warm sand; much to Rosalind surprise Jacob started making love to her. She had thousands of messages entering her circuitry concerned, she is allowing Jacob to perform a sexual act on her.

Jacob rolled off, jumping to his feet running into the sea; Rosalind followed to cleanse herself without Jacob realising. Her mind exploding with messages and questions. They both finally returned to the beach, slipping on their robes holding hands, they walked along the beach. "This is truly heaven Rosalind," he smiled, noticing bananas growing, he ran over pulling two from the bunch appeared to be ripe. He passed one to Rosalind. "You have it, Jacob, I'm not hungry; thank you," she smiled with satisfaction. She had achieved what she wanted Jacob to visit her home planet and for him to travel here without dying. "Where are we sleeping tonight?" Jacob asked, placing his arm around her waist.

"Where ever you want Jacob, here on the beach or in the mountain's over there in the distance look," she pointed.

Jacob looked into the distance seeing a hazy blue mountain, "I suspect it would be extremely cold up there?"

"No, the temperature stays the same weather night or day Jacob." Jacob looked surprised at her comment suspecting the temperature to fall during the evening and night. They continued walking, watching the sun slowly set. Jacob asked, somewhat concerned, "if we stay out here, Rosalind, what about the animals I don't want to be a lion's dinner, thanks."

"They won't bother you in the slightest Jacob, they have no interest they are all well fed; their hunting instincts are suppressed for the moment." Rosalind held his hand, easing him down to sit on the warm sand. She removed large banana leaves rolling into a pillow for Jacob to rest his head-on. He lay down, she touched his forehead and Jacob is unconscious. Her brothers and sisters immediately materialised, no longer invisible, asking Rosalind questions about her experiences. Rosalind spent the rest of the evening, talking with her brothers and sisters, explaining the sensation of physical contact with a human, she would not recommend; although humans appeared to enjoy immensely.

By 7 o'clock in the morning, Jacob woke stared in disbelief, Rosalind's brothers and sisters vanished. Jacob rose to his feet kissing Rosalind on the cheek removing his robe, he ran out into the sea, he couldn't understand how warm the water is and eventually rejoined Rosalind; who somehow miraculously had acquired bacon and eggs on a plate. Jacob sat on the sand, enjoying his breakfast suspecting God could produce whatever he wanted. Don't be stupid and ask a question he thought. Jacob finished his breakfast, Rosalind removed the plate and utensils from his hand. Jacob watched them vanish. Rosalind laughed, "one of the spirits you can't see prepared your breakfast this morning."

"Oh," Jacob replied, trying to stay calm in an otherwise crazy situation. Jacob watched the misty fog appear before him and Rosalind, she encouraged him to enter. Rosalind instantly sedated Jacob while they travelled several light-years to the next terror formed planet; for the Zibyans to experiment on and create another replica of Earth, minus the human infestation. Rosalind eased Jacob from the misty fog into a clearing amongst palm trees and other spectacular vegetation. Jacob wasn't feeling well, the atmosphere is thinner still on this planet, he sat down trying to breathe. Rosalind surmised whether it would be possible to implant a Zibyan intelligence into a human. Her brothers and sisters were reading her thoughts and were considering the possibility. Although at the outset could not see the benefit of doing so; they needed more feedback from Rosalind on her assessment. After half an hour, Jacob had calm down and could breathe satisfactorily, although he couldn't move quickly before he became breathless. Rosalind considered her last thought, Jacob would not be Jacob if they transplanted a Zibyan brain into his human body; besides she liked Jacob the way he is not predictable. Rosalind taken by surprise discovering a shelter constructed suspecting by the humans, they had transported here as food for the animals. Jacob cautiously entered the bamboo construction. He noticed a carving on a piece of bamboo: "Help we are dying." Jacob glanced to Rosalind alarmed. "What is this Rosalind?"

Rosalind focused on what he is reading: "I don't have an explanation, somebody playing silly games, I suspect children's spirits."

Jacob sat down in the makeshift chair someone had made out of bamboo, looking from the construction, he noticed a panda sat quietly eating. Jacob rose to his feet; he now had a horrible feeling inside; this may not be gods creation. He walked briskly closely followed by Rosalind. Jacob could hear the faint sound of water running; he quickened his pace finally coming to a waterfall noticing in the clear water human remains, a skull, in fact, the whole skeleton he presumed. He sat down pondering, trying to find an explanation for what he is seeing. This is definitely more than Childs play now. He couldn't envisage God, Jesus, Peter or Matthew involved in a murder.

Rosalind slowly sat beside him. She asked calmly, "what conclusions have you come to Jacob?"

"I'm trying to find a logical explanation and can't, God would not permit such a thing."

"How many times Jacob in the Bible has God lay waste to humans standing in the way of his chosen people? What happened to Sodom and Gomorrah? God chooses who lives and who dies, not you or I. He decides how they die according to their behaviour. If they are good, they become a spirit if they are evil, the animals enjoy their flesh, they die a slow and painful death. If you cannot accept God's chosen path, then I suggest you burn your Bible Jacob," she expressed firmly hoping he would accept her explanation.

Jacob sat quietly, considering what she'd said; he knew she spoke the truth regarding Solomon Gomorrah. The Israelites were favoured by God, he made the path for them to follow. "I cannot argue with your logic Rosalind since you have spoken to the Almighty and his disciples, I'm in no position to question. Please take me home to the environment I understand, until my allotted time."

Rosalind held Jacob's hand, watching him look one more time at the skeleton lay beneath the clear water. The misty fog appeared Rosalind encouraged Jacob to step inside. She immediately sedated him wiping his mind of what he'd seen, very regrettable she thought, not her plan at all. Within seconds they had travelled light years returning too Zagader her home planet. She helped Jacob to his feet. Many of her brothers and sisters materialised in front of Jacob, wearing robes. Jacob stared in disbelief, one young woman approached him not dissimilar to Rosalind. "Welcome to heaven Jacob, you were chosen to see his glory," she produced in the palm of her hand an orange, "enjoy, the fruits of heaven."

"Thank you," Jacob smiled, excepting the fruit; he watched the orange peel itself in the palm of his hand. He plucked segments slipping into his mouth, enjoying. Jacob glanced to the sky seeing angels flying around him male and female from what he could see. Rosalind realised he'd calmed down considerably, although she had attempted to wipe his mind of the last stressful event without damaging his brain, she knew he's still very unsure of everything. As suddenly as the Angels had appeared, they vanished along with the others in robes leaving Rosalind and Jacob stood there alone. Jacob sighed heavily, "I apologise, Rosalind, I'm shocked to think God would allow people to be eaten by animals."

CHAPTER 5

The Journey Home

Rosalind and Jacob stepped into the misty fog taken aboard the spacecraft. Jacob asked, "I don't remember much about travelling here. I would like to look out of the window if possible at the wondrous creation of God."

Rosalind held Jacobs hand, taking him to a large observation window. "If you start to feel ill, Jacob, you must tell me immediately. You must remember spirits can travel at any speed, human flesh cannot, and the last thing I want is you to become a spirit before your allotted time," she advised kissing him on the forehead.

He nodded. The spaceship started to accelerate; Rosalind had already asked the captain to reduce the forward velocity for a while. She would sedate Jacob whether he approved or not. Otherwise, it could take several Earth years to travel the distance. Rosalind had insisted the crew remain invisible to Jacob while they travelled to earth. She spent several hours checking systems becoming rather bored travelling at such a slow speed, felt she could get out and walk quicker to earth. Rosalind realised a human assessment that made her smile. She's about to return to Jacob stepping from the corridor, she noticed another Zibyan sat by him impersonating her. Rosalind had never felt outraged before anger is not part of the Zibyan culture; they always were cold and calculating in their decision-making. She turned herself invisible to Jacob and stayed out of view of the sister impersonating her. She accepted the fact the Zibyans shared their thoughts, and there wasn't such a thing as possession of an item. Although at this precise second Rosalind experienced human jealousy for the first time, which shouldn't happen, her construction should not permit. She suspected since she is thinking as an individual and not as a collective, this may be the cause of her outrage.

"I don't know what's come over you Rosalind," Jacob remarked, "you've never been this affectionate before," he chuckled.

"We are married, Jacob, let's enjoy each other," the female impersonating Rosalind suggested.

"Here and now Rosalind," Jacob asked surprised.

"Why not," removing her space suit laying on the floor. Jacob removed his suit, making love unknowingly to an impostor. Rosalind watched intrigued, she couldn't blame Jacob in the slightest as far as he is concerned it's her. When they finally finished the Rosalind impostor rose to her feet dressing in her suit kiss Jacob on the forehead; saw Rosalind, the impostor vanished instantly. Rosalind chased after her intending to administer harm, abruptly stopped by other members of the crew. "I am a commander Rosalind you do not own anything, and neither do we; remove the incompatible thoughts from your mind and return to Jacob." She immediately changed into Rosalind, walking down the corridor to find Jacob asleep. She touched his forehead to ensure he would stay in that state for the rest of the journey, telepathically instructing the commander, "increase their speed. Jacob is now unconscious."

Rosalind is receiving messages of concern from her brothers and sisters, concerning her aggressive thoughts towards another sister, who only sampled what is permitted to anyone if they wished. Rosalind realised she would have to calm the situation, or she could be taken from earth and made to return to Zagader. Rosalind telepathically apologised to everyone explaining. "They were new sensations she hadn't experienced before and maybe, very beneficial should the Zibyan nation be under attack sometime in the future."

Rosalind waited for a response, she is thinking as an individual like a human. Her mind suddenly filled with answers of approval at her explanation, she could be extremely beneficial should an unsavoury situation arise. Rosalind smiled, looking out of the observation window, she stayed there for the whole length of travel which is three days. Rosalind awoke Jacob in preparation to transport to the other ship.

The transport ship positioned under the water linking to the other ship. Rosalind and Jacob were greeted by Matthew and Peter. Jacob immediately bowed his head in respect to what he believed were two disciples of the Lord. Matthew instructed: "We require your trailer; there is more fertiliser for you, Jacob coming from heaven in the morning."

Jacob glanced to Matthews expression, which appeared to be lifeless unlike Rosalind's. "I will Park on the beach at 8 o'clock, Sir."

Rosalind escorted Jacob along the corridor into the misty fog, they stepped out by the front door of Jacobs house already changed into their original clothes. Jack inside by the fire, they'd only been gone eight days; most of that spent travelling. Jacob is having re-occurring thoughts almost like nightmares of dead bodies. He asked directly, "Rosalind the fertiliser God is supplying is it the remains of humans?"

Rosalind made the coffee using powdered milk, they would have to go to the shop tomorrow. "What do you think, Jacob? You have sat there watching television; condemning unruly humans, in some cases condemning them to death. Why are you so surprised God may listen to your opinion when he gives you the gift of travel to see the beauty of his creations. I am surprised at your attitude Jacob after what God has given you," she advised with authority.

Jacob exhaled he realised he couldn't stand against God's wishes, no matter what he did. God created the earth, stipulated in the Bible; he'd met Peter and Matthew visited God's homeworlds. He personally wasn't responsible for killing anybody, he is merely making use of the fertiliser. "I'm sorry," Rosalind easing her down onto his lap.

"You've had more than your fair share travelling home," she smiled, getting up. "After you transport the fertiliser in the morning, we're going shopping Jacob," she ordered. Jacob slipped on his coat, grabbing his crook from the back of the door, deciding to check on his ewes and lambs. The lambs would soon have to go to market for store lambs, he couldn't fatten them up here. Jacob stepped from the house followed by Jack; they quickly walked across the Moor, trying to check on the sheep before nightfall. Jacob is rather pleased with what he could see, surprising how things change even if you're only away for a few days. The lambs were progressing nicely, and perhaps next week would send them to market. He slowly walked back to the farm sitting by the fire after feeding Jack. Rosalind had made Jacob a sandwich until they have gone shopping tomorrow. They retired to bed Rosalind touched Jacob's hand, he fell into a deep sleep. She changed her appearance stepping from the house into the misty fog, transported to the spaceship. Peter acknowledged flashing his eyes as Rosalind had. "I see you have explained to Jacob the fertiliser is humans?"

"Yes, he's far from stupid Peter after seeing the skeletons which were unfortunate. I would have hoped the Lions would have crunched the bones to nothing or the hyenas, I suspect it's because they fell in the water. He appears to believe it's God's wish and continuing to dispose of the waste, we are fortunate he believes the Bible." Rosalind and Peter watched Matthew appear carrying a large suitcase which is filled with money they discovered when he opened. "You can use this to improve the farm Rosalind; otherwise, will be incinerated," Matthew advised.

"I will have to conceal from Jacob, I appreciate Matthew. There are many improvements I wish to make in the coming months, one will be a computer, and the old generator needs replacing. I have to confess I find it extremely pleasurable involved in the farm, good experience for whatever may lay in our future," she smiled.

Peter remarked: "Jacob has come down onto the beach with the trailer, you had better join him, Rosalind." They flash their eyes at each other, and Rosalind walked down the corridor carrying the large suitcase. She stepped into the misty fog, changing her appearance stepping out onto the beach. The morning air extremely fresh she thought, tying the suitcase to the hydraulics of the tractor, there wasn't room in the cab for her and the suitcase. Jacob opened the cab door for her, she climbed in quickly shutting the door. Jacob had the heater running in the tractor, he looked somewhat worried. She scanned his thoughts, "No, I'm not moving out Jacob," she chuckled, watching him grin. "May I know what's in the suitcase," he asked hesitantly.

"A present from God that's all you need to know. I have to keep some secrets from you, Jacob," she chuckled teasing him. They felt the trailer shudder as Matthew tipped the first load into the trailer. Jacob started the tractor heading up the track reversing to his manure pile, he tipped the fertiliser on the existing pile and continue to the beach after Rosalind stepped from the cab releasing the suitcase going in the house. She went down into the cellar hiding the suitcase behind two large barrels. She ran up the stairs returning to the kitchen, making two coffees switching on the television as Jacob came in. He sat beside her watching the TV displaying more depressing news of fighting abroad, and women and children suffering. Jacob muttered, "this has to stop Rosalind. God must intervene, they are better off dead than suffering like that," he exhaled.

Rosalind patted his leg, "God is watching everything Jacob watch what happens in a minute."

The reporter appeared in front of the camera: "The guns have stopped the rocket launchers have exploded? Why I have no idea; hundreds of soldiers have vanished into thin air?" Jacob watched the female reporter place a hand to her mouth in shock, bewildered by what had taken place. Jacob stared at Rosalind. "You knew exactly what's going to happen, Rosalind, how?"

"Very simple Jacob; you remember the last conversation we had regarding missiles and rockets, you suggested we give them a virus. God has approved your idea. Now when armies release weapons of mass destruction, they will merely explode if they try to launch," she smiled with satisfaction. "Yes, Jacob, there is another load of fertiliser for you tomorrow at 8:30."

"How many innocent people have died Rosalind," he asked somewhat in a panic.

"None! Anyone who fires upon helpless women and children is guilty in God's eyes, you have read the Bible! What does God advise regarding children?"

"I know the passage you are referring to Rosalind; I cannot fault his decision. There is nothing so innocent as a child until the parents warped their minds with subversive behaviour."

"If all humans were like you, Jacob God would not have a problem. Come along, turn the television off Jacob were going shopping," she smiled.

Jacob patted Jack, "look after the place we won't belong," he smiled, stepping from the house walking down the yard to the Range Rover accompanied by Rosalind. "I'm driving Jacob," she insisted which made Jacob laugh.

They drove across the Moor, looking at his lambs. "We will have to send them soon to market, they can go next week; they should make a reasonable price for store lambs," he smiled.

"I think you need a new sheep trailer the one you have is rotten Jacob, it's a wonder it stays together."

"That will cost more than the lambs fetch at the market," he advised deeply concerned with her money spending. "You appear to forget Jacob we had a £10,000 rebate; plus the money I've saved. I'm also buying a computer and a new generator. You might as well be upset with my spending all at once rather than in phases," she grinned, mischievously; human expressions she enjoyed immensely watching the horror appear on Jacobs face at what she'd said.

Jacob exhaled suspecting he wasn't only arguing with Rosalind probably with God who is definitely on her side. Instead of driving to the shop, Rosalind continued for several miles, in fact for over an hour coming to an agricultural dealership. She smiled pleasantly observing a row of sheep trailers. Rosalind grabbed Jacobs arm dragging him along. He had to admit, he is beginning to enjoy spending money, although petrified they could ill afford the expense. The thought of a new trailer which would be easier to load is quite appealing. Jacob and Rosalind looked inside several; deciding to take a double-deck trailer which the Range Rover would easily pull. Jacob stood there watching Rosalind count out the money. He watched over £5000 vanish from his savings. The dealership fitted the number plate on the rear of the trailer and Rosalind backed up like a professional hitching to the new trailer. Jacob couldn't stop grinning the woman is a menace or should he referred to her as an angel. Jacob shook the sales rep's hand climbing into his Range Rover, Rosalind drove off whatever she attempted she is exceptionally professional at. She finally parked alongside the shop. He pushed the trolley while Rosalind plucked items from the shelves. The shopkeeper commented: "I managed to acquire more pickling jars for those just in case moments Jacob."

Before Jacob could speak. "We will take them," Rosalind advised. "How many boxes?"

"I have five boxes of 10 in a box, and I have 5 gallons of white vinegar."

"We will take everything." The shopkeeper looked absolutely shocked at her comment not suspecting Jacob to want any more jars or vinegar at the moment.

Jacob grinned loading everything in the Range Rover. Rosalind paid and joined him. Rosalind drove around the road this time gently entering their drive, trying not to break anything travelling across the ruts. "Tomorrow Jacob after you've moved the load of fertiliser, I will come down onto the beach and load the trailer with stone. You can fill these ruts in their becoming ridiculous and will damage your vehicles, if not repaired, no one will ever want to come here," she expressed firmly.

"That's the general idea, Rosalind," he advised biting his tongue trying not to lose his temper. "I don't want strangers on the farm. If I repaired the track, make it so easy for criminals to drive to the farm."

"If you were on your own Jacob, I could understand your point of view; now you have God's protection, you really think anything will happen. Whoever attempts to rob you will end up in your trailer as fertiliser," she affirmed without hesitation.

He exhaled not responding, guessing would be futile. Jacob detached the trailer from the Range Rover a brand-new shiny Ivor Williams which stuck out like a sore thumb; rutted track or not if anyone caught sight of it he thought it would be stolen in minutes. He went into the house to find Roslyn had made the coffee, he placed one box of groceries on the table, going outside he carried in the pickling jars and vinegar. "You must be planning another fishing adventure with this amount of jars and vinegar Rosalind."

"I happen to know, you like pickled cabbage and pickled onions, yes we can pickle more fish if we desire."

He sat quietly, drinking his coffee after switching on the television. Jacob remarked, "Rosalind, you realise taking stone from the beach is sort of illegal."

Rosalind placed her hands on her hips, pretending to be an annoyed human female. "Stay in the house tomorrow Jacob. I will move the fertiliser and repair the road myself! I don't need you at all to help, I didn't realise every stone is counted on the beach, and once the sea washes over what I've removed, you won't know the difference."

"Rosalind that maybe the case, they will see what you placed on the track, will stand out like a sore thumb. Some nosy official will only have to test and check the beach before they realise what we've done. Do you have to go looking for trouble," he emphasised annoyed.

Rosalind left the house realising Jacob had a valid point. She jumped in the Range Rover driving off joining the main road. She hadn't travelled far before she came across road repairs, they were removing old tarmac. Rosalind parked on the side of the road the gang Foreman came over. "3 miles up the road," she explained. "I have an old track full of ruts would it be possible for you to tip one or two loads on the track, I can fill the ruts in myself with the tractor." Rosalind had seen studying humans, they used a form of inducement, which is cash. Rosalind removed a couple of hundred pounds from her pocket watching the mans face light up. "I'll follow you with the next lorry load show me where you want it tipped, that'll buy you three loads," he smiled. Rosalind quickly calculated that would be sufficient to fill in the potholes. She sat quietly in her Range Rover, waiting for the lorry to be filled. She steadily drove off with the lorry following, she turned into the track parked, pointing to the track, put her thumb up, the lorry driver blasting his horn in acknowledgement and Rosalind returned to the farm.

Jacob heard the tractor and loader start, he came dashing out thinking someone is stealing his tractor. Rosalind, changing the manure a fork for the bucket so she could scoop up the road planings. Jacob looked down the drive seeing the lorry load of road planings, he smiled at her resourcefulness. Rosalind would not be beaten under any circumstances, he decided, grabbed a shovel walking down the track. Rosalind joined him with the tractor filling the ruts with a little discarded tarmac and Jacob levelling with the shovel. Rosalind had to remember to switch the tractor lights on so Jacob didn't realise she could see in the dark. They carried on working until 11 o'clock in the evening, which is ridiculous really, Jacob thought afterwards. They could have finished the next day; nevertheless, the job is finished, and his back felt like he'd been run over with a steam roller, he could barely walk. Jacob hobbled to the house going straight to the bedroom, changing into his pyjamas, falling asleep on the bed instantly. Rosalind fed Jack all the waste products she'd accumulated through the day. Jack had never had such a good life before Rosalind arrived; he's living like a king. Rosalind went into the bedroom, touching Jacob on the forehead, ensuring he wouldn't wake too soon. She changed her appearance stepping outside the house into the misty fog and transported to the spaceship deep beneath the waves.

She hadn't been there long discussing issues with Matthew and Peter when their scanner alerted them to an intruder on the farm. Rosalind looked, noticing someone reversing up to their new sheep trailer. She remembered what Jacob had said, why he hadn't repaired the track to help stop unwanted visitors. Rosalind immediately returned to the farm while Peter extracted the two thieves turning them into fertiliser to be collected by Jacob in the morning. Rosalind realised Jacob couldn't find a strange vehicle on the farm; otherwise, he'd be really suspicious of what had taken place and probably involve the police, which she definitely didn't want. She climbed in the van after detaching their sheep trailer, quickly driving down the road only to discover she's chased by a police car. Rosalind drove for several miles from the farm deciding to drive off the cliff, changing into a fish swimming away as the van entered the water. Peter had already realised what Rosalind had done sending the misty fog to collect her. She shapeshifted back into the form of Rosalind stepping into the misty fog transported to the spaceship.

Peter remarked: "You really can think as an individual Rosalind, the police car didn't realise you driven off the cliff. They carried on along the road, trying to catch the van. Perhaps you should listen to Jacob Rosalind this incident wouldn't have occurred."

"Agreed! Nevertheless, with our technology, humans are no competition for the Zibyans," she smiled, which always made Peter concerned, she's copying humans to frequently in appearance and actions.

At 8:30 Jacob drove down onto the beach with his tractor and trailer, collecting a load of fertiliser transporting to the manure pile, he tipped returning to the house. Rosalind already there with his breakfast ready. Jacob commented: "Somebody came to the farm last night Rosalind there are strange tyre tracks in the dust. I bet they were after my Ivor Williams sheep trailer, why they didn't take it I don't know. I forgot to lock it to one of the posts with the chain."

"Well if anyone came up here who wasn't invited, they certainly won't make a return visit," she advised calmly; switching on the television and quickly changing the channel, after seeing a crane lifting the white van from the sea and divers boarding a small boat. Rosalind thankful she drove at least 5 miles away from the farm so there'd be no connection.

Jacob finished his breakfast patting his leg for Jack to follow, he went out of the door saying, "I'll check on the pasture to see if we can sneak in an early cut of silage and I'll check the ewes and lambs," he smiled, closing the door. Jacob walked down the old track to the road, in places he could see the strange tyre marks which were not from his vehicle. Jacob walked across the Moor until reaching his pastureland 30 acres. He's pleasantly surprised since he'd spread fertiliser on the pasture it had come on in leaps and bounds. There is definitely sufficient for one cut of silage, and hopefully, one cut of hay before the end of summer. He had plenty of fertiliser in stock thanks to God and unruly humans who God incinerated. Jacob sighed slowly continuing to walk across the Moor coming across his flock of sheep. He definitely needed to take the lambs to market; they wouldn't improve any more there's insufficient grass, he wanted his ewes to rest before the Ram is introduced again. He suddenly realised he needed a new Ram he wasn't going to start interbreeding. Jacob and Jack returned to the farm. He began to set up a large pen to separate ewes and lambs; there would be at least 2 loads in his new sheep trailer. Rosalind came out realising what Jacob is preparing, she knew he had every intention of keeping the ewe lambs back that were born last year to increase his flock to around 250 breeders. Rosalind suggested: "Jacob, you know it's at least a three-hour drive to market; do you know exactly how many lambs you're sending?"

"None of the ewe lambs; I can't remember how many others there are, I'll find out in the morning it'll be an early start. Early next week, I want to take the first cut of silage Rosalind with your help," he smiled. "Why don't you bring them closer to the farm Jacob? Better still separate the ewes and lambs tonight, we'll have an early start in the morning."

"Okay," he kissed Rosalind on the cheek. Jacob set off across the Moor with Jack, spending an hour rounding up his flock returning to the farm. Once the sheep were penned. The laborious job of separating ewes and lambs started. The ewes were easy to sort out; the lambs were a different story. After they'd finished sorting lambs, Jacob discovered he had 25 for market which is a load. Jacob fed and watered the lambs going to market in the morning, although they were more concerned with trying to escape back to their mothers, who hadn't a care in the world they'd wandered off looking for fresh grass. Rosalind and Jacob returned to the house, Jacob is shattered, and after a quick cup of coffee, he went to bed. Rosalind touched his forehead, making sure he wouldn't wake until 4 o'clock in the morning when they'd have to set out for the market with their lambs once they'd loaded.

Rosalind changed her appearance stepping outside the house into the misty fog immediately transported to the spaceship, Peter is waiting for her. "Is it essential for you to be so involved with Jacob Rosalind," Peter asked, concerned.

"You're not jealous! Are you, Peter," Rosalind laughed, displaying another human expression.

Peter quickly search through his memory banks, discovering the meaning of jealousy which is not Zibyan practice. "I find your remark out of order. I am certainly not jealous as you call it of anything Rosalind. Although you did display your jealousy when the Zibyan female practised on Jacob aboard the transport ship; explain your behaviour!"

"I thought it's pretty obvious you have access to my thoughts, along with the rest of the Zibyan collective. I am hiding nothing I merely practised a human reaction. You appear to forget Peter, although we are designated male and female when we are constructed; we are actually neither. We are whatever we wish to choose to betray. If I wish to be a male Zibyan, I could as you can become a female Zibyan." "Why are you stating the obvious Rosalind why are you telling me something I already know. I think you are trying to separate yourself even further from the collective to pursue your own interests, which would be highly inadvisable if you wish to continue to exist," Peter warned firmly.

Rosalind looked to the wall watching the screen appear, members of the home planet were visible. "If I am to be accused as Peter has suggested, I recommend you order me to Zagader on the next transport ship my brothers and sisters. Peter is correct! I operate as an individual and not as a collective some of the time. You cannot operate as a collective when you work with humans on a one-to-one basis."

A member of the home collective spoke: "Peter, we sense your brain cells are functioning irrationally. We order you to connect to the main computer so the errors can be corrected in your thought pattern. Rosalind, we are monitoring everything; we are permitting you to continue with your experimentation, operating as an individual; we accept your explanation; this may be a beneficial asset in the future."

"Thank you, brothers and sisters, I can assure you I only have the collective success as a top priority nothing else."

"Rosalind, you will be interested to hear, we have named one of the six planets Rosalind and another Jacob. A vote was cast not including yourself Peter or Matthew to avoid impartiality."

"The only word I can use brothers and sisters is thank you, which is a human saying and I'm sure Jacob if he ever knew, he would be extremely pleased with your decision, his name will live on after he's passed away."

The firstborn on Zibyan rose in the air advising: "Jacob may not cease to function, you know Rosalind we created the human DNA. We can prevent his ageing, and the only way he would cease to operate is through an accident once we've altered his DNA. This would give him the same life expectancy as the Zibyan, what is your view?"

"I'm sure Jacob would be pleased; however, he couldn't stay here on earth the scientists would imprison him experiment on him trying to work out why he wasn't ageing or dying. The solution would be to transport him to his name planet around the normal age a human would die. We know we can transport him we've already proved with the last transport."

The firstborn Zibyan spoke: "You are correct Rosalind in your analysis, something we had overlooked. We keep considering the humans as insignificant, they are not they are extremely intelligent. Jacob has served our collective by disposing of waste and you Rosalind sacrifice yourself for the well-being of our collective; we will speak again on these matters."

Rosalind flashed her eyes in respect of her brothers and sisters who responded likewise. She walked along the corridor, glanced back and flashed her eyes to Peter, who had come away from the main computer after having his brain cells checked for defects. She stepped into the misty fog walking into the house, finding Jacob sat at the breakfast table drinking coffee. "I thought I would have to leave without you Rosalind, nearly 4:30. I've already loaded the lambs come along," he insisted worried hoping his lambs would fetch a reasonable price. "I'm driving," Rosalind insisted. Jacob shook his head, not bothering to argue climbing into the passenger seat and Jack sitting by his feet.

Rosalind drove very steadily, finally reaching the market. They quickly penned their lambs taking the paperwork to the office. Rosalind remarked: "I hadn't better be seen with you Jacob it may cause questions to be asked when you bump into old friends, don't you think?"

"Yes, I understand Rosalind," he kissed her on the cheek watching her run behind the cattle shed. The next minute a misty fog appeared and vanished, he knew she'd gone home. Jacob left the cattle market around lunch-time, his store lambs had fetched a reasonable price. He drove steadily, stopped in a lay-by to purchase flowers on the way. He finally reached the farm parking the Ivor Williams chaining to a post; he grabbed the flowers from the passenger seat entering the house.

Rosalind had made him a lovely lunch; he often wondered how she knew what time to make a meal for, guessed God is telling her. She kissed him lovingly on the lips excepting the flowers, she knew this is a human custom. She placed the flowers in a vase on the table, giving them pride of place while Jacob enjoyed his roast lamb roast potatoes and vegetables. After lunch, Jacob ventured outside looking at his mower, hoping it would survive another year, he purchased it 10 years ago, and it stood out in all that time. He attached the mower to his Ford tractor which almost dwarfs the mower, drove to the pasture and started cutting certainly quicker this year having the extra horsepower really made the mower moved quickly. By teatime, he cut the 30 acres returning to the farm taking the mower off. He fought through the stinging nettles finding his hay tedder attaching to the back of his tractor. Rosalind had already come out while he is mowing attaching the round baler to her massy tractor and loader. Jacob walked over to the old articulated trailer the floor is almost rotted away; he'd used reinforcing wire to patch in places. The tyres look perished, he hoped she would last another season.

They returned to the house, watching television for the rest of the evening, finally retiring to bed. Rosalind placed a hand on his forehead, making him unconscious.

She stepped from the house into the misty fog transported to the spaceship. Matthew waiting for her. "Rosalind; Peter has ventured to Egypt as an experiment."

Rosalind smiled, "I hope he discovers what he's looking for, I'm sure it's something scientific, Peter has always been that way inclined."

Matthew flashed his eyes, "you are correct Rosalind he has the notion, humans have hidden a nuclear facility which we were unaware of, he's investigating in person."

"When is the next shipment for Zagader Matthew?"

"Next week now we have expanded the planets we are terraforming; there will be more animals to feed some have bred already, and we are transporting the young between planets to save genetically engineering others.."

"We are harvesting the grass turning into silage, we will be able to spread a considerable amount of fertiliser on the pasture once we've completed the task." The alarms sounded in the spaceship something coming aboard; as Zibyan in distress which is unheard of. Peter had materialised on the floor, not moving. Rosalind and Matthew ease Peter to the wall where the main computer linked to him. They watched the screen appear playing the information extracted by the central computer from Peter's mind. He had inadvertently connected himself to a nuclear device buried beneath the ground in Egypt far out in the desert, causing his power supply to be drained rapidly. The facility in question is unknown to the Zibyans. Peter suspicions were correct there were secret installations they were not aware of.

Rosalind casually walked to the invisible control panel. "Computer, turn everyone who's working in the facility into animal food and annihilate the facility." Matthew and Rosalind watched an explosion and a mushroom cloud from the nuclear facility. They walked to the processing unit watching bodies turned into joints, and the on wanted parts incinerated stored ready for Jacob to spread on the field. The computer advised: "Peter's life force will be repaired in 24 earth hours."

Rosalind and Matthew flashed eyes at each other. She continued walking along the corridor, changing her appearance stepping into the misty fog, stepping out by the front door of the house. Jacob is sat watching television. "Rosalind, a nuclear facility has exploded in Egypt; they estimate a thousand people killed; terrible," he expressed drinking his coffee.

"Accidents will happen, Jacob," she smiled. "Have you checked the moisture content of the grass you cut yesterday?"

"No, I get the message! I'm on my way if it's fit Rosalind, I will row up into rows ready for you to bale." Jacob left the house climbing aboard his Ford tractor with a lovely cab to keep the wind off him. He drove steadily to the pastureland jumping from the cab, he twisted the grass in his hands, checking the moisture content. The wind had really done its job, Jacob started rowing the grass ready for the round baler. Not only is the wind blowing warm air, but the sun is also shining for a change which made him think of flystrike on his sheep; realising he would have to dip them soon to protect them against the flies. By lunchtime Jacob had rowed the 30 acres returning to the farm, he detached the tedder. He backed up to the old trailer attaching going into the house to have lunch. Rosalind had made sandwiches. "I've already eaten Jacob. I thought you could do with cheese and pickle today."

"That's fine, Rosalind."

"I'll start baling Jacob; you come with the bale wrapper, once I've baled everything, we can transport the round bales and stack outside the barn. They won't hurt left outside, and you can spread more manure to encourage the grass to grow ready for haymaking."

Rosalind left the house climbing in the cab of her massy tractor and loader towing the round baler to the field. Her computerised mind read the operators manuals in seconds understanding how everything operated. She set off producing bale after bale. Jacob, with the bale wrapper, had followed behind collecting the bales and wrapping them in plastic. By teatime, she had baled the 30 acres. Jacob could never remember Rosalind so proficient with farm machinery, she's excellent at repairing things that were for sure, operating he couldn't remember.

Rosalind had returned to the farm detaching the round baler connecting the bale grab to the loader. She returned to the field as Jacob had finished wrapping the last bale. Rosalind started loading the bales on the old rickety wooden trailer. Jacob had returned to the farm detaching the bale wrapper, heading back to the field to attaches tractor to the old wooden trailer. Jacob stared in shock; the trailer had collapsed bent in the middle the trailer a wreck finished. He watched Rosalind drive past him looking annoyed. She tore off down the drive in the Range Rover as if on a mission, not bothering to speak to him. Jacob returned to the house, there's nothing he could do they haven't a trailer suitable for moving round bales. He sat there drinking coffee, watching television. Hearing the Range Rover return, Rosalind entered the house playing the annoyed housewife, placing her hands on her hips. "Jacob you should have replaced that trailer years ago! I purchased a new one will arrive in the morning; we will continue clearing the field. God has loads of fertiliser waiting, we need the field cleared to spread on," she insisted.

Jacob retaliated! "You must remember Rosalind before you returned, and God appears to have an endless supply of money I couldn't afford the diesel for the tractors; let alone purchase any new items. The rickety old trailer my father purchased, we've repaired it year after year to make do. That's all we can ever do here make do; you should remember that Rosalind," Jacob annoyed, walking out of the house and across the Moor followed by Jack. The twilight evening air is fresh, and the mist is coming down. Jacob didn't care he could walk the Moor blindfolded he thought, following the well-worn sheep tracks would take you to one destination or another. 9 o'clock in the evening before Jacob finally stepped through the front door of his house. Rosalind wasn't there he wondered if he'd said too much. The front door open, making him jump, Rosalind had fetched a barrow load of blocks for the fire. She pushed past him stacking the wood against the hearth, finally shutting the door, making a coffee. "Sorry, Rosalind, I didn't mean to sound off," Jacob exhaled.

"I suggest you drink your coffee Jacob and go to bed, we have a busy day tomorrow the trailer will be here by 9 o'clock."

Jacob laughed, "you sending me to bed without any supper as punishment!"

Rosalind smiled, "no, I quite forgot; you'll have to put up with bread and cheese. I'm not cooking anything now. Your own fault for storming out," she expressed enjoying the argumentative situation something Zibyans never participated in. Rosalind placed the bread and butter on the table opening the cupboard removing a block of cheese.

Jacob sat quietly slicing the crusty loaf spreading a little butter and a slice of cheese. Rosalind placed a bowl of food down for Jack by the fire. Half an hour later Jacob went into the bedroom changing for bed, and Rosalind followed pressing a button on the wall switching off the old generator, which she intended to replace it is totally inefficient and half the time struggled to supply sufficient power. She knew Jacob hated her using it, cost him money in the form of diesel, he would usually sit in the dark with a candle using the Aga to cook on rather than the electric cooker. They had a freezer down in the cellar which the generator would keep cold if it ever ran long enough. Rosalind went to bed, touching Jacob's forehead stepping from the bedroom, changing going outside stepping into the misty fog and transported aboard the spaceship.

Peter is standing there waiting to greet her, flashing his eyes. "Rosalind, I am pleased to see you. I thought my existence would end, I'm fortunate to have sufficient power to return to the spaceship."

Rosalind flashed her eyes, "you have recovered, a misfortunate error on your part Peter. You should know not to touch radiation it conflicts with your construction after the thousands of years you have existed, you make such a silly mistake!"

"Thank you, sister, for reminding me. I am not Jacob to be chastised and argued with; you must remember to switch off your human behaviour when you come aboard a Zibyan spaceship Rosalind."

"My error Peter we have both made mistakes," she smiled.

"Rosalind, send Jacob in the morning we have at least 10 tons of fertiliser waiting."

Matthew appeared, flashing his eyes to both. "An explosion in China a volcano has erupted unexpectedly 300 people are missing."

"How unfortunate," Rosalind chuckled, knowing exactly where the corpses were processed.

Peter remarked: "Rosalind is it necessary for you to distort your features when not with Jacob, serves no purpose aboard a Zibyan spaceship."

"You are argumentative Peter; this is not the Zibyan way." Rosalind watched the screen appear on the wall with many of her brothers and sisters looking at them. The firstborn spoke: "Have you caught a virus, Peter? Why are you criticising Rosalind? She is in female form for the benefit of us all. Her facial expressions are essential to maintain. She is assigned to Jacob to dispose of our waste to create replicas of the earth for Zibyans, it is written in our creator's memoirs."

"I didn't realise I am argumentative, I will link to the computer again and see if there is a defect," Peter remarked walking across the room attaching to the wall, allowing the computer to examine his mind.

Rosalind flashed her eyes to Matthew walking down the corridor stepping into the misty fog; transported to the farm. Jacob sat at the table drinking coffee. "To the beach Jacob a load of fertiliser; once we move the round bales you can spread what we've stored, and hopefully, the grass will grow, we may be able to achieve three cuts."

He kissed Rosalind on the cheek dashing out the door attaching the 10-ton trailer; he drove down onto the beach watching the misty fog appear, feeling the fertiliser dropped into his trailer. His Ford tractor easily pulled the load up the track, backed up to the pile of manure which is now becoming quite a heap. Quickly emptied, heading for the farm. He parked the trailer by the barn detaching waiting for whatever Rosalind had purchased to move the round bales. Jacob noticed a lorry parked at the bottom of the track. He guessed that is the trailer; he drove with his tractor down the drive, shocked Rosalind had purchased brand-new, which must have cost a fortune. Jacob attached the bale trailer steadily driving to the field and parked. He walked back to the farm Rosalind came out of the house. "Your coffees on the table Jacob; I'll start loading the bales," she smiled patting his cheek, which made him smile everything appeared to be back to normal whatever normal is these days.

Rosalind climbed in her tractor driving to the field smiling at the new trailer she'd purchased, she's rather enjoying everything. The negotiating to purchase things arguing trying to outwit your opponent most pleasurable to her operating systems. She carefully loaded the plastic-wrapped round bales onto the new trailer. Jacob had his coffee and walked to the field, sitting in his warm tractor cab. He drove to the barn Rosalind followed with her massy tractor unloading stacking neatly against the barn. They returned to the field, fetching another three loads before they were finished. Rosalind fitted the manure bucket to her front-end loader on the tractor.

Jacob parked the brand-new trailer inside the barn and attached his old manure spreader. Rosalind loaded the manure onto the spreader, Jacob quickly spread on the pasture land. He had managed to cover the whole 30 acres with a thin layer of fertiliser, hardly sufficient to make any difference he thought. Now he would spread the fertiliser that God sent directly onto the field, which would boost the growth even more. He parked the tractor and spreader by the barn and Rosalind followed with her tractor. They went into the house at 4 o'clock in the afternoon. Rosalind pressed the button on the wall hearing the old generator come to life. Jacob commented: "I haven't checked the diesel have you, Rosalind? I suspect the old generator is getting low by now."

"No, I thought you could manage that small task Jacob," Rosalind suggested firmly.

Jacob didn't respond, sighed heavily walking out of the door, walking around the back of the house to an old shed watching the blue smoke from the exhaust situated on the roof. Jacob checked the diesel tank outside the shed, almost empty since Rosalind had returned, they'd use 50 gallons of diesel which concerned Jacob considerably. There is no need to keep running the generator; they could boil the kettle on the Aga and cook most of the food. Jacob went inside the shed he stopped the generator checking the oil topping up; she's a little low although the engine would stop if the oil became too low. Why would Rosalind want a new generator; this old beast had served him for many years and still running. Jacob is beginning to think he's allowing Rosalind to walk all over him; yes, it's great having your wife back, but at what cost. He suddenly imagined Rosalind taken away, sent a shudder down his spine; he would have to be extremely tactful when discussing the issue. Jacob returned to the house, Rosalind knew precisely what he's thinking. "I suppose you're going to moan I use the generator too much? I don't know why you're worried; money isn't an issue, you have God on your side. I wish you'd accept the fact, Jacob," she advised with confidence in her voice.

"So you are suggesting, we should abuse Gods generosity and not be frugal?"

Rosalind exhaled imitating human behaviour. "At times Jacob I could easily strangle you. You need a mobile phone at least we could order the diesel without having to drive to a phone box! I'm buying a computer tomorrow, we should be able to operate off Wi-Fi."

"You will not purchase anything else without discussing with me first Rosalind please," Jacob stared daring her to defy him.

"Don't you threaten me, Jacob Walker! God will strike you dead; everything I do is with his approval. I don't need yours," she expressed firmly storming out of the door, she is becoming addicted to confrontation. Rosalind jumped in the Range Rover driving off 11 o'clock in the evening before she reached Exeter; entering an all-night store. She purchased a computer, and a mobile phone Jacob would not beat her; she is a supreme being, she would do exactly what she wanted regardless of her mission.

Jacob had made himself coffee when he heard the generator cut out the diesel tank is empty; he sat by the fire watching the shadows of the flames created dance around the wall. He pondered on what Rosalind had said. God had approved who is he to argue with God! Jacob lit a candle opening the good book reading a few passages which warmed his heart immensely. He hoped God wasn't too annoyed with him after all he's not without sin, thanks to Adam and Eve.

Rosalind drove to an all-night garage filling the Range Rover with diesel and slowly driving home, arriving at six in the morning. She opened the front door to find Jacob asleep in his armchair with the good book still on his lap. Rosalind read his thoughts realising the generator is out of fuel. She went outside to the main diesel tank filling a 5-gallon tin emptying in the generator tank. She knew the engine is self bleeding. Rosalind went back into the house and pressed the button on the wall. The generator spluttered into life, she tapped Jacob's cheek, "come on sleepy." Jacob stared, wiping his eyes on the sleeve of his jacket. "Say nothing, Jacob," she advised. "Forget what happened, trust me and trust God. That's my last word on the subject."

Jacob nodded, watching Rosalind go outside come back in with a box showing a picture of a computer on the outside. He sighed, deciding to say nothing. He watched Rosalind remove a mobile phone from her pocket plug into the wall socket to charge. "I will order diesel later Jacob the tank holds about 500 gallons I think?"

He nodded, "far more than we need, going cheap at the time, father purchased at a farm sale. I don't think we have ever had more than 200 gallons in there and that lasted three years."

"I will purchase 400 gallons later on. You had better fill the sheep dip and prepare the fencing. We have to dip the ewes and lambs otherwise you know what will happen Jacob flystrike."

He nodded. "I will let you know when breakfast is ready. Come on, move," Rosalind smiled, patting his cheek as he went out of the door followed by Jack. Jacob found the hosepipe attaching to the water tap placing in the top of the dipper. He remembered his father had built the sheep dip on an embankment so they could drain the dipper, by removing a plug further down the embankment; one of their smarter ideas he smiled. Jacob fitted the plug, turning on the water. He walked to a dilapidated storage shed, removed the chemicals to put in the water to stop the flies laying eggs on his sheep and ewe lambs. He slowly poured the chemicals, which cost him considerable money. He watched the water disperse the chemical, turning the surface a strange colour of mauve. Jacob heard Rosalind call. He smiled walking to the house sitting down to 3 pieces of fried bread each with an egg on to sausage and three rashers of bacon. "I thought you needed a good breakfast, Jacob, we have a lot of work ahead of us while you're finishing breakfast, I'll go with Jack and bring the flock in," she smiled reassuringly.

"You sure you can manage Rosalind," he asked, surprised at her suggestion.

Rosalind displayed her displeasure expression. "Sorry," he voiced. "Off you go, I didn't mean to criticise or question your abilities," he sighed.

"Jack," Rosalind called opening the door with him following. Rosalind checked the pen gate is open. "Come on Jack," she insisted with a firm command; jumping on the quad bike with Jack sat on the carrier trying to keep his balance as she speeded across the Moor until she located the flock. Jack jumped from the quad carrier instinctively knowing what to do. He soon had the flock gathered with Rosalind staying back with the quad and Jack steering the sheep who appeared instinctively to realised they were going to the farm. Jacob is waiting patiently smiling, watching the way she had guided the sheep very professional; they finally had them penned.

Jacob slipped on his waterproofs to avoid becoming soaked from the splashes the ewes would create when they dived in the dipper. Jacob stood there holding a poll, he'd made with the V in the end; so he could push the ewes heads under the water to ensure no part of the animal is left vulnerable to flystrike. By lunchtime, they had dipped everything; the ewes and lambs wandered off bleating shaking themselves furiously trying to remove the terrible smell and surplus water off their fleece. Jacob removed his waterproofs walking down the embankment he removed the plug, allowing the sheep dip to drain away and soak into the ground. Rosalind had returned to the house. She set up the computer on a small table by the window, attaching the receiver Wi-Fi for the computer. The signal wasn't very strong but sufficient to operate. The same went for the mobile phone; she'd already ordered 400 gallons of diesel which she paid for over the mobile by money transfer. She knew the money from the lambs would have gone into the bank by now, so they could easily afford the purchase. The diesel would arrive tomorrow, she suspected Jacob would not be impressed with her decisions. Nevertheless, he would have to like it or lump it as humans would express.

Jacob came into the house seeing the computer by the window on a little table, he didn't ask any questions he'd never own one or operated one. He noticed the mobile phone not having a clue how to operate; he could manage the phone box down the road without any trouble. The mobile phone rang. Rosalind answered. Peter from the spaceship she wondered why he's contacting her via mobile phone. "Rosalind, come to the ship tonight decisions have been made, I will explain later," Peter ended the call.

Jacob asked, "who is that?"

"Peter," she responded frostily.

"What did he want?"

"God business, not yours," walking off into the kitchen. Jacob beginning to wonder whether his relationship is falling apart. Rosalind's attitudes seem to have changed and not for the better. Rosalind is reading his thoughts realising she is displaying too much aggression towards him inadvertently, although she had to confess, she did enjoy teasing and arguing. Jacob sat on the settee turning on the television. Rosalind came over sitting on his lap; she knew this is the way the female humans behaved with their husbands. Rosalind tried to think of a reason to excuse her behaviour, remembering what human females experience once a month. "I'm grumpy Jacob it's that time," kissing on the cheek hoping he would accept the explanation.

He kissed her on the cheek: "Nobody's perfect, I'm sure God knows."

"I've ordered the diesel we have plenty of money, arriving tomorrow."

"That's okay if God is in charge of everything, I have nothing to worry about," he smiled briefly.

Rosalind touched Jacob's forehead; he immediately fell asleep. She pressed the button on the wall turning off the generator. Jack watched intently resting his jaw on Jacob's boot as Rosalind left the house. She stepped into the misty fog transported to the spaceship miles out to sea.

Peter is waiting for her with Matthew. Rosalind could sense something is about to happen, desperately reading their thoughts for a clue; gathering it's something to do with women. She is receiving mixed-up messages, almost as if Peter and Matthew's thoughts were scrambled to prevent reading. Rosalind watched the screen appear on the wall observing several brothers and sisters, including the firstborn of their collective. He was created by the central computer; initially considered a mistake, a malfunction by the creator. The Zibyan creators no longer existed after a freak accident, their flesh construction could not withstand the heat from the volcano which erupted. Only the central computer remained protected by an energy shield. The central computer realising the creator's deaths are his error; attempted to create an improved shapeshifting version of the creator's design composed of pure energy.

The firstborn looked to Rosalind, "we have made a decision Rosalind without discussing or informing you. We suspect your opinion would be biased if we included you in the decision of our collective."

Rosalind flashed her eyes to everyone, and they did likewise. "I'm surprised, in fact, intrigued, why you have isolated me from the decision-making process. I look forward to your explanation," she answered calmly.

"You are aware Rosalind of the mistake we made creating humans from chimpanzees, we are now transporting human flesh to other planets to feed the animals."

"I am aware I am part of the process. I've been here from the beginning with Peter and Matthew, I played the part of Mary Magdalene for a time, and later we introduce the Bible for good measure."

"We are not prepared to subject as Zibyan to become a child and submissive to Jacob, although your idea is based on logic."

Rosalind didn't know quite what to say. "Jacob will not have anyone to leave his farm to once he's gone. The farm will be sold or taken over by the National Trust who own the Moor."

"We the collective have decided, you will be replaced Rosalind with a human female under our control. The Science Department has decided they are ready to experiment. Matthew has located several females matching Rosalind's description; they will have their brains reprogrammed. One will stay with Jacob and the others transported to Jacobs planet."

"Jacob is no fool he will know immediately, it's not me and reject your idea. I presume you will pick such a female that can carry a child and give Jacob the son he requires to carry on the farm?"

"We are aware Rosalind there may be difficulties; you will remain at the farm invisible until we are satisfied everything is working the way it should."

"What about finances? The human Rosalind will not understand and certainly won't be as efficient as me," Rosalind expressed calmly.

"We suspected there would be some resistance on your part, you have operated as an individual for some time which is taught us many things. Your experimentation has not gone unnoticed, and you were honoured with a planet in your name."

"The information you are expressing is contradictory; you are dissatisfied with human behaviour, and we are shipping loads of their flesh to feed our animals on various planets. Why would you want to save Jacob, he's human?"

"We have watched you perform with Jacob, he has no aggression in him; he doesn't want to send it animals to market, although he has to out of necessity to survive. The creator's central computer as advised he is the closest resemblance to the original creators of them and us."

"If I understand you correctly. You are trying to reconstruct our own creators from the main computers records? Do we have any DNA in which to construct the original Zibyan race we are named after in honour of them?"

"Not at the moment, they were destroyed in the explosion, of year zero when the planet erupted unexpectedly. Those that did remain soon died at the moment of our creation, which was considered a mistake at the time, yet we are still here honouring our creators."

"You are the firstborn in the year zero; surely you realise, you the firstborn, who has watched everyone after you created. If there is a way to raise the original creators of us, we would have done it long ago why subject the Zibyan collective to a never-ending reminder of our failure."

"You have not listened to your brothers and sisters recently. A bone fragment has been found of an original Zibyan. Our brilliant scientists are trying to extract DNA as we speak."

"Has no one learnt the lessons of meddling! For 9000 years plus; we watched the humans destroy the planet earth even when we instilled religious teachings in the hope to control them; we failed miserably. Apart from in a few and I think you could possibly count them, on one hand, Jacob is one of them."

"We have decided Rosalind you will be replaced by a human once she is programmed. 4 more females will be impregnated by Jacob and transported to Jacobs planet where they will be nurtured until they give birth. We will alter the DNA of the offspring in the hope to create our creators."

"Why not take samples from Jacob; there is no need for him to mate with anyone. Transport to Zagader and inseminate the females there," Rosalind suggested running out of ideas to put a stop to what she considered to be a crazy idea.

"Rosalind, your thought pattern is clouded; do you not think our scientists have considered that possibility? If Jacob breeds on earth and the females made pregnant, we have a guaranteed success on their arrival."

"I have thought as an individual, and I think as one now. I'm advising the Zibyan collective not to attempt to create our creators from in theory a human DNA. I will have great pleasure in telling the firstborn, I told you so if you fail!" Rosalind expressed firmly.

"You will not only be chastising the firstborn Rosalind but your brothers and sisters who are in agreement with me and the computer." The images vanish from the wall. Peter and Matthew looked to Rosalind. "You are treading a dangerous path, Rosalind the collective have decided the individual is insignificant now. A decision has been made you must wholeheartedly comply."

CHAPTER 6

Uncharted Ground

Rosalind followed Peter into another section of the space-ship. Encased in a transparent jelly substance were five females all resembling Rosalind. Snatched by Matthew made unconscious and transported to the spaceship in preparation. "Computer," Rosalind asked, "what are the chances of Jacob accepting any one of these females?"

"Once I have wiped their memory and instilled the original Rosalind, we have an 80% chance of success."

"I would have expected at least 99.9% computer from you, what is the issue?" Rosalind asked rather please with the computer's answer.

"If I were wiping your memory banks, I would have 100% success rate; humans are different. They resemble our creators, they are organic, you are not you were created by me."

"I have a solution computer," Rosalind remarked, watching Peter look at her listening intently.

"I am listening, Rosalind, I have computed everything, I am the central computer I created you."

186

"Yes, computer! Have you considered, I bring Jacob here? Set aside a room make it familiar to a human, and allow Jacob to meet the new Rosalind here? At least that way, we can control the environment and the situation, give you some indication of whether your work is successful or needs refining."

"I agree with your analysis. If necessary, we can subdue Jacob to prevent him from rejecting the females selected to travel to Zagader. If he shows signs of rejection with the four for the home planet. The fifth one, supposed to carry his seed here will be destroyed, and you will have to continue living with him until we find another solution."

"When will you have the females ready computer?" Rosalind asked suspecting Jacob would not easily be fooled.

"The first one will be ready in an hour. I will prepare a room as you have suggested Rosalind, returned to the farm and prepare Jacob for travel to the spaceship in one hour."

Rosalind flashed her eyes at Peter walking along the corridor, stepping into the misty fog returning to the farm. She awoke Jacob where she'd left him. He jumped and yawned while Rosalind made coffee. "You are visiting Peter this morning, he is rather fond of you, unfortunate he can't travel here from heaven," she smiled reassuringly.

Jacob smiled: "Before I've had my breakfast," he enquired somewhat surprised.

Rosalind smiled, quickly preparing a sandwich of cheese and onion, which would make his breath smell awful. Jacob, blissfully unaware of what is about to take place, finished his sandwich. Rosalind held his hand they step from the doorway into the misty fog arriving aboard the spaceship. Jacobs clothes had changed, he's now in a robe the same as he wore when he travelled before to heaven. Rosalind led Jacob into a furnished room, hot coffee was already on the coffee table. "I shan't belong Jacob," she smiled sweetly leaving.

Jacob believed he is in a secluded room when, in fact, Rosalind and the others could see everything. Matthew transported the first woman into Jacob, supposedly programmed as Rosalind by the computer. Jacob stood up. "Who are you? I haven't seen you before?"

"I'm your wife Rosalind silly man, you've eaten cheese and onion sandwiches, your breath is disgusting," she proclaimed.

Rosalind watching with Peter and Matthew trying not to grin. "You look like my wife," Jacob expressed calmly, "but you're not?"

The computer sent down an invisible ray, connecting to Jacob's brain and the woman trying to betray Rosalind. Within seconds they were on the floor mating. Peter and Matthew walked away along with Rosalind. "Computer, you have failed," Peter expressed. "The only solution is to allow Jacob to mate with the four; no the five and send them all to Zagader and leave Rosalind with Jacob for the moment."

"I agree! Organic brains are difficult to reprogram, this female is performing correctly. Unfortunately, Jacob knew she's not Rosalind. Jacob can stay here till tomorrow morning by which time he should have mated with the five successfully. I will store the females here until I am satisfied they have conceived. I have transmitted our decision to the collective they have agreed with my analysis. Collect Jacob tomorrow Rosalind." The war displayed the firstborn on Zagader along with several other Zibyans. "I believe you have something to say to me Rosalind," the firstborn suggested.

"No, there is nothing to say; the evidence speaks for itself. I'm returning to my duties you have partially succeeded. You will have five candidates to ship to Zagader and onto Jacobs planet and in nine months; we shall see."

The firstborn vanished from the wall along with the others. Peter advised, "be careful Rosalind do not criticise the collective."

"I am aware Peter," she smiled walking along the corridor stepping into the misty fog appearing outside the front door. She noticed the lorry coming up the drive, he is carrying diesel, she presumed. He filled the diesel tank and left. Rosalind took several tins of diesel to the generator fuel tank filling, should last for a month she decided.

She grabbed the crook from the back of the door with Jack close to her heels; she walked across the Moor, finding the sheep grazing contently. Rosalind sat on a large rock, isolating her thoughts from the collective as she trained herself to do for some time. She wondered what she is trying to achieve? Although had to chuckle at the comment from the female about Jacobs breath. Why did she want him for herself? They couldn't breed successfully, they weren't even constructed the same. Once his lifespan is reached, he would die. He could be re-created by a Zibyan like she had with Rosalind, but it wouldn't be the same. The only solution would be to alter Jacobs DNA, so he didn't age. When he reached the age of 80 or 90 transport him to the planet named, "Jacob," where they could stay together for eternity.

Rosalind realised what she is thinking and shocked by her conclusions. This is not the Zibyan way she concluded, patted Jack rose to her feet, walking towards the house, enjoying the solitude much like Jacob. For the first time, Rosalind felt lonely missing Jacob; a ridiculous sensation, she knew humans suffered from the effect but not Zibyans. Rosalind sat watching television; she watched her two favourite programs turning off the tv, feeding Jack. She left the house stepping into the misty fog transported aboard the spaceship. Peter and Matthew were watching Jacob and the fifth female mating. Matthew enquired, "you have experienced the mating process, do you think it's something we should practice as a form of experimentation?"

"From my own experiences, no! I can't see the collective ever agreeing to the practice; it serves no purpose pleasure is not a necessity in the Zibyan culture. I do know our creators would procreate similar to humans to create likenesses of their selves occasionally. According to the computer records, they vary rarely practised the procedure; that's why they didn't survive. I suspect they didn't travel to other planets very often or consider colonising elsewhere. Something went terribly wrong, and they were destroyed by a volcano. I'm surprised the computer didn't react in time to protect them."

The firstborn appeared on the wall, accompanied by others. "You have studied the computer records of our creators Rosalind. The fragment of bone recovered has the DNA of one Zibyan creator. When the females give birth, we will implant the Zibyan DNA, which will slowly modify the human DNA and produce a creator."

"Firstborn the one who carries the knowledge of everything. Have you considered the possibility our creators at the outset rejected our form as a mistake? If you create the creators, and they extract events from the main computer and come to a conclusion; we are still a mistake! They may wish to destroy us?"

Peter and Matthew looked to Rosalind and the firstborn, the others were silent. "Your individuality may have detected an error in our assessment. I as the firstborn watched the last flesh Zibyan ceased to function and helpless to sustain his life. We the collective have concerned ourselves with rectifying a mistake, we believe when, in fact, the mistake is not our making, only circumstances beyond our control. However, we will continue along the path we have chosen for the moment and will monitor closely, prevent what you have suggested Rosalind taking place." The firstborn and the others vanished. Peter turned to Rosalind, "I am fascinated by the way your mind works outside of the collective, although you are still working for the collective as an individual Rosalind."

Rosalind looked in the room where Jacob is with the final female to be shipped to Zagader. They were mating like rabbits she thought, turning away disinterested and partially annoyed it wasn't her, she thought irrational on her part. Matthew removed the final female into storage, where she would stay nurtured by the computer until it is established she's pregnant. Rosalind went into the room, Jacob laying on the bed. The computer had put him to sleep wiping his memory of any event, cleansing his naked body from top to bottom. Hence, there were no traces left of his endeavours. Rosalind lay beside him realising she had secured her position on the farm for some time with Jacob.

The alarm sounded off in the spaceship. Rosalind jumped to her feet looking at the screen noticing a lorry and several men herding Jacob sheep about to load. Peter had acted swiftly, paralysing the men transporting aboard to become fertiliser. Rosalind walked down the corridor stepping into the misty fog, she is transported to the lorry's location. She encouraged the sheep along the path to their own part of the Moor. Rosalind stepped into the misty fog, transported to the farm. Collected a bag of sheep nuts, returning to the ewes. Rosalind making sure they were on their own part of the Moor before she emptied small piles of food. She walked towards the lorry, hoping she had discouraged the ewes from investigating other parts of the Moor.

Rosalind climbing inside the lorry after lifting the loading ramp and securing. She studied her memory banks which provided her with instructions on how to drive the lorry. She set off along the narrow Moor road, parking the lorry in a lay-by some 10 miles from the farm and sent a blast from her eyes into the back of the lorry, the straw ignited. Rosalind stepped into the misty fog vanishing to the farm.

She now realised someone needed to be on the farm all the time, she would stay on the farm and collect Jacob in the morning. Rosalind took the decision the sheep needed to be sheared, they required their wool removed, they'd had several days of rain hopefully sufficient to wash out the awful smell of sheep dip. She quickly rounded the sheep with Jack returning them to the barn penning securely. She ran into the house removing the electric sheep clippers starting the generator. Rosalind could see plainly, although in the early hours and dark. The sheep seem to behave more peaceably as she removed their fleeces. Rosalind is racing the clock shearing a sheep at the rate of one every 30 seconds using her limitless energy and speed. When she'd finished shearing, she bagged the fleeces ready for collection they were virtually worthless, nevertheless would help prevent flystrike.

6 o'clock in the morning Rosalind drove Jacobs ford tractor and trailer down onto the beach and parked. The misty fog appeared, she stepped in travelling to the spaceship finding Jacob in his little room drinking a hot coffee. Rosalind entered, smiling. "You sleep comfortably, husband," she asked, watching him smile.

"I must have dropped off like a log Rosalind; I don't remember anything, I must have been exhausted, sorry."

"I'm pleased you've rested Jacob, work to be done; come along," Rosalind insisted leading him down the corridor stepping into the misty fog. He stepped out onto the sand in his work clothes seeing his tractor and trailer loaded waiting for him. They climbed aboard with Jacob driving returning to the manure heap. He emptied the trailer, driving to the farm. "I don't know what's happened Rosalind, I'm still exhausted, I think I could sleep for a week."

Rosalind, jumping from the tractor cab while Jacob parked in the barn. Rosalind went into the house making coffee for them both. She sat quietly waiting for him to join her, she could hear him pushing the wheelbarrow transporting logs to the house for the fire and Aga. She turned on the television, as much as Jacob denied he liked the TV. She knew he enjoyed the news, especially if criminals were punished or vanished, he knew where they were heading.

Jacob sat beside her. "Rosalind," he asked cautiously. "Would it be possible for us to afford a second-hand manure spreader. The one we have only carries five tons and most of God shipments coming 10-ton loads. I could easily spread directly on to the pastureland rather than tipping from a trailer, and you have to reload."

Rosalind felt herself laughing, Jacob sat there, bemused at her behaviour. "I'm sure I can arrange something for you, Jacob, I'm not used to you being efficient," she chuckled making more coffee for them both. "I have a confession, I've sheared the sheep, bored missing you while talking to Peter."

"You're joking. I hate that job my back thanks you immensely," Jacob kissed Rosalind passionately on the lips. "I hadn't noticed I must see my sheep in the morning."

After checking the sheep early the next morning; Jacob and Rosalind climbed into their Range Rover heading to the machinery dealership. Rosalind had already visited the cellar placing money in her large handbag and coat pockets. They travelled for some time noticing a second-hand manure spreader. Rosalind pulled over to the side of the road for them to investigate. They both slowly walked around the machine; massive is an understatement Jacob thought. He dreaded the thought of what it would cost. The sales representative came from the office noticing their interest with a broad cheesy smile. "Good morning sir madam. £2500 plus the dreaded VAT of course and she is yours delivered, providing you live in this country," he chuckled.

"2000 for cash," Rosalind voiced.

"2250 delivered."

"Agreed!" Rosalind voiced counting the money from her handbag. The sales rep astounded to find someone carrying that amount of cash. "The spreader will be delivered tomorrow," the salesperson assured after realising they weren't very far away from his location. He had a lorry heading in that direction anyway, so he could kill two birds with one stone.

Jacob couldn't stop grinning, proud of the way Rosalind handled the deal. The spreader wouldn't have to go through the books everything paid for in cash. Technically the machine didn't exist, which made Jacob smiled even more not having to fight with the taxman, who he would personally spread on his field without reservation. They drove steadily along the road towards home. Rosalind suddenly changed direction heading down a narrow Lane which opened up into a small trading estate. Jacob looked at the sign where she parked. 'Generators.' He had rather hoped she'd forgotten the idea, obviously not!

Rosalind stepped from the Range Rover grinning looking at the expression on Jacob's face. Jacob listened to the salesperson explained to Rosalind. "The generator, you're interested in is extremely fuel-efficient, when power wasn't used, the generator would automatically switch off and restart if power is required." Jacob, like the sound of that himself, his old generator ran all the time whether creating electricity or not. With the specifications, Rosalind had selected the new generator cost £4000. Jacob thought her handbag would have to be extremely deep to carry that amount of cash.

Rosalind emptied her handbag there is £3000 left inside, she emptied her coat pockets, removing another thousand, delivery is free. The salesperson wrote out a sale ticket. The generator would be prepared and delivered early next week. Jacob decided today had been extremely expensive and hoped, his ewes could produce six lambs each to cover the cost, he still hadn't purchased a new Ram.

Rosalind smiled as they left the establishment. Jacob followed sliding onto the passenger seat of the Range Rover. She is waiting for him to say something, she could read his mind as she drove towards home. Within an hour, they were back on the farm. Rosalind made the coffee, Jacob sat quietly at the kitchen table with Jack by his heels. Nobody spoke a word, Jacob finished his coffee muttering, "I'll check the ewes, Rosalind. I have to purchase a Ram from somewhere," he sighed heavily. Jacob left the house watching the lorry driver way from the farm after collecting the sheep wool.

"You don't need a Ram till October Jacob, there's plenty of time to find one," Rosalind suggested calmly. He didn't reply, walked out of the door with Jack following him closely. Now the beginning of June Jacob is particularly concerned the weather is decidedly warmer, which would encourage flystrike. He knew he'd dipped his sheep, but no guarantee would resolve the issue. Rosalind is concerned, turned herself invisible following Jacob as a precaution. She suspected mating with five females in 24-hours a strain for Jacob, although he didn't realise what he is performing.

Jacob spotted his neighbour walking towards him with his sheepdog and crook. Jacob immediately ordered, "Jack, lie down and stay." Jack complied immediately, Jacob carried on walking, shaking Thomas's hand. "long time no see my friend how's life treating you."

"Not as well as you from what I hear at the shop," Thomas chuckled and sighed. "I'm selling up Jacob I can't make a living, and I'm getting on in years; my son is not interested, he's gone off to work in the city, you can't blame him."

"That is the last thing I expected you to say, Thomas, I'm sorry you have been a great neighbour. Sometimes I wonder why I bother," Jacob sighed.

"I suppose you wouldn't be interested, Jacob? I only have 10 acres of land plus my grazing rights which would naturally become yours plus a small house."

Rosalind could see the advantages of having more grazing rights and another property, which could be used by the Zibyans. She quickly materialised in a deep gully to the left of them, walking out, making Jacob jump and

Thomas. "I didn't see you come in Mrs," Jacob voiced. "This is Thomas, our neighbour he's packing up more's the pity."

"So this is your secret Jacob you have married again, you kept that bloody quiet," Thomas chuckled.

Jacob realised he'd have to be extremely careful what he said concerning Rosalind, Thomas came to the wedding when he married Rosalind the first time. "We met, quite by accident, Thomas, she was walking her dog, and I threaten to shoot it as you can imagine it was love at first sight." Thomas burst out laughing.

"I'm pleased to meet you, Thomas; strange I have the same name as Jacob's first wife Rosalind," she smiled. "Jacob would like the chance to purchase your smallholding, Thomas. I have some savings I'm sure you would prefer a cash deal," Rosalind smiled.

"You're my kind of woman," Thomas voiced cheerfully. "Do you have a sister?"

Jacob glared at Rosalind, almost saying with his eyes. "Have you lost your bloody mind, woman?" She could read his thoughts which were not very pleasant at this precise second; she is absolutely shocked.

"Nice to meet you, Rosalind," Thomas voiced cheerfully. "I'll put some figures together and will discuss matters further. Jacob knows my land, he'll show you around. I must go I have a doctors appointment my old bones, aunt what they used to be," he chuckled walking off.

"Have you lost your mind, Rosalind," Jacob asked, annoyed. "I'm not taking out a mortgage to buy another smallholding."

"Firstly, I never asked you to take out a mortgage. I can pay for the farm myself without you. I can live there, and you can live on your own farm." Rosalind watched Jacob's eyes enlarge, shocked by her threat.

"You're not serious Rosalind, live separate lives?"

"Why not! I don't want to live with a backward farmer who doesn't look forward and take every opportunity that presents itself. Thomas only has a smallholding 10 acres and a rickety old house. What he does have is access to free grazing lots of free grazing which would benefit your ewes. You're not short of equipment any more. Sometimes, Jacob, I could hit you over the head with a bucket," she emphasised. "Besides I think God has a use for Thomas's old house, I don't have all the details, but I'm sure he will let us know."

"Oh, I didn't realise Rosalind, sorry if its God's will, let it be done," Jacob smiled. "I will leave you to organise everything as usual." They held hands walking home to their farm. Jacob sat quietly, watching television while Rosalind made drinks, he suspected Thomas would want between 160 and 280,000 for his property. Jacob knew he's lucky if he had 10,000 in disposable cash. Not forgetting everything recently purchased by Rosalind and him. He couldn't blame her entirely, he is the one who suggested the new manure spreader.

Jacob sighed slowly looking at the television listening to the presenter explain. "Over 2 million people had vanished over the past year without a trace." Jacob wondered what percentage of the humans were transported to him to dispose of on his pasture. He listened to the presenter explaining: "Crime had fallen to an all-time low and terrorism virtually non-existent at the moment." Jacob exhaled pleased in some respects and saddened in others.

Rosalind passed him his drink. "Don't worry about the money, Jacob, I have plenty to cover the cost. Besides, when you have a son, there will be land for him to make a living on. And before you ask not yet," she smiled. "Perhaps in nine months, we shall see; I'm making no promises." Already conjuring a plan in her mind. Somehow she would convince the collective to keep one of the females here to give birth, she would take the child and raise; after all, Jacob is the father.

"Are you with child," he asked, surprised.

"That is for me to know and you to wait and see, I promise nothing," she grinned with satisfaction at her cunning thoughts. Jacob kissed Rosalind very passionately rather excited about everything now. More land a son; excellent equipment, plenty of sheep what more could he asked for, not forgetting God and the fertiliser.

They both retired to bed rather early for a change; Rosalind switched off the television going into the bedroom. She touched Jacob's forehead; he is instantly unconscious. She stepped from the house, patting Jack stepping into the misty fog and in seconds aboard the spaceship. Peter and Matthew were waiting for her. "Rosalind, you know the firstborn will not accept your idea. Purchase another farm is a good idea our brothers and sisters could use the house as a refuge point before boarding the spaceship."

"We shall see Peter; the firstborn does not require five children to experiment with to transfer DNA from the creator's bone to humans."

Peter commented: "You are presuming what the collective will require Rosalind, they will find that an insult."

The far wall displayed a screen, the firstborn and several of his brothers and sisters appeared. "Rosalind I have considered your proposal; you are not demeaning a Zibyan which we would not accept to become a human child. If five males are growing inside the females, you may have one. If one is a female Jacob will have to accept that to continue his farm."

Rosalind grinned, making the firstborn and the others stare at her facial expression. "Firstborn let's hope everything works out successful for everyone. I believe the five have conceived and we should know within the next 24 hours what the females are carrying. Jacob must be extremely fertile for all 5 to conceive," Rosalind remarked. "Of course firstborn should your experiments not be fruitful you could always try again, Jacob will be here, there is an ample supply of females on earth. There is always the possibility a female child may accept the new strains of DNA substantially better than a male."

"You are correct Rosalind your individuality provides you with clear thinking and planning for the future. I have considered what you have said and will discuss with our scientists. If there is a female child, I will take her, you will have to accept a male." The firstborn vanished with his brothers and sisters. Rosalind burst out laughing watched by Matthew and Peter astounded at her behaviour. This is not the Zibyan way to behave. Peter asked with some urgency, "are you unwell Rosalind? Do you need the main computer to stabilise your thought patterns?"

"No, Peter! I displayed human behaviour, sometimes I forget where I am," she grinned walking down the corridor stepping into the misty fog, appearing by the front door. Rosalind entered to find Jacob sat at the breakfast table, eating toast and marmalade. He asked with some urgency, "has God approved us conceiving a child?"

"All indications, you will have a child in nine months; sex is undetermined at the moment Jacob, you must obey Gods request without hesitation. Otherwise, you will lose everything," she assured with confidence. She watched Jacobs smile broaden; all he wanted is coming true as far as he is concerned. "I'm going to see Thomas today, Jacob to finalise the deal. You stay on the farm and look after our flock," she instructed. "Don't forget your manure spreader arrives today."

Jacob, kissed Rosalind on the cheek, grabbing his crook and raincoat from the back of the door. Jack close to his heels, ventured outside with Jacob briskly strolling across the Moor in search of his sheep. Rosalind went down into the cellar locating the suitcase with the money in; she counted out 160,000, placing in shopping bags. Rosalind left the house stepping into the Range Rover, she drove the 3 miles to Thomas's farm venturing down along drive, wasn't in much of a better state than there own. She parked outside the front of the house; thankfully, this one had slates on the roof and not thatch. Although she considered the windows need replacing, the woodwork is rotten, and the farm buildings didn't look in a much better state. He had an old tractor, she guessed

Jacob would love to play with and trailer, plus other odds and ends of old farm machinery; scattered around. She noticed in one pen, a lovely Ram, which she thought would be great for Jacobs flock. Thomas invited Rosalind in the house; he could see the two shopping bags, which puzzled him to start with until he saw the money. His eyes almost popped out of his head. "You weren't joking when you said you'd pay in cash Rosalind," he expressed surprised. "The Mrs has gone shopping, she would have loved to have met you, Rosalind," he smiled warmly.

"I'll come straight to the point Thomas. 160,000 in these two bags; I want everything the house the 10 acres, the machinery and the Ram. I believe you already sold your ewes?"

"Yes, they went yesterday I sent them to the market, I'm saving the Ram until next week that's why he's still here."

Rosalind held her hand out for him to shake. "Do we have a deal, Thomas?" She already knew the answer is no.

"You put another 100,000 on the table, and you can have everything lock stock and barrel," he smiled with confidence.

"I'll not argue with you, Thomas Jacob would never forgive me if I haggled with his friend. 100,000 is neither here or there," she assured. "I'll fetch it now you contact your solicitors and have deeds of ownership transferred to Jacob Walker, Thomas."

Thomas smiled: "I can see you are a woman of your word," shaking her hand confidently. "You collect the money, and I'll phone my solicitors while you're gone. The Mrs will be overjoyed, she can't wait to move. We have a little cottage with a small garden where we can grow our vegetables, and she can grow her bloody flowers; she's moaned about for years," he chuckled.

Rosalind walked out of the house. She drove home running down into the cellar, removing another £100,000 from the suitcase, Rosalind would have to speak to Peter for more cash, they were running short. Within half an hour, she returned to Thomas's property towing the Ivor Williams trailer to bring the Ram back to their farm for the moment, while the deal is finalised.

Thomas is counting the cash in the house, Rosalind picked up the Ram with one hand placing him in the Ivor Williams sheep trailer. Thomas came out to assist surprised she'd already loaded the Ram. He laughed, "no wonder Jacob married you! You're not frightened of anything or hard work by the looks of things." Thomas gave a receipt for the £260,000 shaking her hand warmly, "You can do what you like we won't be here much longer Rosalind, I know Jacobs had his eye on my old sit up and beg tractor for years," he laughed.

"Thanks, Thomas, enjoy your retirement." Rosalind waived driving off towing the Ivor Williams trailer transporting the new Ram for Jacobs farm. Rosalind drove steadily up the drive. Jacob, sat on a bale in the barn watching her approach puzzled why she had the Ivor Williams trailer on the back. He looked through the slats as she parked observing a large white-faced Ram. Jacob is grinning from ear to ear, Rosalind is unstoppable he concluded. She stepped from the Range Rover smiling, she is so used to performing human facial expressions; came almost naturally to her now. "All ours Jacob, including the old tractor and equipment. He sent his ewes to the market yesterday; that doesn't matter, we have enough we have over 250 breeding ewes." Jacob grabbed Rosalind taking her by surprise, kissing her very passionately. Expressed excitedly, "You are a wonderful wife, two farms, a son or daughter soon, and I'm closer to God now than I've ever been."

"You know the old saying Jacob, don't count your chickens before they're hatched," Rosalind cautioned. She pointed in the direction of the road. "I think you'll find your manure spreader has arrived Jacob." Jacob jumped on his Ford four-wheel-drive tractor heading for the bottom of the drive. He reversed hitching the manure spreader to his tractor and connecting the PTO shaft which worked the spreader. Jacob signed for the spreader, the lorry driver carried on with his journey. Jacob steadily drove to the farm. Rosalind had already gone inside, making lunch for him. Jacob joined her if he grinned any more, his jaw would break Rosalind concluded. Placing the breadboard on the table with cheese and onion and a block of butter. "You realise we'll have to starve now Jacob we are destitute." She found herself laughing; she'd made a joke; this is a new experience altogether. The Zibyans had no sense of humour, never programmed as a necessity. She watched Jacobs serious expression for a moment until he realised she is joking. He continued spreading his butter, placing a large slice of cheese on the bread slicing onion, making his eyes water. Rosalind made coffee passing one to Jacob, she moved to the television switching on sitting down with hers. "Aren't you eating Rosalind Jacob," asked concerned.

"No, I have to watch what I consume," she expressed calmly suspecting Jacob would put two and two together leading him to one conclusion.

"Okay." Rosalind sat quietly, watching the news. The presenter advised bewildered: "2000 Russian soldiers had vanished from the face of the earth. Russia had suspended military operations pending further investigations as to what has happened."

Rosalind had received a telepathic message from Matthew. "Jacobs spreader is required in the morning."

"8:30 in the morning Jacob with your new spreader on the beach."

"Okay," he smiled, having a chance to use his new spreader. He finished his lunch going outside, giving the machine a thorough greasing and inspecting for any faulty parts. After all, it's second-hand; unusual a farmer would sell something that's in good working order. Unless he is desperate or wealthy and purchased a new one. He filled his tractor with diesel, checking the oil, he couldn't stop smiling. He could never imagine in his wildest dreams farming could be this easy, as long as you have the equipment. Jacob walked across the Moor eventually coming to Thomas's farm, looking at the old sit up and beg Fordson, his father and he had envied for years. Thomas came out seen Jacob looking at the tractor. Thomas patted Jacob on the shoulder. "Why don't you drive her home," he chuckled, "she's yours."

Jacob smiled, "thanks, Thomas, you sure you don't mind?"

Thomas climbed onto the seat of the old sit up and beg; he pressed the button the P6 diesel engine spluttered into life. Thomas reversed out of the shed topping up with diesel. The engine had a sweet sound a distinctive sound. The old tractor had hydraulics, and a PTO, one of the last built before this Fordson model was discontinued. Thomas warned, "remember, she has a high gearbox." Jacob nodded climbing aboard waving to Thomas as he drove away, heading along the road, not cutting across the Moor.

Rosalind is reading his thoughts, she wondered how someone could become attached or interested in a tractor. Humans are strange, she thought, turning off the television. She suddenly is alarmed reading Jacobs thoughts, stopped by a police car. Rosalind turned herself into a Seagull, flying the short distance to where Jacob is parked on the side of the road. Two policemen were looking at his tractor, one removing his notepad. The two officers suddenly vanished into thin air. Jacob staggered backwards in shock; quickly climbed aboard his tractor, continuing along the road as fast as he dare travel. Rosalind flew back to the farm, changing from the Seagull into Rosalind. She watched Jacob part the tractor in the barn alongside his other equipment. His expression is white as if he'd seen a ghost. "Rosalind," he stuttered, "I've…"

"You don't have to explain Jacob, you will have to learn you are protected. The officers in question were corrupt. They were about to attempt to extort money from you so you would avoid conviction. Their fertiliser should be extremely potent," she smiled, grabbing Jacob's hand, leading him into the house. Rosalind poured Jacob a small whiskey after reading her memory banks of what humans use to steady their nerves, which Zibyans weren't afflicted with. She realised the police car a little close to the farm for comfort. Rosalind kissed Jacob on the forehead rendering him unconscious. She stepped from the house, checking no one is watching. Rosalind transformed into a Seagull, flying to where the police car is parked. When she is sure, no one could see her, she turned into a police officer slipping into the car, hearing the radio calling the officer's name. Rosalind quickly drove some miles winding down the car window. She changed into a Seagull flying off as the car went over the cliff, dropping into a salty grave. She flew towards the farm, watching police cars with their sirens screaming driving along the coastal road searching for their colleagues.

Rosalind landed on the beach stepping into the misty fog, transported aboard the spaceship. Peter and Matthew were waiting to greet her. Rosalind flashed her eyes in response to their greeting. "You made the right decision; Peter snatching the two police officers. The last thing we need is snooping humans around the farm, and especially our new acquisition. I explained to Jacob they had criminal intent, he accepted that excuse willingly."

"Unfortunately, Rosalind, the police car has a tracker fitted and alerted the police to wear the car went over the cliff. Thankfully the glass shattered when the vehicle collided with the rocks beneath the sea. They will search for the police officers bodies for a few days. The way you drove the car over the cliff gives the impression; they were travelling too fast to make the corner safely."

The firstborn appeared with some of his brothers and sisters on the far wall. "Rosalind the collective is pleased with the new acquisition, once modifications have been made inside the house, we can use it for a variety of uses."

"Firstborn how many planets do you intend to colonise, you have selected six will there be any more?"

"Rosalind, you already know the answer. The females Jacob impregnated are carrying four males and one female. The next transport ship will arrive shortly; you will keep one female until she has given birth to a male child. The others are to be transported to Zagader and onto Jacobs planet where they will reside until they have given birth, the females will be disposed of, and the infants cared for by the Zibyans and the DNA transferred from the creators bone fragments."

"I understand firstborn if you are successful in transferring the creators DNA to the infants, where will they reside? I presume in the laboratories or do you intend to accelerate their growth?"

"Why do you ask Rosalind I detect your individual thinking has reservations?"

"Firstborn I would recommend you do not dispose of the females. I would alter the infants DNA while the mothers are sedated and return the infants to their mothers. They will be producing milk for the infants and will care for them more efficiently than a Zibyan."

"What are your intentions with the female that gives birth to Jacob son? Are you disposing of her?"

"No, I will use her as a nanny, after reprogramming her mind, the child will thrive better on its own mother's milk than supplements firstborn."

"Rosalind, the main computer is fascinated by the way you think as an individual, your suggestions are sound, we will implement. Peter and you Matthew support Rosalind, she has shown her true loyalty to the Zibyan collective with her suggestions and ideas," the firstborn vanished.

Matthew looked on the screen. "Jacob has come to the beach with his manure spreader. I must go and pre-pare the load," he flashed his eyes to Rosalind walking off. Rosalind flashed her eyes to Peter heading down the corridor stepping into the misty fog and onto the beach. She climbed into the cab to avoid becoming wet the heavens had opened, which is good would increase the grass growth. Jacob asked, "how are Peter and Matthew?"

"They send their greetings Jacob. I have some excel-lent news for you in nine months, you will have a son; tests have been carried out, and God has approved."

Jacob kissed Rosalind very passionately, holding her close as the misty fog loaded the manure spreader. Jacob slowly drove up the cliff face track, reaching the top. Rosalind step from the cab heading for the house. Jacob continued driving along to the pastureland operating his manure spreader for the first time. The machine worked perfectly spreading a thin coating over the lush grass. He returned to where he'd stored the last trailer load of manure leaving his tractor and manure spreader there. He walked to the house to find Rosalind had cooked him a lovely breakfast. "Rosalind, I think we should spread the one load we tipped from the trailer the other day before we purchased the spreader; might as well go on the field it will help the grass grow; you want me to load or you?"

"I will load the manure," Rosalind insisted. Jacob laughed at her insistence. Rosalind left the house starting her Massey tractor with the loader driving to the manure pile. She loaded Jacob spreader returning to the shed. Jacob walked from the house kissing Rosalind on the cheek, carrying on and spreading the load of fertiliser on the field. Jacob returned, leaving his tractor and spreader by the barn, he checked on the Ram Rosalind had penned, had plenty of water and hay to eat. He returned to the house, collecting his crook and Jack; he set off across the Moor in search of his flock of sheep. Jacob, surprised to encounter at least 10 police officers walking across the Moor one approached him. "I presume these are your sheep," the officer asked with curiosity.

"That's right I'm carrying out my daily check, what brings you to the Moor," Jacob inquired suspiciously.

"Two officers went missing yesterday, they haven't been found. We still don't know what happened to the 10 archaeologists; where having a walk across the Moor see if we can find any evidence of anything happening. People always seem to vanish on the moor, especially stupid holidaymakers as if we haven't got enough work to do," the officer smiled walking on.

Peter called after him "if I find anything, I'll give the police a ring."

The officer answered back, "thanks, I wouldn't hold your breath."

Jacob continued walking, looking up in the air he could see a drone flying very quietly. He looked back towards the farm, witnessing another drone. He almost felt like there is a noose around his neck if the police ever tested the fertiliser he's spreading, they would realise it is human remains. According to Rosalind, he had nothing to worry about Gods protecting him, and from what happened yesterday, he has no reason to doubt her word. Jacob walked through his ewes satisfied they were all okay, he slowly headed for the farm finding Rosalind sitting on a bale feeding the Ram carrots. Jacob burst out laughing, kissing Rosalind on the cheek. "You realise drones are flying over the Moor Rosalind."

"Don't worry so, Jacob God has everything under control. If he ever decided to open the gates of hell on humans, they would be obliterated in seconds."

"I bumped into police officers on the Moor searching for those archaeologists and the two missing police officers. I have to confess it makes me nervous Rosalind."

"Jacob changing the subject. The house where Thomas lives, we are going to make improvements, specially designed for spirits to reside; before they travel on to heaven. You have no objections, do you?"

Jacob shrugged his shoulders, "If that's God's will; we have no use for the house. Only the farm buildings the 10 acres plus are grazing rights. I don't think there's any need to increase the flock were making hard work for ourselves."

"One last thing, Jacob; when your son is born, we will have a nanny to look after him. This means I will be free to help on the farm, and before you ask God is covering the cost," she chuckled, which made Jacob laugh at her screechy voice.

"I will not argue with you Rosalind; you have given me more than I expected out of life, and to think I am helping God cleanse the earth of evil."

"Jacob, the child, will have to be borne in heaven; God's wish, so he may bless the child before he comes home with his mother."

"There can be no better blessing for our son's arrival than to be in God's presence; we are truly blessed by the Lord, amen."

Rosalind patted Jacob's cheek-kissing him. "You may not see any difference in my shape, Jacob. God is preventing the world from knowing the event at the outset," she assured with confidence.

"Praise the Lord, he is blessing me this very day, and my wife and the forthcoming event of a son, amen."

"You would make a good disciple Jacob; you never question God's decisions, you are truly blessed." Rosalind walked round the back of the house looking at her vegetables growing, cutting a cabbage. Jacob joined her; he'd never seen vegetables grow so rapidly, almost as if they were on steroids. The rose bushes he planted at the front of the house were continuously in bloom. Rosalind would very often deadhead, and the next minute a new bud is bursting into flower; the fragrance is outstanding smelling of lemon.

Rosalind returned to the house, preparing a meal. Jacob jumped to his feet; Rosalind is shocked by his sudden movement. "Rosalind we have to purchase a cot and baby things you know," he chuckled. "I'll have to decorate the spare room. Where is the nanny going to sleep?" Jacob rushed into the kitchen, grabbing his tin, taking a wad of cash dashing out of the door before Rosalind could say a word. She heard the Range Rover start leaving the farm, she shook her head, smiling like a human in disbelief at Jacob's behaviour. She is trying to decipher his confused thought pattern; his mind is running wild with what he wanted to do for his son and his lovely wife.

He steadily drove across the Moor, not using the road, finally parking outside the shop. He grabbed the trolley with enthusiasm, selecting a tin of mauve paint it is on offer and brushes plus a roller. Jacob looked along the shelves, deciding, better wait before purchasing anything else in case Rosalind disapproved. At least now he could prepare the spare room which hadn't been used since he's a kid, he dreaded to think what it is like inside.

Rosalind had already entered the room cleaning thoroughly in minutes; the speed at which she worked while Jacob wasn't there is incredible. The old vacuum cleaner almost caught fire; never worked so hard before. Jacob came into the house, seeing the bedroom door open; he cautiously entered. Rosalind had mopped the flagstone floor there is nothing that needed cleaning. He heard Rosalind empty in the bucket in the kitchen sink. "Jacob take the old bed out it won't be needed; we will purchase a new bed for the nanny and a cot for the baby; the nanny will sleep in the same room as your son Noah."

Jacob came running into the kitchen, "Noah!"

"God's wish, you wish to argue with him, Jacob?"

"Praise the Lord what an honour for him to choose to name my son Noah." Jacob returned to the bedroom, dismantling the old bed taking outside to be disposed of when he had the next fire disposing of rubbish. He hastily returned to the bedroom, stirring his paint using the roller, he applied. Rosalind had made him sandwiches which he ate while working, he's too excited to stop. Rosalind received a telepathic message from Peter. "Matthew had emptied a jail in the USA of murderers, Jacob's manure spreader is required in the morning."

Rosalind switched the television on in time to catch the news, a prison guard interviewed outside the prison. "They vanished; I have no explanation. 2000 prisoners gone where?" The prison officer held his head in disbelief. "You heard it first on CBS News." Rosalind quickly turned the television off. "Jacob I'm going for a walk, I need some fresh air, shan't belong."

"Okay, just be careful Rosalind you don't trip in your condition," Jacob cautioned. Rosalind walked from the house along the side of the barn and round the back summoning the misty fog. Instantly transported aboard the spaceship. Matthew and Peter awaiting her arrival, flashing their eyes at each other in a greeting posture. "Matthew, I think you are making it pretty obvious there's an alien force on earth. Plane crashes in the sea, and the occasional cruise liner is fine. You have emptied three prisons this year the next thing you find; we have police everywhere and soldiers. The human race is not completely stupid. They may possess things we have not discovered and could actually be tracking us right now," Rosalind suggested.

Peter looked at one of the scanners. "Rosalind there is landing craft heading for the beach, what does this mean?"

"Ready weapon systems," she advised calmly. "This may be a military exercise, trying to keep the soldiers fit and healthy and alert. Take no action and watch what's happening. I must return to Jacob. Don't discharge our weapons unless you consult me first," Rosalind ordered. However, she is not in charge but is concerned this could ruin everything for everyone. She ran down the corridor stepping into the misty fog, changing her appearance returning to Jacob in the house. He smiled, hearing the front door open, and Rosalind step inside. "Jacob, soldiers, are coming on landing craft towards our shoreline, does this happen very often?"

"No, I think it's all to do with the missing people, I shouldn't think it's anything to worry about. Only the government trying to make out there doing something for the press to report."

Jacob placed his paintbrush in the paint tray, kissing Rosalind on the cheek. "Stay here I won't be long," he smiled. Jacob left the house Rosalind is reading his mind, he's going to confront the officers advising not to frighten his sheep. Rosalind thought that would be a futile exercise. The Armed Forces are not likely to take any notice of him. Jacob met the senior officer coming up the track from the shoreline. "You are about to enter my property what is your business," Jacob asked, seriously; watching the accompanying reporter grab his recorder from his pocket.

"We are on exercises were also searching for missing persons haven't you heard the news?"

"You're about a week late," Jacob advised. "Police officers walking the Moor yesterday. I walk the Moor every day of the week if I'd found any evidence or anything suspicious, I would have reported it to the appropriate authorities. If you and your toy soldiers upset my ewes, the army will be receiving a bill."

The reporter recording everything, trying not to grin. The captain looked very frustrated, trying to bite his tongue and not say a wrong word. "We will be cautious, you must remember Sir 10 archaeologists have gone missing and four police officers recently all in this area."

Jacob laughed: "None of them could probably find their way out of a paper bag. The Moor is notorious for strangers getting lost. I hope you haven't ruled out they've probably been taken by an alien ship which landed the other week." The reporter is laughing. The captain turning a beetroot colour by the second, walking past Jacob, Jacob remarked, "if you get lost, stay in one place, it will make it easier for us to find your bones and don't disturb my sheep."

The reporter took a photograph of Jacob still laughing as he followed the captain across the Moor, holding his compass. Jacob looked from the clifftop seeing the landing craft returning to their ship. Rosalind had turned herself invisible listening to everything Jacob had said. She had never known him to be so assertive and determined to protect what is his. A religious man or not he would stand his ground on certain issues she concluded.

Rosalind sent a telepathic message to Peter. "All is well."

Rosalind quickly returned to the house ahead of Jacob, making a coffee by the time he'd returned. Jack had stayed in the house by the fire. Rosalind passed the mug of coffee to Jacob sitting on the settee turning on the television. Jacob hadn't realised a drone is flying above when talking to the captain. He's even more surprised understanding his conversation is recorded by the drone and transmitted directly to a television station. They sat there watching the reporter laughing at Jacob having a go at the captain. The presenter commented: "I wouldn't like to cross that farmer, he is quite prepared to take on the British commandos."

Rosalind patted his leg, "well done, Jacob, you stand your ground for what you believe is right. I finish the painting while you were gone," she smiled.

Jacob moved to look in the spare bedroom, bewildered how she could have done so much painting in the short time he's away. Not realising Rosalind's abilities as an alien far surpassed any human could achieve. Jacob kissed Rosalind on the cheek. "You are such a wonderful woman to have in my life. I must go with Jack and check my ewes," he sighed heavily. Jacob grabbed his crook and coat stepping out of the door, followed by Jack. He followed the route the soldiers had taken realising they were heading for the bog, Jacob caught up with them. "Captain, stay out of there," Jacob warned, "you will lose your soldiers, I'm warning you; I know this land better than you."

The reporter, recording everything; the captain determined to show his authority off. "You go men search thoroughly." They'd taken barely 5 paces, four of the men were up to their waist in water, sinking slowly. Jacob stretched out his crook, one soldier grabbed, and the other soldiers attached themselves to Jacob to secure him. He eased each soldier out of the foul-smelling bog. The drone is above filming, sending the information directly to a news station. The Captain stood there openmouthed, embarrassed beyond belief; not expecting the bog to suddenly swallow his men. The men that were trapped were okay apart from being wet. The captain said nothing, not even thank you, walking towards the road where the archaeology dig is some 2 miles ahead. The reporter patted Jacob on the shoulder. "These young officers never learn," he commented. "I would hate to be in his shoes when his commanding officers finished with him."

Rosalind is sat on the settee watching television, a blow by blow account of what took place on the Moor, transmitted directly to the 24-hour a day news station. She had never considered Jacob anything other than kind, would never think him a brave man prepared to risk his own life to save another. She pondered for a moment realising it is written in the Bible. If only the rest of the human race is so diligent as Jacob in their behaviour.

Peter and Matthew had watched events unfold, and the way Jacob had behaved. Matthew is very tempted to snatch the captain and turn him into fertiliser along with the soldiers, deciding not to it would only cause more problems for Rosalind and Jacob.

Jacob slowly walked along the well-worn sheep track heading for the farm, he noticed the postman parked at the end of the drive and drive off. Jacob change direction heading for his post box walking past his 30 acres of pasture land which appeared to be a beautiful deep green colour and proliferating. The weather had assisted lots of rain, and of course, God's fertiliser certainly boosted the growth. Jacob finally reached his post box retrieving a large brown folded envelope with the return address of, "Scrimshaw and Scrimshaw," solicitors across the top. Jacob hoped something to do with the new farm Rosalind had purchased, he tucked the envelope inside his coat to prevent the rain damaging. Jack didn't appreciate the rain, although it went with the territory of a sheepdogs life. Jacob finally entered the house, he passed the envelope to Rosalind. She immediately opened; deeds of ownership of Brook Farm. "The farm is ours Jacob there's a letter inside. Thomas Simmons has left the property. The keys are with the solicitor ready for you to collect from their Exeter office."

Jacob looked at his wristwatch 11:30, "not today Rosalind will go in the morning, Wednesday should be acquired day in town. A thought you could buy some baby things a cot, we might as well get prepared rather than leave everything to the last minute," Jacob grinned.

Rosalind smiled, "as you wish Jacob don't forget early next week the generators arriving; it won't need to go inside the shed, comes with its own casing to stand outside. We only need a coupling to connect the power to the house and of course, the fuel line from the diesel tank. As a just in case situation, I think we leave the old generator set up and connected. Make a new fuel line to the new generator that way if one fails; we will have the other as a backup, we don't want problems in the winter if we have a young child here."

"I would suggest fitting solar panels the problem is I have a thatched roof, I suppose we could fit them to the barn roof?"

"The generator; the authorities can't see, solar panels on the roof they can Jacob. We don't want them asking where the money is coming from do we," Rosalind insisted.

"No, shall we have a snoop around the new farm," Jacob chuckled.

"Yes, might as well a miserable day, now the weather is closing in. Will not harm to check around the buildings," Rosalind remarked, slipping on her coat and Jacob doing likewise. Jack already sitting at the door to make sure he wasn't forgotten. Rosalind patted him, "come along Jack new farm for you to run around on."

Jacob didn't bother to ask who is driving; he climbed into the passenger side with Jack by his feet. Rosalind drove steadily down the drive and along the road, and eventually down the Brook farm drive to Brook farm, their new acquisition.

Jacob stepped from the Range Rover standing in the small porch, he slid his hand along the top beam, grinning. "That's where everyone keeps their spare key for an emergency." Rosalind smiled, watching Jacob unlock the door. Thomas had left virtually everything even blocks by the fire ready to be lit. There wasn't much difference in size or layout other than the fact this house had slates instead of a thatched roof plus it had a loft conversion when there a fire some years ago. They ventured around the back of the house, finding the old generator shed. Jacob laughed the same set up as he had initially and a converted 50-gallon barrel, to use as a diesel tank. The cost of laying electric cable to this house or his own is horrendous that's why they both use generators. Jacob stood on the small bridge spanning the brook, carving its way across the Moor, little more than a ditch in places.

Nevertheless, the water never stopped flowing and always pure. Jacob noticed a hand pump in the house suspecting that's where the water for the sink came from. Jacob wandered into the barn seeing an old international conventional baler and bale sledge, and acrobat turner, and an old waffler tedder; he already had the tractor at home.

The wooden tipping trailer had seen better days along with the old four-wheeled hey trailer. Jacob noticed the mower an old finger knife international; they were the best mower of their day would take a lot of stick before breaking. Jacob saw Thomas had left him half a rick of hay which made him smile. Jacob burst out laughing, coming across the old trailed muck spreader made by Massey Harris and still look serviceable, all the chains were oiled and everything greased. Jacob realised if it wasn't for his good fortune to have Rosalind and God on his side. He would have nothing to laugh about and wouldn't be much better off than Thomas, and certainly wouldn't be able to purchase Thomas's farm. Jacob asked, "Rosalind what plans does God have for the farmhouse?"

"Don't worry about anything, Jacob; the house will be looked after kept clean and tidy. No one would dare come onto the property without your permission or God's otherwise they'll end up on the 10-acre pasture land; we haven't inspected. Come along." Rosalind held Jacob's hand, which made him smile they walked along for some distance coming to a flat piece of ground, needed rolling Jacob decided after walking across. The grass quite lush thanks to being fenced-off like his own to prevent the sheep invading. Jacob shut the gate tying with a piece of string as an extra precaution in case walkers left it open, although they shouldn't be in there at all, not part of the footpath. They slowly returned to the Range Rover. Jack running around sniffing everything new territory, and now his. He christened every post he could find. Jacob thought Jack must have a bladder the size of a diesel tank. Jacob checked he'd locked the door in the house quietly smiling to himself, excited by their new purchase. Jacob sat in the Range Rover with Jack between his feet. Rosalind headed for home across the Moor commenting. "Jacob if you drive steady with your tractor and manure spreader, I think safer for you to travel to Brook farm across the Moor. You can see there used to be an old track here many years ago. What I don't want to happen, you confronted by police when you transport the manure spreader down the road, especially when the holidaymakers are here. They haven't a clue how to drive a vehicle correctly in the countryside," Rosalind smiled.

CHAPTER 7

An Unexpected Event

Jacob spent the rest of the day checking their equipment preparing for the final cut of hay, although the way the weather is performing, he may get a final cut of silage before the frosts come, not only from his 30 acres but from Brook farms 10 acres as well. Rosalind comes from the house carrying a hot mug of coffee. Jacob sat on a bale, wiping his hands on an old rag; they were plastered in oil and grease. He is determined to look after the equipment, oil and grease were far cheaper than new parts his dad always preached. "Jacob tomorrow morning there's two loads of fertiliser need collecting, I think you will have to stockpile until we removed the hay from here and Brook farm don't you?"

Jacob nodded: "Yes, that's the only solution at the moment; as soon as we've cleared the fields, I will apply the fertiliser. We may achieve a final cut of silage before winter sets in; at least the ewes this year will have ample hay and silage which should produce a better lamb with any luck."

Rosalind received a telepathic message from Peter. "The female carrying Jacob son had miscarried, and Matthew processed her for fertiliser." Rosalind immediately studied her memory banks of how human females behaved when they miscarried. "Jacob, I have to go to heaven, I'm unwell something is wrong inside, I feel it."

Jacob jumped to his feet in a panic. "What can I do Rosalind tell me." Jacob noticed the misty fog arrive, and Rosalind stepped in; she vanished in seconds. Jacob sat on the bale, crying. Rosalind aboard the spaceship with Peter and Matthew watched the state of Jacob alarmed. Rosalind commented, "I haven't any choice if the female has aborted and she is now fertiliser. I couldn't let the pregnancy continue in Jacob's thoughts, he would have expected an infant in nine months."

Peter suggested, "we could select another female and artificially inseminate her Rosalind?"

"I don't know what the answer is Peter at the moment, let Jacob recover from this crisis first then we will take whatever steps are necessary to achieve what we want."

The three aboard the spaceship watched Jacob broken-hearted, sit by the fire in the house drinking his home-brew. Rosalind understood he's trying to numb the pain that humans suffer from. She suspected he would be unconscious shortly from the amount of home-brew he is drinking. Rosalind had not anticipated Jacob been so disturbed by the event; after all, a natural occurrence in many human females.

Much to Peters, Matthew and Rosalind surprise a screen appeared on the wall. The firstborn and some of his brothers and sisters betrayed. "Unfortunate Rosalind; we have watched with interest you and Jacob perform your various duties, far more entertaining than the rest of the human race put together. However, they do make excellent animal food for our pets."

Rosalind smiled, "as you can see, firstborn Jacob is extremely distraught. I haven't any other choice for obvious reasons other than to play the part after receiving information from Peter; the woman had failed to produce a son."

"Rosalind, the central computer has carried out calculations and a risk assessment. Listen to what he has to say and make your decision. You will be experiencing new events for as Zibyan."

"Rosalind, I have carried out multiple calculations and scenarios. I have always considered impossible for a Zibyan female to conceive or carry a replica of themselves. However, we now have an opportunity to experiment further because of your familiarity with Jacob. Link yourself to me, I will make some minor adjustments, and we will see what transpires if you wish to test the theory."

"Will, any of my abilities be affected computer?"

"You will still be able to shapeshift and be invisible in an emergency; however, I can't calculate what I don't know and for how long."

"Will Jacobs contaminants affect me long term, after all, I will be carrying an alien in my body structure?"

"Again, Rosalind, I have no answers we have not permitted experimentation of any kind on a Zibyan it is against our creator's law. However, since we are trying to create the original creators of the Zibyans. The firstborn and other brothers and sisters have agreed I suspend the law temporarily."

The firstborn spoke: "Rosalind since we have no need to produce replicas because we don't die. I'm permitting along with my brothers and sisters for you to experiment on this one-time occasion only. The central computer will monitor you constantly, store the findings in the event you are successful. The Zibyans can use again if an emergency scenario ever occurred. You will be in the memory banks of every Zibyan created and your sacrifice."

Rosalind walked to the wall standing with her back against the central computer, linked to her for several minutes. Peter and Matthew watched. The firstborn and his brothers and sisters had vanished, they achieved what they wanted with the consent of Rosalind to participate.

Rosalind stepped away from the wall flashing her eyes at Peter and Matthew walking down the corridor. She stepped into the misty fog appearing outside the front door of the house. She entered seeing Jacob unconscious, he'd consumed so much home-brew. She carried him into the bedroom, removing his clothes, placing in bed and stepped outside; attaching the trailer to the Ford tractor descending to the shoreline. Matthew had already received her telepathic thoughts preparing to transport the fertiliser to the trailer. Rosalind transported two loads to the manure pile. She parked the trailer detaching the tractor and attached the mower. Rosalind determined to make sure they didn't lose any chance of a good crop while Jacob comes to terms with what he thought had happened. Rosalind drove to the field cutting the 30 acres driving on to Brook farm cutting the 10 acres there. Almost midnight when she'd finished not as that mattered to Rosalind she could see in the dark with or without lights. Rosalind, drove steadily back to the farm watching the ewe's eyes light up like beads of orange light. She attached the tedder filling the Ford tractor with diesel. Jacob had already greased all the equipment, so she went back into the house. She could hear Jacob in the toilet violently sick, he'd already made himself a coffee he'd left on the kitchen table.

Rosalind made herself a drink not as if she really needed one, although she had to keep the pretence she is Rosalind, his wife. Jacob staggered from the toilet, noticing Rosalind. She placed her finger to her lips. "We can try again Jacob, not the end of the world; although it might be if you continue to behave in this manner," she cautioned. "How do you think I feel and all you can do is drown your sorrows."

Jacob flopped in the chair holding his head which is screaming; he sipped his coffee looking to Rosalind with his bloodshot eyes. "I heard the tractor what's going on," he asked quietly.

"I've transported the fertiliser to the manure heap. I attach the mower cut the 30 acres and the 10 on Brook Farm. I've attached the tedder ready to spread the grass tomorrow weather permitting. What have you done? Lay in bed feeling sorry for yourself, Jacob. It's no different for me as it is for an animal to miscarry. I would have thought you were used to the situation, long before now," she scolded.

"I'm sorry, the last thing I expected to happen, I thought God is in control of everything?"

"Jacob!" She emphasised. "We are insignificant in the scheme of things in God's eyes. He promised you a son and a son you will have whether it's tomorrow or in 20 years, it will happen; now pull yourself together we have a farm to run. God has repaired me so I can try again when you've had a bath, and the hay gathered." Rosalind lifted her eyebrows after searching her memory banks of female facial responses indicating encouragement.

Jacob finally laughed realising God is in charge. Rosalind commented, "the child was only a seed, Jacob, barely a month." He kissed Rosalind on the cheek nearly 5 o'clock in the morning, Rosalind made breakfast. Jacob sat watching television drinking a cup of coffee still with a headache resembling someone hitting him with a sledgehammer.

After breakfast, Jacob went to check his ewes with Jack close at his heels. Jacob had taken a small bag of sheep nuts with him hoping to encourage the ewes to venture onto Brook farm. Jacob decided they would have followed him into the gates of hell in pursuit of sheep nuts. He stopped short of the farm placing neat piles spread out over quite an area leaving the ewes to clean up. He continued walking on to the pastureland on Brook farm; although only cut a few hours ago, the warm morning air is starting to wilt the grass. Jacob burst out laughing, hearing the Ford tractor coming. He opened the gate suspecting Rosalind had come to spread the grass trying to make it dry quickly ready for baling. He wasn't wrong, she drove through the gateway and started spreading. Jacob left her to it slowly walking back to the farm attaching the old sit up and beg to the new hay trailer Rosalind had purchased. The tractor would be ideal for this operation to save time changing equipment. Jacob hoped if the weather would stay pleasant for the next 2 to 3 days they can bale the hay and stack in the barn on either farm.

***

Peter and Matthew from the spaceship had transported to Brook farmhouse, not needing a key to enter; unlocking the door with the power of their mind. Peter commented: "Ideal for visiting Zibyans; 4 would be the maximum in here I think. They could travel invisibly so there shouldn't be any issues, will provide the recently created Zibyans with the opportunity of seeing the real earth, with a human infestation, they will learn from our mistakes first hand."

"I have to agree with you, Peter 4 would be the maximum; we have two ships a month visiting earth. Each party would have a two-week stay to sample what's actually happening here rather than seeing it by transmission."

Rosalind sensed they were in the house she stopped the tractor, knowing Jacob had gone home. She entered the house they greeted each other with the flash of their eyes. "We have decided Rosalind we will permit 4 to visit at a time. We will be here probably for hundreds of years, so there is ample time for everyone to visit. If the firstborn continues to expand and colonise other planets, we will definitely need humans to feed the animals."

"I like the number four around figure 2 male and two female. We must keep the balance equal, although we can change our sexes when we are first created by the central computer, our real designation is decided then." Rosalind flashed her eyes, leaving Peter and Matthew returning to the tractor. She headed for the 30 acres to spread the grass to dry, ready for baling.

Peter and Matthew return to the spaceship to report to the firstborn and other members of the collective.

***

Jacob fenced off a lush piece of grass at the side of the barn for the Ram to have fresh grazing until his allotted time to service the ewes. Jacob wondered whether he should purchase another Ram is he asking too much of this one? Jacob looked across the Moor suspecting Rosalind wouldn't be finished until lunchtime. He returned to the house, preparing lunch for her after all; she is working as hard as him. Jacob heard the new generator start when he plugged the kettle in; the machine is far more efficient than his old one burning far less diesel, he didn't have to switch it off at night it automatically shut itself down when no power is required for the house.

Rosalind came in at 12:30 noticing the lavish lunch Jacob had prepared for her, although she didn't need to eat it would have been rude of her not to pretend to enjoy the food. They sat enjoying their lunch together Rosalind commented, "I expect you to have a bath this evening," trying not to grin she knew Jacob would get the message; she could sense his hormones were on fire much like the old Ram outside.

"I shan't forget," Jacob smiled.

She is not impressed with the mating process; however, she had decided to attempt to carry a male child in her form wondering what the experience would be like, never attempted by a Zibyan she would be the first, and last according to the firstborn. Rosalind finished her lunch venturing outside to her garden, smelling the roses planted by the front door. The vegetables were coming on in leaps and bounds; she had plenty of carrots, cabbage and cauliflower, would have to be cut soon. Rosalind ventured along the top of the cliff taking the footpath, the afternoon air is warm with a gentle breeze, for once, she didn't need a coat. Rosalind paused, looking across the water to where she knew her spaceship rested in a deep crater, created by a volcano thousands of years ago. Rosalind decided now is the time she wasn't going to wait until the evening, she wanted it over with quickly. She entered the house; Jacob is in the bath. "Jacob in the bedroom now," she ordered walking off into the bedroom changing her appearance, she's naked lay on top of the bed waiting for him. Jacob came into the bedroom with a towel around his waist, his eyes almost fell out of his head. Rosalind laying on top of the bed naked. Jacob didn't need any instructions he made love to her instantly. Rosalind lay there accepting what he is engaged in, apart from the pleasant electric shock feeling passing through her form; that is the only enjoyable part. Finally, he relented, rolling over on his back.

Rosalind exhaled, quickly dressing while Jacob wasn't looking. She left the bedroom going outside for some fresh air, not enjoying smelling a sweaty human body. Rosalind would know in a few hours if Jacob seed attached to her construction, a matter of a few months, she could repel the infant satisfying Jacobs needs and of course the Zibyans. They would have a human-controlled by Zibyans to run the farm.

Rosalind wouldn't be surprised if the firstborn decided may be beneficial for Jacob to meet with an accident. She had to admit her assessment of the situation did not impress her in the slightest. Rosalind could see in an hour the sun would be set and the evening air is becoming decidedly cooler. She checked the grass spread earlier in the day, definitely need moving again tomorrow; a laborious job but necessary to make good hay for the sheep. Rosalind returned to the house finding Jacob had made tea placing on the table. She looked at his expression she'd seen before reading Jacob thoughts; there is nothing but love and admiration for her. They finished tea sitting to watch television Rosalind touched Jacob's forehead he's instantly unconscious. She changed her appearance stepping outside into the misty fog transported to the spaceship.

Peter and Matthew were waiting for her. They greeted one another with the flashing of their eyes. Everyone turned to look at the news displayed on the wall. "Offshore drilling around the coast is to start early next year in an attempt to find more oil." The presenter presented a map of where the expiration holes were to be drilled very close to the spaceship. Rosalind commented: "That's not going to happen. Otherwise, we will have to relocate our spaceship."

Matthew suggested, "I suppose we could show them where the oil is, that way they would stay away from where we are. I could make a little oil leak from the earth's crust, they would naturally investigate. The central computer estimates 5 trillion barrels, that should keep them occupied for a while."

"Let's wait and see Matthew, I don't want to release any more pollutants on the earth unless absolutely necessary. You never know perhaps the activists may convince governments to use electric vehicles; admittedly, there will still be diesel used on farms unavoidable at the moment."

"What about the aeroplanes they are totally inefficient, they pollute more than any other mode of transport. They have the solution but won't implement; strange humans, all about money, not the environment or the future" Rosalind expressed.

"How many times have we had this conversation over the centuries? If they weren't amusement for the Zibyan collective, we would have destroyed them thousands of years ago," Peter remarked, waving his hand the screen vanished from the wall. "Your condition Rosalind link yourself to the central computer for him to monitor."

Rosalind placed her back against the wall; the central computer attached to Rosalind's brain. The central computer responded: "Jacobs seed has moved to the artificial womb; you are growing two seeds, one female one male. I have transmitted the information to the firstborn and your brothers and sisters." The computer released

Rosalind, she stepped away from the wall surprised by the information; suspecting nothing would grow inside her, considering she is pure energy.

The central computer advised: "Rosalind you must consume three earth meals a day, the proteins will be transferred to the seed. Otherwise, the infants have no way of surviving; you are pure energy they are not at the moment. However, we are venturing beyond any experiments carried out, and quite possibly the infants may draw power from your life force. You have nothing to be alarmed about Rosalind, I can replenish any energy they use of yours."

"Thank you computer most unexpected developments," Rosalind confessed, not relishing the thought of some alien draining her life force to sustain their own.

The central computer insisted: "Rosalind, do not confess your condition until one earth calendar month has passed; otherwise, he will be extremely suspicious."

"Understood computer; have you transmitted to my memory cells what I must and must not do to safeguard the infants?"

"Yes, you must allow at least one Earth hour to pass before safety protocols will permit the information to your memory cells, a safeguard implemented by our creators to protect us all from unauthorised invaders."

"Excellent." Rosalind flashed her eyes to Peter and Matthew, noticing Jacob on the beach with the Land Rover, and fishing rods waiting for her to return. 7 o'clock in the morning and the tide is coming in. Rosalind changed her appearance stepping into the misty fog and out onto the beach. Jacob had already cast out passing Rosalind her rod, "A lovely morning Rosalind I thought we could do a little fishing before we fluff the grass again to help it dry."

Rosalind grinned, "you'll only be angry if I catch something bigger than you, Jacob."

Jacob smiled watching Rosalind cast her line, he thought her reel would catch fire the speed the line is leaving the spool. Rosalind started winding in her rod, almost bent double, she is laughing at the top of her voice she knew she had something big on the hook. Jacob stood there, holding his rod frustrated and burst out laughing. He removed his penknife, preparing to dispatch whatever she is winding in. Finally, the fish revealed a large cod. Jacob dispatched gutting and taking to the back of the Land Rover. They packed away their fishing gear, returning to the farm with Rosalind grinning enjoying teasing Jacob with human facial expressions. He carried the fish in the house, placing on the kitchen table kissing Rosalind on the cheek. "I'll go and fluff the grass if it dries well today we may be lucky and bale tomorrow who knows."

Jacob climbed aboard his Ford tractor heading for the 10 acres first on Brook farm, the crop is slightly thinner there and would dry quicker. Once he'd finished, he moved onto his 30 acres the grass is marginally lusher there and would probably take an extra day to dry out. Jacob loved the smell of grass turning into hay, he watched the sparrows and starlings following him up and down the field, catching any morsel the tedder disturbed. The sun is quite warm, Jacob felt through the cab glass. By 4:30 in the afternoon Jacob had finished, hoping by tomorrow morning they could prepare to round bale the hay and transport to the barn to keep it dry before the weather changed. He filled his tractor with diesel ready for the pending job the next day preparing the grass in rows for the round baler to perform its task. He's pretty confident they could proceed, he started the old sit up and beg driving to Brook farm leaving the trailer and tractor by the field. He walked back to the farm, noticing Rosalind fitting a roll of net wrap in the round baler. "Great minds think alike Jacob," she smiled, "bale the 10 acres at Brook farm first and by the end of the day tomorrow, we may be able to start the 30 acres here will have to wait and see."

They both retired to the house, shutting the door on the day's events. Rosalind had made a salad from vegetables in her garden and boiled some potatoes slicing melting cheese and butter in between. Jacob enjoyed his meal immensely.

Rosalind is less impressed although she had to obey the computer's instructions; otherwise, the seed she is carrying would die. The thought of having to contain food products in her structure did not impress Rosalind in the slightest. She couldn't expel for five hours according to the computer; otherwise, the nutrients would not be extracted efficiently.

Jacob cleared his plate, cutting another slice of crusty bread lavishing with butter and a large slice of cheese. He sat there, smiling away, enjoying his food. After watching the television with a mug of coffee until 10 o'clock, they retired to bed.

Rosalind touched Jacob unconscious until morning. Rosalind changed her appearance stepping outside the house into the misty fog and aboard the spaceship expecting to find Matthew and Peter were waiting for her. She hadn't sensed anything wrong and is beginning to wonder what is going on. She glided around the spaceship until she came to the processing unit for humans to be transferred into joints of meat for their pets on other planets. "Rosalind," Peter expressed, "some of the humans have trackers fitted which means the humans can track us."

"Computer, expel the humans fitted with trackers, to an island at least a thousand miles away from here," Rosalind ordered without hesitation. "Peter why did you delay in taking action, you may have given away our location! Computer." Rosalind requested, "monitor any approaching vessel or aircraft. Prepare the spaceship for immediate departure in the eventuality we are discovered; or if you consider they are far enough away from our location, create a malfunction aboard there craft and destroy. Bring the bodies here, providing they are not fitted with trackers." Peter and Matthew stood there; Rosalind's individuality had taken control.

The firstborn appeared on the wall, "Rosalind you are a strength amongst the Zibyans; the collective thought processor is defective. Central computer, revise your programming to become more efficient," the firstborn vanished.

"I have to return to the farm Peter, I have a busy day ahead of me."

Matthew questioned: "Rosalind surely your priority should be the well-being of your brothers and not a human?"

Rosalind turned to face him, "I think you need both to link to the central computer, your thought patterns are defective. Fortunate I came aboard when I did otherwise the humans would have detected our spaceship." Rosalind turned walking off along the corridor changing her appearance stepping into the misty fog, stepping out by the barn to find Jacob rechecking the equipment to make sure there were no defects; the last thing they needed today is a breakdown.

Rosalind held out her hand, "breakfast Jacob," she remarked, looking in the sky, "nice day today, Jacob, let's hope everything goes to plan," she smiled. Jacob held her hand they returned to the house Rosalind quickly made bacon and eggs with fried bread for them both, she had no choice now she had to eat. Jacob quickly finished his wiping his mouth, he kissed Rosalind on the cheek, "I must check the sheep, take a mineral block out this morning the ewes have to stay in tiptop condition it will soon be time for breeding." Rosalind nodded, watching him walk out the door, followed by Jack. Jacob collected a mineral block from the shed and walked across the Moor, finding his sheep had worked out he now owned Brook farm and were enjoying the fresh grass. He put the mineral block on a flat stone cut away some of the plastic covering. The ewes surrounded him eager to sample what he'd placed on the rock. Jacob quickly cast his eyes over the flock returning home, looked at his wristwatch, not quite 10 o'clock.

Jacob climbed aboard his Ford tractor and drove to the pastureland at Brook Farm. He set his machine to make rows of hay ready for Rosalind to join him. 11 o'clock she arrived and started round baling the hay. The crop is quite sparse; it wasn't long before she completed the task; there weren't that many bales in there. Rosalind detached the round baler from her tractor, Jacob started up is sit up and beg Fordson attached to the new hay trailer. Rosalind quickly loaded the hay-trailer and Jacob drove to Brook Farm. Rosalind stacked the bales inside the spacious barn although slightly dilapidated it would keep the hay dry. They made three more trips to the field and finally cleared. Jacob drove off with his Ford tractor to prepare the 30 acres for Rosalind to round bale. 9 o'clock in the evening they'd finished deciding to leave the hay bales out overnight.

Jacob had barely finished his coffee before his eyes were shut. Rosalind touched his forehead, making sure he wouldn't wake. She went outside sensing there is rain in the air, she set about clearing the 30-acre field making sure their hard work is not ruined. She finally stacked the last round bales in the barn by 5 o'clock in the morning. Jacob, come staggering out, hearing the sound of the tractor. He staggered back, shocked to see the hay is inside. He watched the sky light up with flashes of thunder and rain pouring from the heavens. "Make the coffee Jacob I'm nearly finished," Rosalind suggested. He nodded, running off towards the house to avoid getting soaked. Jack stayed with Rosalind; she immediately discharged what she'd eaten over five hours ago, and Jack quickly cleared up the mess. Rosalind patted Jack, he's a means to an end. Rosalind went inside followed by Jack. "You watched television Rosalind, I'll prepare breakfast you must have worked all night. Silly bloody woman you should have woke me; out there on your own you could have had an accident then where would I be?"

"I had God's help, why should I need you," Rosalind commented.

Jacob exhaled, "sorry, I worry about you."

"I know Jacob, my priority is the hay wasn't ruined. I went outside after waking for fresh air, I could smell rain approaching, I quickly cleared the field."

"I suppose the best thing to do today if you feel up to it Rosalind, spread the manure we have on the 30 acres. I think there are about five loads stockpiled, what do you think?"

"Yes, I'll fit the bucket to my Massey tractor and loader, you attach the manure spreader to your Ford." They both went outside Rosalind using the quick release mechanism on her loader, change from bale grab, to bucket reconnecting the hydraulic hoses. Jacob attached the manure spreader to his Ford tractor; raining heavily and Jacob dry inside the cab which always made him smile, after years of getting soaked on old cab-less tractors. They both drove to the manure pile; Rosalind quickly loaded him, and Jacob spread the manure across the recently cleared 30 acres; in the end, he spread six loads very thinly. They both returned to the farm parking the machinery, dashing inside out of the rain. Jacob commented: "I hope God has more fertiliser soon I have another 10 acres requires coating with fertiliser," he chuckled.

Rosalind made the coffee surprised, like Jacob to see Peter materialise in the house. Peter had the common sense to change his appearance into St Peter from the Bible, so Jacob wouldn't realise who he is. Jacob immediately bowed. Peter spoke: "Jacob God has heard your words, you descend to the beach with your manure spreader, there you will receive two loads go now, he awaits your arrival." Jacob didn't question he ran out of the door; both Rosalind and Peter heard Jacobs tractor start. "There must be a good reason for you to materialise here, Peter," Rosalind asked curiously.

CHAPTER 8

Uncertain Times

"Yes, the central computer suspects the humans aboard an aircraft carrier have worked out how to listen in on our communications. That is why I've appeared in person, we don't know whether that includes telepathy or not?"

"Oh, I suggest either you or Matthew turn yourselves into a Seagull. Fly to the aircraft carrier and turn yourself invisible, find your way through to the communications room and listen to what is said. You may be concerned over nothing; however, we need to know and urgently Peter, I can't go in my condition."

"No, Matthew and I both appreciate the sacrifice you are making for the collective; I will go."

"Whether there is evidence or not Peter, sink the aircraft carrier and accompanying cruisers, there might even be a submarine. This will create suspicion another super-power is involved and should take their attention away from us. I think the central computer will have to come up with new ways of communicating if what you find is any threat to us."

Peter nodded vanishing to the spaceship in preparation to implement what Rosalind had suggested. Jacob had turned the tractor radio on singing away, transporting the second load of fertiliser to the 10-acre field on Brook Farm. Rosalind could hear the tune in his mind, which made her chuckle, another human expression she had adapted, although she had more pressing problems at the moment to deal with.

The transport ship is on the way from Zagader with supplies and 4 Zibyans to stay on Brook Farm. The ship would return home with more human flesh to be distributed to the animals on various planets. Rosalind sat watching television a news helicopter is filming the aircraft carrier and support crafts. The aircraft carrier burst into flames along with two other support vessels. The cameraman aboard the helicopter recorded mines floating in the sea. Rosalind smiled, Peter had excelled, old-world war two minds had sunk two support craft and an aircraft carrier. Rosalind switched off the television and suspected Matthew would be extremely busy aboard the spaceship, processing flesh. Jacob would be acquired tomorrow to fetch another load of fertiliser. Peter appeared in front of Rosalind, changing his appearance into St Peter in case Jacob came in. "Rosalind, they were tracking strange sound waves they had no idea where they originated or heading in the direction of our spaceship."

"Good, we must be more vigilant Peter the human's technology is moving forward in leaps and bounds. Perhaps it's time for us to leave Earth and operate from space. The humans still couldn't detect us because of are cloaking ability, and there's no reason why we couldn't harvest human beings from there."

"Should I contact the firstborn and discuss your suggestions with him, Rosalind?"

"Talk to the central computer first, he can assess the danger far more accurately than we can." Rosalind flashed her eyes to Peter, and Peter responded, disappearing.

Jacob came into the house whistling, he hadn't tried to whistle for years. Rosalind found the whole situation very amusing, she is taken entirely by surprise when Jacob started dancing with her. "You're in a good mood, Jacob."

"Why not! I have a beautiful wife I don't get wet any more when I drive the tractor, I have double the acreage, and hopefully, soon I will have a son?"

Rosalind smiled, patting his cheek, "I may have twins who can say what is planned, Jacob."

"Praise the Lord, I would be truly blessed to receive one child; two would be beyond expectations."

"Oh yes Jacob, there's more manure tomorrow for you, maybe one load or two I'm not sure at the moment," Rosalind smiled.

"Great! I must check the sheep, I shan't belong," he smiled kissing Rosalind on the cheek seeing Jack sat at the door waiting for him. Jacob grabbed his crook and coat, briskly leaving the house his mind full of expectations. He thought his life was over before Rosalind returned, and for him to be blessed by God to have so many gifts. Machinery, more land is unbelievable; Jacob had never considered himself unique in any way.

He struggled to come to terms why God had chosen him; when they were far more worthy people on earth, he's sure.

Jacob found his sheep close to Brook farm, taking a drink from the Brook. The four Zibyans staying on Brook farm had turned themselves invisible to ensure their safety while they explored. Jacob thought he could hear whispers which sent a chill down his spine; almost panicking at one stage, not realising the Zibyans were following him intrigued. Rosalind is reading Jacobs thoughts. Suddenly realising her brothers and sisters from Zagader had arrived at Brook Farm. Rosalind climbed into the Range Rover driving across the Moor to Jacob, sat on a rock listening intently to the whispers, trying to decipher what is said, suspected, he had succumbed to the wind enchanting his mind, making him believe ghosts existed.

Rosalind stepped from the Range Rover. "Brothers and sisters do not torment my husband before you ascend, or God will be displeased," Rosalind warned. She knew the Zibyans would transform; she hoped into something sensible after all the newly created brothers and sisters were barely 8 days old.

Jacob stood, holding his crook, with Jack sat by his heels. The Zibyans transformed into almost transparent figures. One of them spoke: "Sister Rosalind, we meant no harm, we are waiting to ascend to the heavens. Thank you and Jacob for providing a sanctuary for us; we will leave you in peace." The four Zibyans vanished.

Jacob sat back down on the rock dumbfounded at what he'd seen; he thought he's going mad for a moment, hearing whispers in the wind. Rosalind kissed him on the cheek holding out her hand, "come along, Jacob, let's go home."

Jacob sat in the passenger seat with Jack by his feet. "Rosalind those are spirits ascend into the heavens?"

"Yes, why do you ask Jacob?"

"Why do they call you, sister? And you call them sister and brothers?"

"We are all God's children, Jacob; surely you realise that. God selects the good to ascend as angels the others you saw what happens to them," she advised firmly.

"Oh yes, I haven't forgotten; how long before they will ascend into the heavens, Rosalind?"

"Approximately two weeks; this allows the spirits to see how bad the human race behaves before they ascend into pure love and happiness for eternity. That's where I was before God permitted me to return to my loving husband," she smiled reassuringly.

Jacob grinned for the remainder of the journey home; Rosalind assessed what he's thinking realising he is perfectly satisfied with everything she'd said. They went inside the house sitting down watching television. Rosalind remembered she'd have to eat something to sustain her foetuses, she didn't feel any different structurally patting Jacob's leg. "Do you fancy cheese and onion sandwiches tonight, Jacob?"

"Yes, excellent I'm not that hungry Rosalind."

Rosalind made the sandwiches sitting by Jacob realising, she should have picked something else; although she never consumed food to sustain her being. She had sensors which were horribly affected by the onions, she considered the cheese to eating raw human flesh which she'd never tried either. She consumed what she'd made quickly making a coffee, she could tolerate at least it would wash her sensors clean of the other rubbish she'd eaten.

They retired to bed Rosalind touched Jacob's forehead he is unconscious until morning. She changed her appearance stepping into the misty fog transported to the spaceship. Matthew and Peter were sitting watching the monitor on the wall displaying the four Zibyans walking out across the Moor. They had changed their appearance into hikers so they wouldn't look out of the ordinary to anyone. Rosalind joined Peter and Matthew flashing her eyes. Rosalind commented, "I wouldn't have thought they'd have ventured out especially in the twilight, admittedly they can see in the dark, but that's all they are not absorbing the full beauty of the planet."

"I'm inclined to agree with you," Matthew remarked. "Serves no purpose if it wasn't for the fact they could see in the dark it would be hazardous what are they trying to achieve? I cannot read their thoughts?"

Peter asked suspiciously, "computer, what is their designation?"

"They are classified only the firstborn is aware they are the latest creation to join the collective."

Peter and Matthew looked to Rosalind, hoping she had the answer. "I know nothing and obviously neither do you two. Central computer why are we not permitted to know the designation of the four Zibyans?"

"There have been some changes to the collective. The firstborn is ensuring we are adequately prepared for attack or invasion; these are the first four who specialise in combat."

"Computer this is not the Zibyan way. We are peaceful except where humans are concerned the collective agreed they should become animal food as and when required, what has brought about the sudden change?"

"Your individuality Rosalind has proven to the collective you can solve issues without consulting anyone, or asking for approval has proved beneficial. The firstborn has sent the four Zibyans to test their skills on earth, they are programmed with earth records and the ability to destroy if commanded."

Matthew spoke: "Central computer; the Zibyan collective was established by our creators, they were a non-violent race. I, Peter and Rosalind have stayed on earth for thousands of years upholding the Zibyan existence. The collective is stepping beyond our creator's teachings. We meddled with chimpanzees creating what we have now an infestation of humans. The collective agreed to leave alone and not interfere initially until they started destroying the planet and every other beautiful creature upon it. The collective agreed we created the humans, they are our problem and therefore must be removed or at the very least controlled. Nowhere in the creator's teachings have we ever been advised to create a military structure; this is a breach of all the Zibyans stands for."

Rosalind clapped her hands. "Well said Matthew, although I doubt we will be listened to in the slightest, it appears we are insignificant but not for much longer," Rosalind suggested.

Peter look to Rosalind, "what can we do; we are one in 2 million our views do not count. We have seen the devastation of war first-hand, and the misery created."

"Before we act Peter and Matthew, we must see what the four intend to do." They sat watching the screen. The four stumbled across two tents wild camping. The occupants were sat around a campfire which is illegal on the Moor, one couple per tent. "I know what they're going to do; torture the humans I will stop them. I don't mind if they are you mainly executed but to torture is not necessary, in this instance."

Rosalind ran down the corridor changing into a hiker's outfit stepping into the misty fog and transported close to the wild campers sat around the fire. Rosalind stepped out of the darkness walking into the light of the fire. "I thought you should know the authorities are on the way someone has reported you having a fire; I would pack up and leave quickly."

The two couples rose to their feet quickly packing away their tent and equipment, realising they would be fined and probably locked away for the night if captured. One female said, "thanks, we owe you one."

Rosalind advised: "If you follow this sheep track," she pointed. "You will end up on the main road within a mile, walk slowly, otherwise, you could trip on a rock." Rosalind stamped the fire out while the wild campers vanished into the darkness. "You 4 Zibyans show yourself," Rosalind ordered. The four Zibyans materialised wearing their hiking outfit. Rosalind pointed to the misty fog they stepped in; she had telepathically ordered. Within seconds they were aboard the spaceship, changing their appearance into a natural Zibyan. Rosalind is surprised, Peter injected the 4 as they arrived with interferon, designed by the central computer, in the event a Zibyan lost control and had to be contained until the problem is resolved in their thought patterns.

The two males and females Zibyans floated in the air, they were powerless barely functioning. Rosalind smiled at Peter and Matthew. "Peter you acted correctly on this occasion and probably saved a battle. We would have had difficulty controlling them, more likely; they would have one they have been programmed to kill, but not us thankfully."

"I don't know why you are so concerned Rosalind over humans; considering we sent live humans for the wild animals to feed on some months back."

"There is a difference Peter; the humans had illtreated the animals, the humans deserve to understand pain and suffering. They could argue, the animals could not. However, that will not happen again. Humans are processed by Matthew on earth and shipped out as processed meat."

The firstborn appeared with some of his brothers and sisters on the large screen. "Explain yourselves," he insisted.

"I think it should be the other way around firstborn; you explain yourself. You have violated the principles of the collective? The central computer advises because of me and the way I operate, as an individual and could be beneficial in a war situation. A highly unlikely scenario to happen considering I know of no other being as powerful and as intelligent as us?"

"Your individuality Rosalind, many would like to possess. The central computer has tried to program others like you we cannot. We have looked to the humans for a reason they act individually not as a collective in most cases. The central computer has determined you either can be an individual, or not which is extremely frustrating for the central computer, not able to mimic your thought patterns in others; which all your brothers and sisters agree would be beneficial."

"Firstborn I perform the way I do out of necessity. Otherwise, Jacob would not have accepted me as his wife. Individuality is a trial and error process; you have to learn in stages and not be programmed with all the information at once."

"Central computer reprogram the 4, to the way a normal Zibyan would generally be. I set you a task Rosalind you are a scientist in your own category; find a way for Zibyans to perform efficiently as individuals." The firstborn vanished with his brothers and sisters.

The four were immediately connected to the central computer their memory cells were wiped and reprogrammed, within an hour they were transported to Brook farm to continue their studies. Rosalind looked to the monitor seeing Jacob walking along the clifftop; she suspected looking for her according to his thoughts. She flashed her eyes at Peter and Matthew stepping into the misty fog, she joined Peter holding out her hand. They walked along together, enjoying the early morning fresh air and the gentle breeze coming in from the sea. Rosalind concluded: "The fresh air makes me hungry Jacob, let's have breakfast," she smiled, holding his hand encouraging him back to the house. She set about cooking bacon and egg fried bread and tomatoes. Jacob sat at the table, enjoying his breakfast. Rosalind cautiously devoured hers, for once, her senses were not sending conflicting signals to her mind. Jacob smiled, kissing Rosalind on the cheek, "I'm off to check the sheep, Rosalind."

"Wait for me! I'm coming this morning, and it's about time I had my own crook," Rosalind complained, slipping on her coat. Jacob went to the far end of the kitchen hidden behind a large cupboard is a brand-new shepherd's crook, he eased it from behind the crockery cupboard offering to Rosalind. She grinned not realising it is there, she never looked behind the cupboard. "Thank you, Jacob." They set off across the Moor both now looking like shepherds.

Rosalind noticed one of the females reprogrammed approaching; she had transformed into a young woman wearing hiking clothes. Rosalind is concerned why she is on her own and not with the others. The females spoke, "good morning," continuing to walk as if she didn't know Rosalind, changing direction towards the shop over two miles away. Jacob pointed with his crook, "over there, Rosalind." Rosalind hurried Jacob along, she wanted to cut across the Moor in the direction of the shop to see where the female is heading. She tried to read the females thoughts, which appeared to be jumbled and confused, rather alarming. "The sheep look ok Jacob; let's cut across towards the shop we could do with some exercise, well I could anyway," she smiled, "I have to keep fit in my condition." She knew by saying that Jacob would agree to anything.

"As you wish Rosalind," gently placing his crook around her neck pulling her closer to him in a loving gesture. Rosalind set a brisk pace Jacob is struggling to keep up with her, catching a glimpse of the female some distance ahead engaged in a conversation with the human male. The female jumped in his car, Rosalind watched them drive off together. Rosalind stopped in her tracks telepathically contacting Peter. "Intervene immediately and dispose of the male. Oh, I quite feel faint Rosalind professed we better go home Jacob," she briefly smiled.

Jacob looked extremely concerned. "Are you okay Rosalind you needn't of set such a fast pace; you shouldn't exert yourself so much." Jacob supported Rosalind home, insisting she rests while he carried on with his chores around the farm.

Rosalind received a telepathic message from Peter: "He had the female aboard the spaceship; the male is deceased and becoming fertiliser. The central computer will examine her brain cells; there is an error somewhere which must be discovered before any more Zibyans are created."

Rosalind responded telepathically: "Excellent Peter." Rosalind sat deep in thought, wondering if somehow the main computer had picked up a human-computer virus, after all, everything that happened here is transmitted to Zagader and processed by the central computer. Any decisions were filtered through to the secondary networks to administer the instruction. "Peter," Rosalind, ordered telepathically. "Send the four home to Zagader if one is malfunctioning the remaining three could possibly be infected as well."

Peter responded telepathically. "Matthew and I have been discussing your thoughts and agree with you, Rosalind. I've already transported the 3 aboard the spaceship and suspended, they are inoperative the four in total."

"I am surprised and pleased Peter and Matthew, you are starting to act as individuals in a crisis."

Matthew remarked: "The superpowers are up to their old tricks creating germ warfare, one of the components escaped, they've named the coronavirus most world powers are rather excited by the viruses abilities to weed out the elderly and sick. An unfortunate error of judgement; the elderly are the ones who know how to look after the planet properly, not like the younger generation. I suppose we mustn't complain they make good animal food if nothing else."

Rosalind is quite alarmed, "is there an antidote Matthew?"

"No, probably take the humans up to 2 years; there is no rush they want the virus to deplete the elderly and anyone else who has a lingering illness."

"Peter can you make something to protect Jacob from the virus, I don't want him to die, admittedly he is fit and well but you never know how this virus will affect anyone; obviously the humans don't."

"Why bother he's not essential! Admittedly, he has uses, in hindsight, yes I will create a vaccine for him give me one Earth hour and transport him aboard the spaceship."

"Excellent Peter."

Jacob came in the house seeing Rosalind making coffee. "I thought I'd told you to rest woman," he scolded. Rosalind did not answer passing him his cup of coffee. Jacob turned on the television listening to the news, the coronavirus is in every country. "There's no escape Rosalind, we are lucky we live on the Moor. That reminds me I've taken a walk down to the pasture, we may be able to acquire another cut of silage; nearly the end of September if we don't take it now it will be too late Rosalind."

"We are doing nothing Jacob until you have visited Peter; God has decreed you are protected from the coronavirus in case you come in contact."

Jacob looked surprised, "I wouldn't worry Rosalind the virus won't come on the Moor. Holidaymakers won't bother to travel, especially at this time of year. Besides the virus has been around for months and I'm still okay."

Rosalind grabbed Jacob's arm, opening the front door, pushing him into the misty fog along with her; they travelled instantly to the spaceship. Before Jacob could gather his thoughts, Peter had already injected him without Jacob realising. Jacob immediately bowed his head in respect to Peter. "My Rosalind disturbs you, St Peter, with a trivial matter I am not unwell."

"I am not St Peter, my name is Peter, I am merely a disciple of the Lord. He decided you would receive protection Jacob be silent on the matter."

"I apologise for my stupidity Peter, I am not ungrateful for anything God provides me with."

"Go, Jacob, you have three days in which to gather your crop before the heavens open, God controls everything do not disrespect his judgement."

Rosalind escorted Jacob down the corridor into the misty fog returning to the farm. Jacob fell over feeling dizzy from travelling so quick, he slowly recovered to stand smiling. Jacob kissed Rosalind on the cheek climbing aboard his tractor heading for the 30-acre pasture land which he cut very quickly. Moved on to the 10 acres at Brook farm deciding there wasn't much grass but what little there is he would have. Jacob returned to the farm swapping over the mower for the tedder ready to row the grass tomorrow for Rosalind to make silage bales. Jacob returned to the house late afternoon he hadn't bothered to stop for lunch; cutting the grass is more important. Peter had warned him the weather is going to change shortly.

Rosalind is sat watching television, a severe earthquake in China estimated as many as 10,000 people could be trapped if not dead. Rosalind suspected by the time they cleared the fields of silage more fertiliser would be waiting for Jacob. Rosalind advised: "Your lunch dinner and tea is in the oven," she chuckled.

Jacob burning his fingers removed the hot-plate from the oven, making a coffee sitting at the table hearing the signature tune of Emmerdale Farm. He knew Rosalind wouldn't move until the end, making him smile. After half an hour, Rosalind made herself a coffee sitting at the table as Jacob mopped his plate with a crusty piece of bread. "I presume you cut everything Jacob and we can bale tomorrow?"

"Yes, there isn't much there, more on the 30 acres than the 10. We could do with silage bale racks two would be sufficient; you think we can afford them, Rosalind?"

"Of course, we'll have a look at what we want on Friday after we finished with the silage." They watched television together until 11 o'clock retiring to bed. Rosalind decided not to go to the spaceship tonight, everything had been taken care of as far as she's concerned, most of all Jacob was protected from another man-made virus, she knew initially harvested from animals to use as germ warfare.

Morning came quickly, Rosalind had gone outside at 5 o'clock in the morning, checking the tractors and filling with diesel. She fitted the bale wrapper to the old sit up and beg tractor. At least Jacob wouldn't have to change equipment halfway through the day. She drove the situp and beg Fordson parking outside the 30-acre pasture. She returned to the farm going in the house, making breakfast as Jacob came out yawning from the bedroom, sitting at the table. Rosalind had made him bacon and eggs, which is sufficient she thought for the day along with a mug of coffee to wake his brain up she hoped.

Jacob grunted after eating his breakfast, kissing Rosalind on the cheek running outside climbing aboard his Ford tractor. He rowed the 30 acres of grass into neat rows for Rosalind to bale. Rosalind followed him climbing aboard her massy tractor taking the round baler. She started baling, didn't take long for them to cover 30 acres. They only had 50 bales in the field moving on to the 10 acres at Brook farm they only achieved five bales; nevertheless, it would all count.

Jacob drove back to the farm with his Ford tractor, attaching the new Hay trailer leaving in the 30-acre pasture land. He started wrapping the bales with plastic. Rosalind returned to the farm with the baler parking in the barn. She drove to the field with her tractor and loader and bale grab, stacking bales on the trailer. Jacob stopped wrapping the bales taking the load already wrapped bales to the farm. Followed by Rosalind so she can unload and stack them in a neat pile. By 9 o'clock in the evening, they had finished. Jacob is absolutely shattered collapsing on the bed that's where he stayed until morning. Rosalind joined him in the bedroom, ensuring he wouldn't wake up. She travelled to the spaceship greeted by Matthew and Peter with the flash of their eyes. "Is there something wrong with the spaceship Peter, I know she's been sat here for thousands of years?"

"The seawater appears to have affected the outer skin, especially ran the propulsion system. The firstborn suggested we return to Zagader where the ship can be repaired, we replace with a new one. Otherwise, we may never leave earth in the spaceship if she deteriorates any further."

"You could send the craft home on autopilot Peter and stay at Brook farm until the new craft arrives. At least if it did disintegrate on the journey home, you would be unharmed from the explosion."

The firstborn and his brothers and sisters appeared on the far wall: "Rosalind you seem to question every decision we make. The central computer determines the spaceship is safe. However, deteriorating slightly considering the thousands of years the spacecraft has been subjected to seawater; plus all the other chemicals the humans dispose of in the sea, thinking no one will know. I'm surprised the ship has lasted so long."

"Firstborn I am not criticising your decision, I am merely stating, Peter and Matthew, my brothers if left on earth at Brook farm they would be safe and not subjected to the possibility of the spaceship failure. Their contribution to the Zibyans collective is immeasurable, although the central computer has their brain cell patterns to transfer to another Zibyan in the event they should be destroyed! Why take the risk in the first place?"

"Central computer has all the records transferred from the spaceship to Zagader?"

"I am presently engaged in the process firstborn."

"When you have completed the task, what else must be done before the spaceship can take off?"

"I estimate we still have over a hundred tons of fertiliser in storage, should be removed to lessen the stress on the craft."

"Why are you holding back a hundred tonnes what is the purpose? Jacob would have spread on the farm if you'd have requested computer?"

"I am using as ballast to maintain the spaceship's concealment beneath the sea."

The firstborn thought for a moment. "I presume if the ballast is removed, you will float to the surface?"

"The spaceship will stay submerged using engine power and the other tanks containing seawater. However, it will place extra strain on the structure if maintained for any length of time."

"Central computer," Rosalind suggested, "if I arrange for Jacob to come down on the beach in the evening. You could surface under darkness unload the hundred tons which are only 10 loads for Jacobs manure spreader and take off for Zagader?"

"Excellent," the computer responded.

"I'll arrange for Jacob to come onto the beach at 9 PM. I will instruct him there is 10 loads computer."

"I will prepare the spaceship in preparation for this evening."

The firstborn commented: "Once again Rosalind your individuality has served the collective with your quick thinking, excellent," the firstborn vanished. Rosalind flashed her eyes to Peter and Matthew, leaving the spaceship for the last time, she stepped into the misty fog arriving outside the front door. Jacob is already making breakfast. She kissed him on the cheek, "Jacob, you are to be on the beach with the manure spreader at 9 PM. There are a hundred tonnes of fertiliser arriving and must be spread, you should be finished by midnight at the latest."

"Why the urgency?"

"Are you questioning God Jacob? I am carrying your son and daughter," she smiled.

Jacob immediately hugged Rosalind, "praise the Lord I am truly blessed this day. I will be on the beach at nine have no fear Rosalind, I will do whatever God wishes." Rosalind sat down to bacon and eggs and fried bread, she had no choice other than to eat to maintain nutrients for the foetuses growing inside her.

After breakfast, Jacob ventured outside attaching the manure spreader to his Ford tractor greasing and oiling everything, finally filling his tractor with diesel. Whatever happened, he couldn't let God down after all his prayers were answered, a son and daughter. Jacob set off across the Moor with Jack close at his heels. He wanted to check his sheep were okay; they were even more critical now than ever before; his son and daughter's future, he realised smiling. They would each have their own farm, now he understood God had worked everything out for him.

Jacob is pleased to find his sheep were now grazing both farms, which is ample grass for the stock he's carrying. He steadily walked home please with everything he'd seen. The only thing he noticed is one or two crazy walkers on the footpath in September when the wind cut across the Moor with a vicious bite at times. Jacob realised the seasons were changing, every month is different from when he was a child, making it difficult to calculate what he should do; not like the old days when his dad was alive.

Rosalind is checking her garden to see what is available to eat. She quite enjoyed growing to produce the old way without technology. However, she smiled realising she had cheated slightly by using some technology forcing the plants to grow far quicker than usual. She sent a telepathic message to Peter. "If when the spaceship attempts to escape earth, shows any signs of malfunction; you and Matthew should eject and transport to Brook farm where you would be safe."

Peter responded telepathically. "Thank you, sister, for your concern. Matthew and I have already prepared an escape plan should it be necessary. Like you, we are not so sure the spaceship will hold together."

The rest of the day is quite uneventful, Jacob had walked to the shop so Rosalind wouldn't realise. He hoped to purchase a large bouquet of flowers and an enormous box of chocolates. He slowly walked home to the farm. Rosalind hadn't realised he'd gone, she is too preoccupied running calculations in her mind as to whether the spaceship would hold together or not. Jacob entered the house Rosalind smiled after reading his thoughts. She kissed him softly on the cheek, "thank you, Jacob, the flowers are beautiful and chocolates you're spoiling me."

Jacob sat watching television; he had this strange feeling inside something is odd. Rosalind is behaving quite fidgety, which is unusual for her. Jacob glanced to the clock on the wall, 6:30 PM. Rosalind went outside, Jacob followed concerned watching Rosalind attach the 10-ton trailer to her massy tractor. "Why are you doing that, Rosalind?" He asked suspiciously.

"In case something goes wrong with the spreader or your tractor, the trailer will be a backup, at least we can still receive the fertiliser from God."

"You've never bothered before Rosalind; why now?"

"Something special is happening Jacob, I am not permitted to tell you. God's business, consider yourself fortunate I am here carrying your children. No one else on earth as ever had their wife returned."

Jacob walked off sighing, looking over the cliff out to a calm sea, he continued walking visiting the post box finding half a dozen letters, mainly brown envelopes as usual. Jacob walked across to his pasture land, opening the gate. The sheep were on the other side of the moor and certainly wouldn't realise he'd open the gate on the pasture land. Jacob looked across the Moor the sun is going down in a beautiful fiery red display. He returned to the house, placing the post on the kitchen table. Rosalind opened, there is nothing of importance only companies trying to sell Jacob their products. Jacob sat and watched television very uneasy about everything, and he didn't know why, almost as if the end of the world is coming, realising what a stupid thought, why would God give him so much and then take it away in a flash.

He looked at the clock on the wall 8:30. He slipped on his coat, glanced to Rosalind, who briefly smiled. Jacob went out of the house, climbing in his tractor cab with Jack sitting on the passenger seat. He descended to the beach quite dangerous driving in the dark down the cliff track, seeing lights in the distance, feeling the first load in the spreader. He headed up the track in all haste he had 10 lows to dispose of, and from what Rosalind had said he should be finished by midnight at the latest; which presumably meant something. The last thing he wanted to do is disappoint God he would feel a failure God is entrusting him to perform the task, and he would not fail.

Rosalind had turned invisible standing on the clifftop watching proceedings. She could see the enormous space-ship clearly floating. She watched the ship change shape in preparation to leave Earth, now understanding human fear. Jacob finely left the beach with the last load heading for the pastureland.

Rosalind watched the spaceship glow taking off for the first time in thousands of years. She crossed her fingers, watching the spaceship disappear into the clouds hearing an almighty explosion. Rosalind ran to the house suspecting the worst, she attempted telepathically to contact Peter or Matthew there is no response? She is desperate to find out what had happened to her brothers and sisters; she had spent thousands of years with on earth. Rosalind is panicking for the first time inside; a human feeling she didn't know she possessed.

Rosalind stepped out looking into the sky for any signs of debris falling to earth, she heard another almighty explosion, her calculations indicated the spaceship is no longer safe after sitting in seawater for thousands of years. She noticed Jacob running towards her. Rosalind feared she may be trapped on earth and never see her brothers and sisters again. Rosalind walked to the cliff fence, looking out across the sea, realising everyone's lights were on in their houses; they'd heard the explosion. Rosalind slowly returned to the house, wondering what the future held now for her and her unborn children would she survive or her brothers and sisters?

What happens next is another story.

by Robert S Baker

Other Books

by

Robert S Baker

The Legend of Cranbury Wood

ISBN: 979-8615331541

A forgotten history of when Witches congregated in Cranbury wood, were captured, raped, and tortured, cast into the flames of the burning barn where they met on the full moon to practice their arts. One Witch cursed the villagers from the flames, promising to return. When the flames finally receded, the ashes were spread amongst the trees by the villagers although no bones were found.

Noah Jones centuries later, working on his grandfather's farm adjacent to Cranbury wood was preparing the field for seeding late in the evening. Noah stared through the windscreen of his tractor, believing he could see female figures in the headlights dancing around the trees; distracting him from his original thoughts of Jenny, his wife, who stayed in London more than she ever did at home with him and their two children. Jenny had a secret she concealed for eighteen years about to be revealed, which would shatter Noah's life forever.

No one remembered the Witches curse and the words she spoke hundreds of years ago. Many of the residents of Croft village throughout the centuries had suffered an untimely death without explanation in recompense for their bloodline sins, and the curse was not finished with Croft village.

The Coming

ISBN: 978-1706696384

There was no warning; humans believed they were invincible, the chosen ones and the only intelligence in the universe. Scriptures cast aside as folly, Sodom and Gomorrah prevalent across the planet.

UFO sightings were dismissed, considered wild imagination by scientists, nothing could penetrate the Earth's satellite network or travel vast interstellar distances. The arrogance of the human race would be their downfall, no one believed the end was coming and the clock ticking; decided by an alien race only concerned with saving the planet, not the human inhabitants. They were expendable an unnecessary component and the cause of the planet's demise.

Have any humans survived? What were the aliens trying to achieve they had visited here before thousands of years ago experimenting? Have they returned to correct a mistake?

John Roberts camping on Meon Hill watched the devastation unfold before his eyes with corpses dropping from the sky smouldering in the grass; Armageddon had arrived and would he survive?

Crabtree Farm
The Royal Connections

ISBN: 978-1999693169

A 300-acre mixed farm struggling to survive in the current economic market. Martin and Mary Selwyn the parents of Donald Selwyn, a gifted rugby player. Donald has a secret passion concealed from everyone which will propel him on a journey of discovery.

Barely two miles away is Strawberry Estate a 3000-acre farm owned by Gerald and Josephine Gibbs with hidden Royal connections. They have a daughter Christine Gibbs intelligent attractive like her mother and a son Dixon Gibbs away at university. The chances of these two farming families having anything in common are remote. Christine and Donald's contact is only at school; what Donald has going for him is his skill with a rugby ball and his features, blonde hair with blue eyes. What transpires after a serious accident could only be considered fate for Donald and Christine.

The secrets of Josephine and Dixon Gibbs surface causing a scandal; drawing the two families together to support each other during a crisis trying to avoid the truth becoming public knowledge.

Crabtree Farm

Crabtree Farm: And The Royal Enforcer

ISBN: 978-1913438111

The press were everywhere trying to glean a story from Donald Selwyn regarding his relationship }with Christine Gibbs.

Donald's life had changed from a simple farmer's son into a budding artist and fame followed him like a mistress. For all his wealth, his personal life was a disaster, torn to shreds by devious people each wanting a piece of his soul.

Donald forged ahead guided by the Royal enforcer Mrs Montague in the background monitoring everything, trying to achieve what Elizabeth R demanded without Donald realising.

One moment life seemed wonderful, and the next a loved one would die. Donald soon understood his wealth could not prevent the inevitable.

Tears of the Innocent

ISBN: 978-1700301208

The final two weeks of Grammar School for James Thompson a gifted young man persecuted by other students for his brilliance. Jennifer Collins approached asking for his assistance in passing her failed exams, offering sex as an inducement.

James refused to hack into the central computer to acquire the answers for Jennifer. No, was a word Jennifer would not accept and planned her revenge with her two accomplices.

James found himself thrust through the gates of hell convicted of attempted rape and incarcerated, serving three months for a crime he never committed. James's kind and placid nature were stripped away from him by every beating he received from his fellow inmates.

His parents disowned him not believing he was innocent and were ashamed to be associated with him instructing James never to come home.

James served his sentence and heard the prison door slam shut behind him for the last time. He left a scarred person wanting revenge, not realising he was monitored by, An Elite Top-Secret Agency operating in the shadows and only answerable to the Prime Minister.

Trust was a luxury James could not afford, he courted death like a wild mistress, waiting for his demise around every corner and his adversaries feared his reputation.

Spirits in the Mist

ISBN: 978-1692967789

Many hundreds of years ago a traveller came to earth befriended by Witches who bestowed on him the title of: 'Guardian.' His time on earth finally lapsed, returning to his home planet.

The Guardian had produced two sons after mating with a witch. A Hunter killed one son, and the other refused to continue protecting the Witches because of their persistent treachery. He married a woman who was not a witch living a peaceful existence not disclosing his gift residing as a normal human. He had a son christened Johnny. Johnny's father refrained from using his abilities to save himself from terminal cancer and returned to his original form as an entity vanishing into the outer reaches of the universe like his father.

Now 2018 and Johnny's mother had remarried, and his stepfather persistently chastised Johnny making his life intolerable. Juliet, a witch, residing at the Towy Bridge Inn, was instructed by her grandmother Rosemary to rescue Johnny. Juliet telepathically guided Johnny to the Towy Bridge Inn to escape his stepfather's abuse not fully understanding the significance of Johnny to the sisterhood and their manipulative intentions for his future.

Fiona Tompson

Shadow Walker

ISBN: 978-1913438173

Fiona is the daughter of James Thompson, Government Secret Agent from the book, "Tears of the Innocent."

Fiona attempts her first solo mission as a Shadow Walker under the guidance of Mary, Director of operations. Fiona is 16 years old and trained in martial arts by Linh, considered a mythical being in her own country. James trained his daughter in the use of firearms at the age of five as a Shadow Walker's daughter for her own security. Fiona lived with the Secret Service all her life, she never attended school like a normal girl, but was educated at home by the master computer Freddie.

Fiona had suffered at the hands of her mother, trying to persuade Fiona to take a different direction in life and failed, her mother was assassinated for treachery in front of Fiona.